Praise for
Who Did You Tell?

"Instantly immersive, then intriguing, then insanely suspense-ful, then . . . the truth. Believe me, Lesley Kara knows what she's doing."
—LEE CHILD

"Lesley Kara does an excellent job of making readers' heads spin as we are forced constantly to change our minds about who is ally and who enemy."
—*Sunday Express*

"I couldn't put it down! If you loved *The Rumor*, you'll love this one too."
—LAUREN NORTH, author of
The Perfect Son

Praise for
The Rumor

"In this chilling tale of paranoia, suspicion, and accusation, Les-ley Kara keeps you guessing until the final page."
—PAULA HAWKINS, #1 *New York Times* bestselling
author of *The Girl on the Train*

"A great debut with a slyly clever premise and a roller-coaster ride to the very last sentence."
—FIONA BARTON, *New York Times* bestselling
author of *The Widow* and *The Child*

"An intriguing premise, a creeping sense of dread, and a twist you won't see coming . . . Everyone is going to be talking about *The Rumor*."
—SHARI LAPENA, *New York Times* bestselling
author of *The Couple Next Door*

"A brilliant premise with a killer twist, *The Rumor* depicts the prejudices and secrets that simmer in a small seaside town to devastating effect."

— COLETTE MCBETH, author of *An Act of Silence*

"Lesley Kara's gripping debut offers a series of red herrings and twists. . . . The evocation of the way in which idle chatter can spiral into something potentially deadly is beautifully done and fans of page-turning suspense novels should lap it up."

— *The Guardian*

"Well-developed characters and a twisty plot will keep readers turning the pages. Those who stay to the very last sentence will be doubly surprised. Kara is off to a promising start."

— *Publishers Weekly*

"This mystery has an unusual and resonant theme — how a single rumor can morph into a completely unmanageable, deadly force. [There's] psychological acuity throughout and [an] astonishing ending."

— *Booklist*

BY LESLEY KARA

The Rumor

Who Did You Tell?

The Dare

THE DARE

THE
DARE

A NOVEL

LESLEY KARA

BALLANTINE BOOKS
NEW YORK

A Ballantine Books Trade Paperback Original

Copyright © 2021 by Lesley Kara

All rights reserved.

Published in the United States by Ballantine Books, an imprint of Random House, a division of Penguin Random House LLC, New York.

BALLANTINE and the HOUSE colophon are registered trademarks of Penguin Random House LLC.

Originally published in hardcover in the United Kingdom by Bantam Press, an imprint of Transworld Publishers, a division of Penguin Random House LLC, in 2021.

LIBRARY OF CONGRESS CATALOGING-IN-PUBLICATION DATA
Names: Kara, Lesley, author.
Title: The dare : a novel / Lesley Kara.
Description: New York : Ballantine Books, 2021.
Identifiers: LCCN 2021003316 (print) | LCCN 2021003317 (ebook) |
ISBN 9780593356135 (trade paperback) | ISBN 9780593356142 (ebook)
Subjects: GSAFD: Suspense fiction.
Classification: LCC PR6111.A73 D37 2021 (print) |
LCC PR6111.A73 (ebook) | DDC 823/.92—dc23
LC record available at https://lccn.loc.gov/2021003316
LC ebook record available at https://lccn.loc.gov/2021003317

Printed in the United States of America on acid-free paper

randomhousebooks.com

2 4 6 8 9 7 5 3 1

Title-page image: © iStock.com/mbbirdy

Book design by Sara Bereta

To Dawn, for going on "the walk" with me

PART ONE

Secrets, silent, stony sit in the dark palaces of both our hearts: secrets weary of their tyranny: tyrants willing to be dethroned.

—James Joyce

She'd created a little altar on the chest of drawers in her bedroom. A solitary white tulip in a fluted glass vase. An illustrated children's Bible and a bowl of water with blood-red rose petals floating on the surface.

She lit first a candle and then a stick of incense. We watched as the thin plume of blue-gray smoke writhed into the air, filling the room with its cloying scent. My nostrils flared.

"Now we must join hands over the Bible," she said. My heart thumped. "We must swear not to breathe a word of this to a living soul." Her eyes flashed wide. "Not now. Not ever."

I didn't dare tell her what my mother told me once, that Jesus says it's wrong to swear oaths.

"Are you ready?" she said. I nodded so hard my head hurt. She could have asked me to sign my name in our intermingled blood and I'd have agreed.

I took her outstretched hands in mine and together we read the words she had painstakingly written out on a small piece of white card, our voices solemn and tremulous. Then she held the card above *the flame of the candle and we watched as it blackened and curled and crumbled into a small pile of gray ash.*

"And now we bury this in the garden," she said.

I nodded again and she scooped the ash into the palm of her left hand and closed her fingers around it. I followed her out of the room and down the stairs, then out the back door and across the yellowing lawn, tucked so closely behind her that our shadows almost merged. And I knew that it would always be like this, that I would always follow her. Wherever she went. Whatever she did.

1

THEN

THURSDAY, JULY 19, 2007

There are two reasons to celebrate today. First, it's not raining. It's been raining for weeks and though Mum says that rain is God's blessing and we should be grateful for every single drop, even she's getting fed up with it now. I heard her tell Dad yesterday that God's blessed us quite enough lately, thank you very much.

The second reason to celebrate is that it's the first day of the summer holidays, which means six long weeks of NO SCHOOL.

I open my bedroom window and sniff the air. Alice and I have just *got* to go on "The Walk." It's our favorite route and one we've done so many times we know each and every landmark: the kissing gate, the gap in the hedge, the little stream with the rickety footbridge, the field with the scarecrow that looks like a dead man on a stick, the line of poplars, the six stiles, and finally, the railway line, where we always wait till we hear the tracks sing, and count the seconds till the train hurtles by.

That's the best bit, in my opinion. I think it's Alice's best bit, too, although we've never admitted that. We tell each other that it's our favorite walk because if we don't dawdle and we don't rush, it takes us two hours from my front door and back again. Just the right amount of time to discuss everything that needs to be discussed before our legs start to ache and our stomachs to grumble. But deep down, I think we both know that it's our favorite walk because of the railway line and the thrill of the open crossing.

I go downstairs and dial Alice's number on the phone in the kitchen. I've only got a bit of credit left on my crappy old mobile. Alice's sister, Catherine, answers. She doesn't even say hello, just shouts for Alice in that snotty way she has. She's a whole nine years older than us so she really should know better. Alice says she's got "issues." She's got *something*, that's for sure. Once, she even slapped Alice round the face in front of me. All Alice had done was spray a tiny bit of her sister's perfume onto my wrist.

Anyway, I'm not going to let Catherine Dawson's rudeness affect me today. I'm going to put on my Teflon coat, as Mum calls it, the same one I put on at school when Melissa Davenport and the others start having a go.

"Shall we go on The Walk?" Alice says.

"Dur! Why do you think I'm phoning?"

"I'll get the bus to yours," she says. "See you soon."

The fifth stile is different from all the others. Higher. My foot slides clumsily on the second step and its sharp edge jabs into my calf muscle. Alice pretends not to notice. She never makes fun of me. Not ever. I'm there for Alice when her mum takes to her bed with depression. I'm there for her when she can't do her French homework or when she has an argument with her sister. And Alice is there for me when I have a seizure, or when Melissa Davenport and Co. fall about, twitching their limbs and rolling their eyes behind my back.

But just as I'm straightening up out of the clumsy squat in which I've landed, I see the flicker of a smile on Alice's lips. A strange little smile that seems to say, "I know something you don't." She's been doing it on and off ever since we set off this morning. She opens her mouth to say something, then bites her bottom lip and looks all worried.

"What? What were you going to say?"

"Oh, nothing really," she says. Then, after a long pause: "It was just something someone said."

She blushes, and I can guess straightaway who this someone is. Dave Farley. He must have asked her out. I don't think I'll be able to bear it if he has.

"You can't not tell me."

Alice presses her lips together.

My heart drums in my throat and neck. "Why are you being so mean? Why won't you tell me?"

"Because I can't. I just can't."

Something horrible happens to my insides when she says that. Best friends shouldn't have secrets. At least, not from each other. Best friends tell each other everything. Like we always have.

Suddenly, I hate Alice Dawson. I hate her because she isn't telling me something. I hate her because she's pretty and doesn't wear glasses or have frizzy red hair or epilepsy. I hate her so much I can barely breathe.

I accuse her of being two-faced—the ultimate insult—and we start screaming at each other. Alice marches off toward the next stile and it's as much as I can do to keep up with her. We're arguing the whole time: me hurling insults at Alice's back, Alice stopping every so often to glare at me over her shoulder and lobbing them straight back. By the time we reach the crossing, we're running out of horrible things to say to each other.

We've had rows before, where one or the other of us has stormed off—usually me, to be honest—but we've always made up in the end. Even after the really bad one we had last month. This time seems different. More final.

And that's when everything starts to shimmer. When the clear blue of the sky and the vivid greens of the grass and trees collide in a messy blur and the only sound in my ears is the vibration of the track.

The crescendo of that long metallic note filling my head with un-bearable noise.

The next thing I know, I'm sitting in a puddle of wee by the side of the track and a train has stopped. But trains never stop here. It's the middle of a field.

I'm feeling all groggy. Where's Alice? What's happened?

Then I see one of the sleeves of her denim jacket, caught up in the branches of a bush. Only . . . only it's not just a sleeve.

Hot bile rushes out of my mouth and everything goes black.

2

NOW

WEDNESDAY, MARCH 13, 2019

Something in the room has changed. Maybe it's the news presenter's tone of voice. That serious one they use when something awful has happened. Or maybe it's the words themselves that force their way through whatever filters have been working in my head.

My shoulders stiffen. A fatal accident on a railway crossing. A young girl.

Her face flashes up in the corner of the screen before I have a chance to look away. A cheeky little smile. Dimples in her cheeks. She was only eleven. Two years younger than Alice. Her name is Elodie. *Was* Elodie. Such a pretty name.

I grab the remote control and turn the TV off, but the picture is still there, the words echoing in my head. Except it isn't the picture I've just seen on the screen, the one of the cordoned-off railway crossing, the police cars, the solemn-faced journalist delivering the news. It's the picture that's always there, behind my eyes, waiting to catch me off guard, to materialize in front of me and suck me back in.

Ross looks up, surprised.

"It's too much," I tell him. "All this bad news."

He scrapes the last of his boiled egg with a teaspoon. "She wouldn't have known a thing about it. I guess that's the only consolation for her parents. Even at relatively low speeds, a train has so much mass and energy, the body's usually destroyed pretty much straightaway."

I take my empty mug to the kitchen and rinse it out. My chest feels tight, as if my lungs are constricted. I want to ask him if he really believes that, if knowing their daughter has been smashed to pieces pretty much straightaway is a *consolation* for her parents, but I let the comment pass, unchallenged, because I don't want to have a conversation about it. Not right now. Not ever.

I try not to think, but it's impossible. Another life wiped out in seconds. Another bereaved family.

Ross follows me out and gives me a sheepish grin. "Sorry, it's just the way my brain works."

I shake my head at him. "Tell me about it."

What Ross doesn't realize is that I know exactly what happens to a body when it's hit by a train. I looked it up once, a long time ago. Couldn't stop myself. It depends how fast the train is traveling, and whether the body is upright or lying on the ground at the time of impact, but basically all the vital organs are smashed, the major blood vessels broken. Sometimes the body is flung into the air; sometimes it gets rolled up under the wheels and ground into little pieces. Broken bones. Mangled flesh. Severed limbs.

I had to know. I just had to. And then I filed the information away and didn't access it again. Buried it deep. But it's always there, ready to infiltrate my conscious mind whenever a train-related tragedy occurs. Especially when children are involved. Especially when it's a young girl. Like Alice.

I blink to dispel the image that's just landed in my head and scrutinize Ross as he stands at the kitchen door, gazing out at the garden and the crop of daffodils that have sprung up through the grass. He's still wearing his tracksuit bottoms and T-shirt, and the early-morning sunlight illuminates his fair skin. There's a malleable quality about him this morning, as if he could quite easily be a student, a sales assistant, a lad behind a bar. But in less than half an hour he will have transformed himself into a GP, his mind already fixed on the day ahead. He will have solidified into a "pillar of the community," as I jokily call him.

I keep meaning to tell him about Alice—he is my fiancé, after all—but somehow it never seems like the right time. Besides, if I tell him, he might ask me questions I can't answer.

"Take your time and tell us exactly what happened." That's what the police said. But it didn't matter how many times they asked me, my answer was always the same.

"I don't know. I can't remember."

Various neurologists have tried to explain it to me over the years, how there isn't always time for what happens immediately before a seizure to be fully incorporated into the memory system. Sometimes I wonder what it would be like if all my lost memories came back. Like missing pieces of a jigsaw, slotting into place. Making me whole again.

Other times, I wonder if it's better I *don't* remember.

Ross drains his coffee. "By the way, I've spoken to our practice manager about that part-time job on reception. She said to give her a ring if you're interested."

I clear the rest of our breakfast things away, relieved he's changed the subject. "I've been thinking about that," I tell him. "Maybe I should look for something full time instead. Something a bit more interesting."

Ross frowns. "Are you sure that's wise? You don't want to push yourself."

"But that's just it. I *do*. If I hang about here all day, I'll go mad."

If only I'd gone to university and got a degree, I might have had a proper career by now. I missed so much schooling because of my epilepsy, ended up taking my GCSEs and A levels two years later than everyone else. The last thing I wanted to do after all that was more studying. Now, though, I'm beginning to wish I had. The only jobs I've had since leaving school have been tedious admin or reception posts. I'm not sure I can bear the thought of another one, and yet I have to do *something*. I think of that advert I saw in the local paper recently, for an open day at Greenwich University. Maybe I ought to go and investigate.

Ross puts his arms round me from behind while I'm washing up and kisses the back of my neck. His hands start creeping up from my waist and I flick soapy water over my shoulder at him with the washing-up brush.

"Spoilsport!" he says, wiping bubbles from his eye. "Anyway, you wouldn't *be* hanging about here all day if you got the job at the surgery. And you'd be able to catch tantalizing glimpses of the gorgeous Dr. Ross Murray when he comes into the waiting room."

I snort with laughter. "Is that one of the perks of the job, then?"

"You bet."

"But seriously," I say. "The pay's rubbish. You said so yourself."

"It's not about the pay, though, is it? It's about your health. We can manage perfectly well on my salary."

I sigh. Not this again. "My health is good now, Ross. It's the best it's ever been. I haven't had a major seizure in almost two years."

I don't usually say that out loud because I don't want to tempt fate, especially now that I'm finally getting a life. Not that I believe in fate. Not really. Even so, I tap the wooden countertop just to be on the safe side.

I still get partials from time to time—brief absence seizures. Fleeting moments of absence that don't really bother me, to be honest. It's other people who tend to notice them, not me. My eyelids flutter and I zone out for a few seconds. At least, that's what I've been told.

"It's the best it's ever been because you're relaxed and looking after yourself properly," Ross says. "You mustn't overdo things."

I scrub the eggy plates with the brush, just a little too hard. He's right. Of course he is. That last job I did was a mistake. I was still at home with Mum and Dad then and commuting into the city every day. I should have listened to them. It was too much for me—I was exhausted. But now that I'm living in London with Ross it'll be so much easier. I'm on exactly the right combination of drugs, too, just enough to stop the really big seizures, the ones where I fall down and make a spectacle of myself, but not so much that my brain is continually foggy.

"I'm just sick of everything always being about my epilepsy. I'm not an invalid!"

Ross spins me round by the shoulders and looks deep into my eyes. "Quite true. You are a gorgeous, sexy woman, who's also as stubborn as a mule."

We kiss for so long, by the time we've finished we've forgotten what we were arguing about. Or rather, we've pretended to forget.

We met in a café, in the small seaside town of Dovercourt, near Harwich, where my parents and I moved after Alice's death. He bumped into me and slopped his coffee on my suede boots, apologized about five times, and ended up buying me a Coke and a flapjack, which I regretted as soon as I picked it up because crumbs spattered all over the table and made him laugh. I'd thought he was the same age as me, so when he turned out to be in his thirties, and about to become a fully qualified GP, I was gobsmacked.

Right from that very first moment he made me feel special, as if I were the only person he wanted to be with. He was all my daydreams rolled into one. Love at first sight might be a romantic myth—in fact, knowing Ross, he'd probably say it's just a cocktail of sex hormones and neurotransmitters—but that's what it felt like, as though meeting each other was all part of some predestined plan. He made my heart beat faster. Still does.

"What time are your parents due?" he says now.

I look at my watch. "They're probably getting ready to leave now. Said they'd be here by eleven."

Ross nods. "Why don't you take them to that new restaurant in Blackheath? Mario's, I think it's called. Our new practice nurse said it's really good."

I check his face. That's the second time he's mentioned her in the past week. An image of a pretty nurse in a navy uniform pops into my mind. I picture her as a petite blonde, hair scraped into a high, tight ponytail, and imagine him bantering with her in between patients. His last girlfriend was a nurse and I'm under no illusion that there haven't been others, especially when he was at medical school. Going out with nurses is an occupational hazard, he once joked.

But not anymore. We're getting married next year. We've agreed on a fairly long engagement to give us plenty of time to think about the sort of wedding we'd both like, and to plan ahead. I know my parents would have preferred us to get married *before* living together—especially Mum; she's a bit old-fashioned in that respect— but when I met Ross he was already in the process of buying this place, thanks to a small inheritance from his late aunt, and it seems much more sensible to focus our energies on getting the house sorted out before all the stress of arranging a wedding.

It's a little two-up two-down in a quiet street, just off the A201 between Woolwich and Charlton. Five minutes in the car to the Plumtree Lodge Surgery, where Ross works, and easy enough for me to walk or get the bus to wherever I need to go. And it's got a little garden. Okay, so it's basically a narrow strip of weed-infested grass, bordered on either side by fence panels that have seen better days, but at least we *have* a garden. Most people my age live in rented accommodation, or with their parents still.

I watch from the living room window as Ross climbs into his car and drives off. Then I turn my attention to the boxes still stacked against the wall. Maybe I've got time to unpack a few more before Mum and Dad arrive.

I switch the telly back on, but they're still talking about the death on the level crossing. Or rather, they're talking about it *again*. That's the trouble with breakfast TV; everything gets repeated on a loop and, if it's something tragic, even more so. I turn it over to a different channel, but little Elodie's face won't leave my mind. It's churned everything up again. I hate it when that happens.

3

The phone rings, but when I pick up and say hello, there's no reply. Just a weird muffled noise in the background. The line goes dead. A minute later, it rings again.

"Hi, Lizzie, we're just out of the Blackwall Tunnel. See you in a few minutes." It's Mum.

"Was that you just now?" I ask her, but the line starts breaking up so we say goodbye. It must have been her.

I wander from room to room, trying to picture the house through my parents' eyes. They're going to love it, I know they are.

Having spent the last twenty-odd years arranging their lives around my epilepsy, traipsing from one hospital appointment to another, endlessly waiting for test results and listening to the differing opinions of neurologists and epileptologists, it's been hard for them to let go. It was hard for me, too, no matter how ready I was to strike out on my own. But they liked Ross as soon as they met him. His profession helped, of course. I've lost count of the number of times one or the other of them has said how pleased they are that I'm in "safe hands."

Ross and I always laugh about that phrase. He'll hold his hands out in front of him, palms up, and wriggle his fingers in a lewd gesture, as if he's feeling me up. "Oh yes," he says. "You're definitely in safe hands with me." But sometimes their use of it annoys me. It's as if they think I'm a fragile parcel being handed from one owner to another. Maybe that's another reason I don't want to get married straightaway.

The sound of a car pulling up outside has me racing to the front door like a little girl. I'm surprised they managed to find a parking space so close to the house. Ross sometimes has to park all the way down the street. I watch them climb out of the car. They look as if they're coming for a fortnight. Mum is festooned with an assortment of carrier bags and Dad's opening the boot to bring out yet more stuff.

I walk down the path to greet them, glad that their visit coincides with this mild and sunny spring day, when everything looks so much brighter and nicer.

"What on earth is all this you've brought?"

Dad shakes his head as if none of it was his idea, and to be fair, it probably wasn't. "Your mum sent me up the loft to see if there were any more of your things up there. And guess what?"

He leans into the boot and lifts out an enormous, slightly battered-looking box. My heart sinks. As if there aren't enough boxes in our house already.

"I told her you probably wouldn't want all this junk," he says, "but you know what she's like."

Mum clears her throat. "Who's 'she'? The cat's mother?"

I kiss her cheeks. They're soft and velvety beneath my lips and I can smell her face powder. It's only been a few weeks since I left home and already Mum seems older somehow, smaller.

"It's all your old schoolwork, love," she says. Her eyes momentarily darken and my heart skips a beat. I try not to think about my schooldays if I can help it. The memories always unsettle me and, for the second time this morning, I have the feeling that something bad is coming. A looming, indiscriminate threat.

Now she's back to her chatty self and I chide myself for being melodramatic. "It's mainly project files, school reports, that sort of thing," she says. "Your dad was all for throwing it away, but I said you'd be cross if we did that."

As we step inside, Mum stops and gasps in delight. "Oh, Lizzie, the hallway is lovely."

"Apparently, it's called Mindful Gray."

"Hark at you! Already a DIY expert," Dad says. He's finally managed to maneuver the box through the front door and lower it onto the floor. He straightens up and rubs the small of his back. At first glance he looks the same as ever—tall and rangy in his smart casual slacks and long-sleeved, brushed-cotton shirt. His usual uniform. But now I notice an air of fragility hovering just below the surface.

I've always thought it an advantage, having older parents. They seemed so much kinder and calmer than other people's, so much more generous with their time. Mum was almost forty-four when she had me—they'd been trying for ages. But the awful truth is that I'll lose them sooner.

"Right, then," Dad says, clapping his hands together. The sharp noise brings me out of my gloomy reverie. "Give us a kiss, Pumpkin, and then we'll have the grand tour."

His stubbly face grazes my chin as he leans in to peck me on the cheek. He's called me Pumpkin for as long as I can remember. I don't mind it like I used to, when I was a bolshie teenager. Bolshier than most, probably, because I couldn't rebel like I wanted to. Couldn't stay out late and get drunk in case I had a seizure and put myself at risk. Some of the friends I've met in online support groups tell me they did all sorts of things at that age. Refused to listen to their parents and their doctors. But I was never courageous enough for all that.

"By the way," Dad says, "did Ross sort that dripping tap out? Only I've brought my tools just in case."

Good old Dad. Ever the handyman. Ross might be able to diagnose a case of pleurisy or treat a urinary-tract infection, but I've already worked out that when it comes to asking him to fix anything on the domestic front, I might as well be asking him to fly a rocket to Mars.

Dad drives us to Blackheath Village, although it's hardly a village. I guess it was once, a long time ago. It does have a small-town feel to it, though, with its little shops and eateries, its farmers' market on a Sunday, and the green, open space of the heath. Before moving to London, I used to think of it as one place—a huge, sprawling city—when really it's hundreds of different neighborhoods, all bleeding into each other but unique in their own way. Blackheath is definitely posher than Charlton or Lewisham, for instance. I might be a newcomer to the area, but that much is obvious, and not just from the prices in estate agents' windows.

Mario's is the perfect blend of style and informality. Crisp white tablecloths and immaculate waiting staff, but a relaxed, café-type atmosphere. Mum and I both have a small glass of white wine while Dad drinks sparkling water. I savor every sip. Alcohol can be a trigger for my seizures, along with caffeine and flashing lights, not to mention stress and tiredness, so knowing I can only have the occasional glass makes me appreciate it so much more. I'm enjoying the taste of it on my tongue when Mum says:

"That box we've brought, love, it's bound to stir up a few memories."

Mum glances at Dad and I'm aware of him stiffening beside me. We all know what she's referring to, and it's something we just don't do. At least, not till now.

Dad lays down his knife and fork and takes a long draft of water before speaking. "I said we shouldn't bring it. We can always take it home again. Or straight to the tip."

"No." My voice sounds unnaturally fierce. "No," I repeat, a little more gently this time. "I'm glad you've brought it. Funnily enough, I've been thinking about things recently. What with . . . the news . . ."

Once again, I see the reporter's face and the police tape fluttering behind her. The picture of little Elodie at the top right of the screen.

Then another image, monochrome and stark, superimposes itself over the first. I take another sip of wine.

Mum nods. "We wondered if . . ."

"Dessert, anyone?" Dad says, his eyes flaring like beacons, and suddenly Mum's twittering away about tiramisu and affogato and the moment has passed.

Later that afternoon, as I wave at their retreating car, I think about all the other times a conversation about the past has been thwarted by something as simple as a look, a word, a barely perceptible movement of the head. All those weighted silences. As I walk back into the house and see the box Dad's left in the hall, there's a strange sensation in my gut. The unease is building.

I drag it into the living room, unable to block the myth of Pandora's box from swirling around in my mind. This is different, though. Pandora had no idea what was in the box Zeus gave her, whereas I know exactly what I'll find in here. An icy shiver coils down my spine as the first thing I see is a black tassel sticking out from inside a book. It's time I laid my ghosts to rest.

4

THEN: AFTER

FRIDAY, AUGUST 24, 2007

It's warm outside, but here in the church it's cold and dark. I'm sitting in between Mum and Dad, right at the back by the door. We can hardly see Alice's family from here, just the backs of their bowed heads. We can hear them sniffing, though, and stifling their sobs.

I lift the Order of Service from the slot in the back of the pew in front and draw it toward me. The cream-colored card is stiff in my hand. It has black thread running all the way down the fold and ending in a tassel. There is a photo of Alice on the front. I focus on the knot of her school tie because it's easier than looking at her face. I can't look at her face.

Mr. Davis, the headmaster, and several teachers from school are here, too. So are lots of girls from our class, Melissa Davenport among them. She and her parents are sitting in the same row as Mr. Davis. Why are they sitting there, when we're all the way back here? It's not as if Melissa was even friends with Alice. They were both on the netball team, but they never hung out with each other. Not unless it was a match day. That was the thing about Alice, though—everyone seemed to like her.

When the pallbearers bring the coffin in, there's a terrible wailing from Alice's mum. It reverberates around the high, vaulted roof of the church. An alien noise that makes my insides fold over. Mum's hands are clasped so tight on her lap the knuckles are white. She is swaying backward and forward. Dad's left arm snakes behind our backs, enclosing us both. I rest my head on his shoulder and shut my eyes, but the tears still manage to escape from under the lids.

I can't believe Alice is dead. I mean, I know she *is*. That's why we're here, at her funeral. That's why they've just brought her coffin in. The coffin is white with gold handles and there are flowers and teddies and dolls heaped on top, as if she were a little girl, not a teen-ager, and I can't help thinking that Alice would be embarrassed by the teddies.

The vicar is speaking now. I straighten up and open the Order of Service that lies on my lap, let my eyes travel down the list of readings and hymns, and see that Alice's favorite is here. It's my favorite, too. "Morning Has Broken." We used to sing it in choir practice. Really belt it out.

When we get to that one, I try to sing, but my voice is all weak and trembly, so I mouth the words instead. Mum and Dad are good, strong singers and their voices ring out, like they do every Sunday at church. A couple of heads turn round and look in our direction, but somehow I don't get the feeling they're impressed. One of the heads belongs to Alice's sister, Catherine, and I wish for once that Mum and Dad would *pretend* to sing, like I'm doing, and not draw atten-tion to themselves.

In between the hymns and the readings are pieces of recorded music, chosen by Alice's family. Catherine has chosen "Come Some Rainy Day" by Wynonna Judd, and when that one is played, almost everyone is weeping. It's the sort of song that makes you cry even if you're *not* sad. But when you're sad to start with, it's heartbreaking. Even Dad's shoulders have begun to jerk up and down.

After the service, only Alice's immediate family go to the grave-side. I'm relieved we don't have to. No way could I watch her coffin being lowered into the ground. I keep picturing all the smashed and broken bits of her body in that cramped, dark space. I try not to think of what I saw that day, snagged in the bush.

I stand with Mum and Dad by the church gate and watch as Alice's parents and her sister pick their way through the long grass. Catherine and her dad are either side of her mum, each linking their arm in one of hers, supporting her. She looks so tiny and frail, it's as if Catherine and her dad are the parents and Mrs. Dawson is their little girl. She's wearing a black skirt and jacket, and a little pillbox hat with a black chiffon veil. It's one of the few times I've seen her all dressed up. Usually she's in an old baggy tracksuit, or pajamas and a dressing gown.

When Alice's grandparents and then her uncles, aunts, and cousins approach the grave, I stare at my feet. It seems wrong, somehow, to look at them. Then again, it seems wrong *not* to look. Disrespectful almost.

But as I raise my head Catherine turns round and looks straight at us, like she did in the church. There's something slow and deliberate about the movement of her neck. I tell myself I'm imagining it and that she's going to do that thing people do with their faces when words are useless. But it isn't *us* she's looking at, it's *me*. Her eyes bore into me and a chord of fear vibrates down my spine. She might as well be pointing her finger and saying, "How dare you still be standing there while my little sister is dead! How *dare* you!"

I turn my head and count to ten, wait for the horrible feeling in my chest to go away, the one that makes me ask that very same question. But when I look back, Catherine Dawson hasn't moved. She's still glaring at me, and I wonder if Mum and Dad have noticed, too, but they're both studying their shoes.

Afterward, when everyone else goes back to Alice's house for the wake, we go home. When Dad starts up the car, I see Catherine huddled with Melissa Davenport and some of the other girls from my class. They are all holding each other's shoulders and crying. A lump forms at the back of my throat. I should be there, too, crying with them, being supported. Alice was *my* best friend, not Melissa's. As we drive past the church, Catherine lifts her eyes and fixes that same withering stare on me once more.

It's like . . . it's like she knows it's my fault.

———————————
———————————

After we buried the ash in the garden, we sat on the canvas swing chair, our bare legs dangling.

"Look," she said, pointing upward. "Isn't it beautiful?"

The sun was poised on the horizon—a shimmering red sphere. I tried to see it as beautiful, but all I could think of were flames and gases and unbearable, searing heat. The clouds weren't white and fluffy anymore. They were long, jagged streaks, tinged with violet and pink. An epic sky, like a warning from God. It made me tremble to see it and I had to look away. Because I knew what was coming.

We stayed on that chair for what seemed like hours, swinging gently back and forth, chatting and giggling, as if nothing had changed. We stayed there till the night crept round us and goosebumps pricked our arms. We stayed till her mother drifted toward us like a wraith.

It was time for me to leave.

5

NOW

After supper, Ross and I sit on the sofa watching the telly, but I can't focus on anything. My eyes keep straying to the box Mum and Dad brought over. Dad was right. They should have taken it straight to the tip.

It doesn't sit well with me, not telling Ross about Alice. We shouldn't have secrets from each other. I know there are things in his past he doesn't like to talk about—the dark period after his mum died—but at least I know that happened. I have the bare bones of it. Whereas this pivotal event in my life—my best friend getting killed by a train, me being there when it happened—I should have told him by now.

When the adverts come on, Ross turns the volume down and shifts position so that he's facing me.

"What do you think about having a housewarming party?" he says.

The suggestion throws me. I stare at the muted screen, trying to think of what to say. I'm not a great fan of parties. Standing around in a room full of strangers. Watching everyone else get drunk while I'm sipping yet another soft drink. Frankly, I'm amazed he's even suggested it. What with one of the partners at the surgery being on long-term sick leave and a succession of unreliable locums, he's been rushed off his feet and stressed out by work ever since we moved in. I didn't think he'd have the time or energy to contemplate having a party.

"I thought it might be nice," he says, and there's such an eager expression on his face that for a few seconds I see the little boy he once was—the little boy who lost his mother. "I could invite my colleagues from the practice. And some of the old gang, of course."

The old gang—the guys he trained with at Imperial College and played rugby with. I try to picture them all squeezed into this room, laughing and telling embarrassing medical anecdotes, or worse still, reliving their laddish exploits. I could do without all that, to be honest, but it's about time I met the people he works with. About time they met *me*. It won't do any harm for all those nurses and receptionists and secretaries to meet Dr. Murray's fiancée. Do they even know we're engaged? Because if not, it's about time they did.

"All right," I say, before I can change my mind. "Let's do it!"

Later, though, as we're climbing into bed, I'm already starting to regret the idea.

"When exactly were you thinking of having it?"

"I dunno. Next Saturday?"

I think of all the boxes still cluttering up the living room, and one in particular. The one that's been exerting its siren call on me ever since it arrived in the house.

"But that only gives us a week, and we haven't unpacked half our stuff yet."

Ross laughs. "Lizzie, it's a housewarming party. People will expect a few boxes."

Visions of drunken strangers helping us unpack flit through my mind: cardboard and newspaper scattered all over the floor, our possessions being plonked in strange and hilarious places. Sometimes I wish I was less uptight about these things. A fun-loving party girl. Someone who could down tequila slammers and Jägerbombs.

"Tell you what," he says, leaning over to switch his lamp off, "we'll have it in a few weeks. What about the first Saturday in April? That'll give us time to go to Ikea and buy some more glasses. I can let people know tomorrow."

I go to switch my lamp off, too, but before I can reach it Ross straddles me and his hands are in my hair.

I giggle and raise my arms above my head, let him slip my top off and fling it on the floor. "Now then, Miss Molyneux," he says, in his best impersonation of Sean Connery's James Bond talking to Miss Moneypenny, "please lie very still while I carry out a totally unnecessary breast examination. It's an innovative technique, part of the new NICE guidelines," he adds, deadly serious. "I shall be using only my mouth."

I lie on my back, sweat cooling on my skin, till the nightmare fades. The one where a train is bearing down on me and I can't move my feet. Can't run away in time. I've had it before, lots of times, but not for ages. I always wake a split second before the impact, the deafening whine of the engine still roaring in my ears. I must have fallen into a deep sleep as soon as Ross left for work this morning. That'll teach me to close my eyes again.

I go to the bathroom for a shower, let the water drum down fast and furious on my head. Things will return to normal soon. The news of poor little Elodie's death will disappear from the headlines. Another story will take its place and the demons will hunker back down in whatever recess of my mind they inhabit. Until the next time some poor child dies on a railway line.

After I've had my breakfast and taken my medication, I potter about the house and make a halfhearted attempt to tidy things up. I'm procrastinating, I know I am. Putting off dealing with the contents of that box. There are still so many other boxes to unpack, so many things to find a place for, but right now, I can't face any of it. I feel restless and out of sorts. It's that nightmare. It must be.

When the phone rings I go into the bedroom to answer it. Recording an answerphone message is yet another thing I need to do. But all I can hear when I pick up is a weird muffled sound before the line goes dead. It's like the one I had yesterday, which I assumed was Mum. Although I'm sure I heard a faint voice in the background this time, almost like a voice on a PA system. How strange. I dial 1471, but it's a withheld number. Oh, well, if it's important, I'm sure they'll ring back.

I'm just about to do a bit more unpacking when a much better idea occurs to me. I retrieve the local paper from the small pile of junk I've left by the front door and turn to the advert I was thinking about yesterday. The one for the open day at Greenwich University. It's taking place this afternoon. I read it again. Maybe noticing this was a sign. Serendipity, isn't that what it's called?

My epilepsy's under control now and it's time to make something of my life. Perhaps I could even do a PhD one day. Then there'll be *two* doctors in the house. I smile. Getting ahead of myself, as usual. But I'll definitely go along later and see what it's like. It's good to have something other than the past to focus on. It's good to have a plan.

6

I've passed through Greenwich lots of times on the bus, enjoying the sight of the elegant quadrants and colonnaded facades of the Old Royal Naval College, but now that I'm actually walking through the campus I can't shake the idea of studying here from my head. Sometimes I get a strong feeling about a place. An affinity for it. As if I know, without a shadow of a doubt, that I'll come back, or that it will have some special significance for me. All this grand baroque architecture, all this history. I feel inspired just *being* here.

"No wonder they use this location for so many films," says the girl walking next to me. We've just bonded over a croissant and coffee in the café under the chapel in Queen Mary Court.

"I know, I keep expecting Johnny Depp in full Captain Jack costume to leap out from behind one of these pillars."

I'm delighted at how easily we've fallen into conversation. How fast we've clicked. It was the right decision to come here today. I've got a stack of information already and I get the distinct impression from the tutor I've just spoken to that, with my A-level grades and the fact that I'm a mature student—*mature*, it makes me sound like a ripe cheese—I'll be in with a good chance of being offered a place. What's more, if I study part time, I can even apply direct, without all the rigmarole of going through UCAS.

It'll be expensive, of course, but Mum and Dad have always said they'd help me out financially if I wanted to do a course. I can apply for a student loan as well. It'll mean giving up on the idea of a full-time job, for the time being at least, but ultimately, I'll be better qualified. And Ross is hardly likely to complain, not after the conversation we had the other day.

The sun twinkles on the River Thames and the sound of violins floats out of the open windows of King Charles Court, where the Trinity Laban music students are doing their practice. It's a beautiful piece of music, something classical I vaguely recognize but can't name. The type of music that fits this setting perfectly. It's like having my own personal soundtrack, and I imagine walking back from the library with my fellow students, books under our arms, exchanging confidences between lectures, discussing what we're reading and the assignments we've been set.

As we pass the Painted Hall, one of the violinists plays a discordant note and the music comes to an abrupt stop. The noise is so ugly and jarring, so thoroughly unexpected, that I recoil almost as if I've been shot, suddenly feeling as fragile as a blown egg. My new friend turns to me, one eyebrow raised, a wry look of amusement on her face, and I feel foolish and embarrassed about my extreme reaction.

"You must be a nightmare to watch a scary film with," she says.

I don't tell her that I never watch scary films, that there's enough horror in my head to last a lifetime, thank you very much. No, I don't tell her that. I just laugh and say, "Yes, I am."

When I get off at the bus stop on Little Heath and turn in to the side street that leads to our house, I ring Mum and tell her about my plans. She puts me on loudspeaker so Dad can hear, too. She sounds really pleased—they both do.

"Your dad's always said you'd make a good academic. We always wanted you to go to uni, but you were so adamant you didn't want to."

I can't help smiling at her version of events. What actually happened was that they did everything they could to persuade me to go to the local university so that I could still live at home with them. They were terrified I'd go to Edinburgh or Aberystwyth or somewhere miles away and they wouldn't be there to protect me. In the end, I decided not to go at all. I wasn't ready.

We chat for a little longer about this and that. Mum's plans for turning my old bedroom into her craft room. Dad's new shed.

I laugh. "How many sheds does one man need?"

"Three," Dad says in the background. "Ross has got a lot of catching up to do."

We say goodbye and I tuck my phone into the top pocket of my coat. The warm spring weather has brought the cherry blossom out early and transformed the gray uniformity of our street into something pink and hopeful and pretty. It's that time of year when anything seems possible. A time of new beginnings. New growth.

When I used to come down to London on the train to visit Ross in his old flat, I couldn't imagine living here. But now that I am, I'm seeing things in a different light. I'm starting to appreciate that wonderful sense of anonymity as I go about my business. It's so different from the small-town life I'm used to.

As I approach the house, I notice that someone has balanced a toy truck—one of those little metal ones—on top of the low brick wall enclosing the strip of concrete that passes for our front garden. For some reason, our wall seems to have been designated as the home for the street's lost property. The day we moved in, it was a man's leather glove.

Ross once joked that whatever you leave outside your house in London, someone will invariably take it, and that sometimes it's cheaper than going to the tip. Which might explain the chest of drawers that's been plonked on the pavement at the other end of the street.

It's only when I come a little closer that I realize this isn't a toy truck.

My stomach clenches. It's a little train.

7

THEN: AFTER

MONDAY, AUGUST 27, 2007

It's been three days since Alice's funeral, and I haven't left the house. There's nothing to leave it *for*. Not now Alice is gone.

Dad suggested we drive to the seaside. Walk along the promenade and have an ice cream. Sit on the beach. But Mum's had a migraine since yesterday and I said I didn't want to eat ice cream and pretend everything was normal, because it isn't. How can it be normal when I've spent the last few weeks being interviewed by the police and going to see a counselor? How can it be normal when Mum and Dad keep talking in hushed voices whenever I leave the room and stop the minute I come in?

How will anything be normal ever again?

It's nighttime now and I'm lying in bed, trying to sleep. Mum brought me some hot chocolate to drink about an hour ago. She lay on the bed with me and stroked my arms with the tips of her fingernails, the way she used to when I was a little girl. Scratchy tickle, I used to call it. "You're still my little girl," she said. "And I hate seeing you so sad."

I hate seeing *her* sad, too. And Dad. It's as if all the stuffing's gone out of them. They look old and ill. A horrible woman in the super-market told Mum that if I was her daughter she'd spank the living daylights out of me until I told the truth, and that Mick and Sheena Dawson have a right to know why Alice died.

Mum doesn't know I know this. I heard her telling Dad in the kitchen when they thought I was upstairs. Dad got really angry and made her tell him who it was, but she didn't know. "What did she look like?" he said, and the way Mum described her, I thought it sounded like Melissa Davenport's mum. "Why are people so igno-rant?" he said.

My fingers curl into fists and my nails dig into the soft flesh of my palms. What's it going to be like going back to school? Everyone star-ing at me and whispering behind my back. Someone put a note through the door yesterday. It was in a little flowery envelope ad-dressed to me and, idiot that I am, I thought it was a sympathy card. Someone saying how sorry they were that I'd lost my best friend. But inside was a page torn roughly from a notebook, and on it the words *"You killed Alice, you epileptic ginger freak"* in big red letters.

I should have shown it to Mum and Dad, but I was too ashamed. Couldn't bear to see their shocked faces. Didn't want to hear Mum telling me all the usual stuff, like "You have to feel sorry for people like that, Lizzie. You have to pray for them."

No *way* am I going to pray for the person who sent me that note. And no way was I going to upset my parents even more by showing it to them. I put it through Dad's shredder so I didn't have to look at it anymore. But the words are still in my head. They always will be now. Along with everything else I don't want to think about.

Eventually, my limbs grow heavy and I feel myself sinking deep into the mattress. Suddenly, I jolt awake. Something has just hit my bedroom window. It sounded like a stone.

I get up and peer out at the dark, empty street. Maybe I was dream-ing. I'm about to let the curtain fall when a figure emerges from be-hind the hedge. I drop the curtain, heart thumping in fear. Someone really *is* out there.

I move to the side of the window and peer round the very edge of the curtain. The figure is still there, staring up at me, and for one heart-stopping moment I think it's Alice, come back from the grave, but whoever this is, she's taller than Alice. She's dressed in jeans and a shirt, a long scarf wrapped round her neck and the lower half of her face.

She stares up at the window, slowly unwinding the scarf with one hand. My breath freezes at the back of my throat. It's Catherine Dawson, her hair fanning out in the breeze, her accusing eyes drilling into my face, just like they did at the funeral. Did she send me that note as well? What kind of adult does that to a child?

I want to open the window and yell at her to leave me alone, but all I can do is stand and stare, transfixed by those terrible, hate-filled eyes. At last, she turns and walks away without a backward glance. I hear the *clack clack clack* of her high heels on the pavement, stand there listening to the sound get fainter and fainter. I won't sleep again tonight.

8

NOW

I pick up the toy train and examine it, trying to ignore the sick little feeling in my stomach. It must once have been bright blue but is now patinated with scrapes that reveal the gray of the diecast metal. By the looks of it, more than one generation of children have rolled this little train along the ground and sent it careening into walls.

I place it back where it was and scan the street in both directions in the hope of seeing the child who might have dropped it. The sick feeling intensifies. What's wrong with me lately? I pull my key out of my handbag and go inside, determined to tackle that box of memories Mum and Dad brought over. Maybe then I won't see a kid's toy train as some kind of ominous portent. Won't have this vague sense of dread hovering over me all the time.

Five minutes later, I'm kneeling on the floor of the living room, drawing out a well-thumbed copy of *A Little Princess*. I flick through its brittle, yellowing pages, remembering how closely I identified with poor Sara Crewe, humiliated by the vile Miss Minchin, taunted by Lavinia and the other horrid girls. I knew exactly how *that* felt.

The Order of Service for Alice's funeral is where I left it yesterday, wedged down the side. I prize it out and tear it up before I can change my mind. The black-and-white pieces of card flutter into the bin bag like charred confetti. Then I pile the books onto the floor and reach down to the layer of colored exercise books underneath. *Don't even think about opening them,* says a voice inside my head.

I grab a handful, trying not to read my tiny, neat handwriting on the front of each one. Not that I need to. The topics come back to me easily. Yellow for history, orange for maths, red for English, and pink for German. Then there was gray for French and purple for geography. But the green ones—what were they? I rack my brain, but it's no good. I lift a cover and peek inside.

Science. Of course. I turn the pages and find the summary I wrote on dissecting a heart, my childish handwriting so familiar and yet so different from the way I write now. It's funny, reading this again. The time Mr. Chatterjee asked us all to choose a partner and bring a pig's heart in so we could dissect it in pairs. Except Alice's dad, who was a butcher, thought he'd go one better and gave us an ox heart.

I couldn't believe it when Alice took it out of the plastic bag and brandished it in front of me. I had to hold on to the bench for support while she stuck her latex-gloved fingers into the slab of wet, raw heart that was three times the size of everyone else's.

"There's still some dried blood in the chambers, sir," Alice had said. She always loved the practicals.

"Well, rinse it out, then," Mr. Chatterjee snapped, and since Alice was doing all the cutting, it was me who had to carry the huge, slippery mound over to the sink and hold it under the tap. As the pink water swirled down the plug hole, I retched over it. Nearly fainted. Alice couldn't stop laughing and Mr. Chatterjee got really cross.

We laughed so much, the two of us. If only I could blank out all the dreadful things that followed. The terrible way Alice died. The hatred in her sister's eyes. The rumors and the bullying.

My heart beats furiously at the back of my throat. One moment of idle curiosity about what lay between the covers of an old school exercise book, and the past has come reeling back. I drop the book into the bin bag along with the others and squash the memories down. This ends *now*.

Outside, it's sunny and bright. I tip the contents of the bag into the blue wheelie bin that stands outside the front door like a sentry box. Soon, all those sentences and diagrams and sums, all those verb conjugations and clumsily sketched maps will be carted away and turned into pulp, ready for spreading and rolling out and starting all over again. If only memories could be recycled so easily.

Above the hum of traffic I hear birdsong and a peal of distant laughter. In the garden of one of the slightly bigger houses on the other side of the street, a magnolia tree is just coming into bloom, the tightly coiled flower buds like pink flames against the sky. I take a minute to stand on the doorstep and fill my lungs with air. Now that I've got rid of this lot, I feel freer. Lighter. I turn to enter the house, galvanized by my decision to apply for a place at uni. I'm going to surprise Ross and make a nice chili for supper. We've been eating too many ready-meals lately.

I almost don't answer the phone. But in the end, I do. Just in case it's something important.

Damn. There it is again. That odd muffled sound, only this time it's getting louder. Alarm flutters in my chest like a trapped bird. My skull vibrates. This time it sounds like . . .

I drop the phone to the floor. This time it sounds like a train.

9

My hand is clammy with sweat as I pick up the receiver from the floor. The line is dead. With trembling fingers, I stab the numbers on the dial pad: 1471. "The caller withheld their number."

I yank the plug out of the wall, my pulse still thudding in my ears. There must be a logical explanation for this. There *must* be. It's got nothing to do with that toy train on the wall. The two things are *not* connected. Of course they're not. Someone was phoning me from a station and a train went by. That's all it was. Probably the same person who's called before a couple of times. They've realized they keep phoning the wrong number and are too embarrassed to say anything. I've done that myself in the past.

Maybe it *wasn't* a train. It could have been something else. Another sort of engine. I didn't even listen to it properly. I dropped the phone. Why do I always jump to the worst possible conclusion?

After a while, I feel brave enough to plug the unit back in. Ross usually calls me on my mobile, but what if my parents have an emergency? I can't have the phone out of action. Ross has left the instruction booklet out and I flip the pages to the index at the back, find the page number for setting up the answerphone. If it rings again, I won't answer it unless it's someone I know.

As soon as this is done, I try to calm myself down by starting on the chili. Ross taught me how to make it when we first got together, along with spaghetti bolognese and shepherd's pie. Maybe one of these days I'll move on to recipes that don't involve mince.

As I chop the onions into tiny chunks and fry them till they're soft and translucent, my heartbeat returns to normal. By the time I've laid the table and lit a candle, I've made a decision. I need to tell Ross about Alice. I've been stupid, keeping it from him. This is the man I love. We're going to get married.

I should speak to my parents, too. We can't keep skating round the subject for the rest of our lives, as if it never happened. That awkward moment in the restaurant yesterday was totally unnecessary. My best friend died. I was there when it happened. Except I wasn't, was I? My body might have been, but my mind wasn't. It was an accident. The coroner said so, didn't she?

When half past seven comes and goes with no sign of Ross, I turn the gas off. He's probably catching up on his paperwork. Even so, he could have rung. I drift into the living room with a cream cracker. Now that I've made up my mind to tell him, I want to do it right away. I don't want to waste any more time.

By eight o'clock, my stomach is rumbling. Where the hell is he? I ring his mobile but it switches straight to voicemail. I can't bring myself to leave a message. I don't want to sound like the nagging girlfriend, checking up on him. Surely he'll notice the missed call and ring back?

By half past eight, I've munched my way through four crackers. By nine, I've rung him five times. If I don't eat soon, I'll be ravenous, and that's not good for my epilepsy. Being seizure-free for the last two years isn't just down to my medication. It's about me being disci- plined and monitoring my health as closely as I can, not taking any

unnecessary risks. Avoiding triggers. Like stress and hunger. Hmm.
I'm not doing very well today.

I hear his key in the door just as I'm spooning some rice onto a
plate and heating up a portion of the chili in a small pan just for me,
which is what I should have done two hours ago. He breezes into the
kitchen, and it's a real struggle to keep the anger and disappointment
from my face.

His eyes take in the pans on the stove and widen in surprise. "Hey,
you've made a chili."

He washes his hands at the sink. "I did tell you, didn't I? That I was
doing home visits this evening?"

I stare at him. "No, you didn't. I wouldn't have made this otherwise."

"Shit. I've had so much work stuff on my mind lately. I was *sure* I'd
told you." He dries his hands on the tea towel. "Never mind, it'll last,
won't it, in the fridge? We can have it tomorrow."

"Don't you want any now, then?"

He gives me a sheepish look. "I'm really sorry, but . . . I ate something earlier."

He goes to the fridge for a beer. "The new practice nurse had to
attend one of my visits as a chaperone." I stop stirring the chili. "We
had chicken and chips to keep us going."

My hand tightens round the wooden spoon. "You definitely didn't
say anything this morning about having to do home visits."

"I should have rung you. I'm sorry. The chicken and chips were
shit as well. I'd much rather have had your chili." He grins. "It smells
almost as good as one of mine." He puts his beer on the counter and
draws me to his chest. "You're not angry with me, are you?"

"Of course not. It's no big deal."

Actually, I'm livid, especially at the thought of him grabbing a bite
to eat with a nurse while I've been stuck at home checking my phone
every five minutes, but there's no way I'm telling him that. He's right.
It's all just a misunderstanding and I've overreacted.

He picks up his beer. "Come on, I'll sit with you while you eat. You must be starving if you've waited this long."

We go and sit on the sofa in the living room, using one of the unpacked boxes as a table. The evening can still be salvaged. Although I don't think I'm strong enough to tell him about Alice now. There's been quite enough emotion for one day.

"I went to Greenwich University this afternoon," I say instead. "They had an open day."

Ross looks at me, surprised. "You didn't say anything about that," he says.

Just like you didn't say anything about working late, I almost say, but stop myself just in time. He warned me when we first got together how overworked GPs are. He's bound to forget things sometimes and I know how difficult it is for him to have to do home visits on top of his already heavy workload. Plus, there's even more for him to worry about now that he's decided to go for the new partnership position that's coming up.

"It was advertised in the local paper. I only looked at it properly this morning."

"And?"

"And I really like the sound of doing an English degree."

Ross takes a swig from his beer. "Just so long as you don't meet a good-looking, earnest young man who wants to read you poetry and get in your knickers. Because you've already got one of those at home."

"I don't remember you ever reading me poetry?"

"True, but I am good-looking." He gives me a worried look. "Would you *like* me to read you poetry?"

I laugh. "No, you're all right, thanks. I appreciate the offer, though."

Later, when we're in bed, I picture myself at the Greenwich Maritime campus, sprawled on the grass by the river, nose deep in a nineteenth-century novel. I feel myself drifting off. Then someone walks by the house in high heels. My eyes snap open and it's like I'm thirteen years old all over again, fistfuls of duvet tight round my neck, waiting for Catherine Dawson to get bored with tormenting me and walk away.

I snuggle up to Ross. His muscular body is warm to the touch and the strength of it comforts me. I close my eyes. All the bad things are in the past. Catherine can't hurt me now.

10

THEN: AFTER

TUESDAY, SEPTEMBER 4, 2007

We've been told to assemble in the refectory to meet our form teachers and collect our timetables. I usually enjoy the first day back after the summer holiday. Now I'm dreading it. Walking through the school gates on my own. Seeing Melissa Davenport and the others for the first time since Alice's funeral. Everyone looking at me. And the worst thing of all is that I've lost my friend and ally. The one person who made everything all right. Who made me feel normal. I can't believe she's gone and that the last words I spoke to her were full of spite.

This time two years ago, we were giggling behind our hands at the form teacher's wacky dress sense, getting lost together in the endless corridors as we searched for the art department or the science labs, bonding over our packed lunches. When Alice's mum was ill, her dad just chucked a load of random items into her lunch box: half a packet of peanuts, a roughly peeled carrot, and a chocolate biscuit, or a Marmite sandwich made with two crusts. On Alice's "bad lunch days," we always shared mine.

I swallow the knot in my throat. I can't believe we'll never sit at the picnic benches in the playground again, trying to split a Mr. Kipling Bakewell tart in half with the handle of a plastic spoon. It doesn't seem possible that she's dead.

I see the girls in my class long before they see me. They're halfway along the wide concrete path that leads to the main block and reception, gathered in a big group outside one of the prefabs.

"Try not to take any notice if they say anything silly or hurtful," Mum said this morning, before I left the house. "Rise above it."

I'm getting closer to them now, but they still haven't seen me. They're too busy talking and messing around with a couple of boys from the year above us. Then one of them spots me and says something I can't hear. They all stare at me as I walk past. I think of Mum's advice and imagine myself rising above them, far up into the sky like an angel, my delicate wings fluttering in the breeze. But it doesn't work. I knew it wouldn't. My cheeks go red.

"Here she is. The girl who pushed Alice Dawson in front of a train."

I stop dead and swing round to face Melissa Davenport. I can't let her get away with that. I just can't.

"No, I didn't! Alice was my best friend! I had a seizure, you *know* I did."

"So you say," she taunts. "We've only got your word for that."

"Why would I lie?"

"Because you don't want to go to prison," she says.

Tears of anger prick the backs of my eyes. "You're talking bollocks!" I say, and they all pretend to be shocked at my language, even though they say far worse things than that all the time.

Melissa steps toward me, a horrible mean expression on her face, but I stand my ground. I won't let her get to me.

"Wash your mouth out with soap, you ginger freak!" she snarls in my face. Someone in the group sniggers and one of the older boys meows like a cat.

"Alice's sister knows what kind of person you are." Melissa sneers at me. "She says you're evil. She knew it from the first time she set

eyes on you. You were jealous of Alice coz she was prettier than you.
She didn't want to be friends with you anymore so you killed her. You
might think you got away with it, but we know the truth. And so does
he." She points her index finger toward the sky.

I launch myself forward and yank her finger right back as far as it
goes. She lets out a bloodcurdling scream and stumbles back. "She's
broken my finger. The evil bitch has broken my finger!"

"No, I fucking haven't!"

"She has! She really has!"

The headmaster's office always smells. Alice once joked it smelled of
fart and aftershave, and the memory makes me smile.

"What's so funny, Lizzie?"

"Nothing, sir. I was just thinking of something Alice used to say."

He sighs deeply and laces his fingers together on top of his desk.
"The last couple of months must have been awful for you," he says, and
before I know what's happening, tears are streaming down my face.

Mr. Davis pushes a box of tissues toward me and waits while I
wipe my eyes and blow my nose.

"Luckily, there's no damage to Melissa's finger, but I want you to
promise me that you won't do anything like that again."

"But she said I killed Alice! It's not fair. Why aren't you making
her promise she won't say things like that again?"

"I'll be talking to Melissa in a moment. But whatever she did or
didn't say, attacking someone is never the right thing to do."

"I didn't attack her, I . . ."

I look down at my shoes. I *did* attack her and I can't pretend otherwise. It's a miracle I didn't snap her finger right off. Now I've made
things a whole lot worse for myself. Everyone's going to think I've got
violent tendencies. Melissa will tell her parents and they'll talk to the
Dawsons, and then the police will want to talk to me again and
maybe the coroner will change her verdict and I'll have to go to court
and it'll be in the papers, and it's all Catherine Dawson's fault. Catherine Dawson is the evil one. Not me.

11

NOW

On Saturday morning, I'm already up when Ross comes down in his lounge pants and T-shirt. He peers over my shoulder as I scroll through the Greenwich University website.

"If you're going to do a degree," he says, "you'll need somewhere to do your assignments. Maybe we could put a desk in the spare room."

He's right. We might call this room *the* study, but we both know it's really his. Just like the house. When Ross first suggested that I move in with him, I told him I'd feel guilty about not being able to contribute to the bills, at least not until I'd found a job. "But we're a couple, aren't we?" he said. "And couples look after each other. Besides, it's going to be your house, too. As soon as we're married, we'll get the deeds put in our joint names."

He leans across me to reach for his diary and, as he does, his eyes settle on the photo of his mother that he's slid under the edge of the notice-board frame to avoid putting a pin in it. She's wearing a long black raincoat and smiling, shyly, at the camera. It's one of the few pictures he has of her.

"You should get a frame for that."

"I know," he says. "I keep meaning to."

"I wish I'd met her," I say, and make a mental note to buy a frame for it myself. Surprise him with it.

"You'd have loved her," he says, his voice gravelly with emotion.

He leans forward to take a closer look. "I remember taking this picture," he says. "It was the week after my birthday and the camera was a present—one of those cheap disposable things. She was walking me to school." He clears his throat. "That was when we talked the most, when she escaped the house. And my dad."

It's the first time he's mentioned his father in ages and I wonder whether now might be a good time to suggest a visit. Surely it's time the two of them made their peace. I don't care if he *is* the cantankerous old bully Ross says he is. He's still Ross's dad. And he's in a nursing home now.

"About your dad," I say, but before I can finish my sentence he's shaking his head and reaching for his briefcase.

"I know what you're going to say, Lizzie, but you don't know what he's like. He made Mum's life a misery. And mine." He pulls out an overstuffed buff folder and plonks it on the desk.

"I tried to persuade him to move nearer London, but he insisted on staying in Aberdeen. There's no way I'm trekking all the way up there to sit and listen to his self-pitying rants."

He breaks into an impersonation of his father. "Ah dinnae wantae die in Englan."

I can't help smiling. Most of the time I forget about Ross's Scottish roots. He's lived in England so long he's lost most of his accent. I only hear traces of it now when he's watching Aberdeen play Rangers.

"Isn't he lonely, up there on his own?"

Ross gives one of those sneering laughs through his teeth. "The Jim Murrays of this world are never short of companions. Other blokes talking shite." He takes a deep breath. "It's real friends and family they can't keep hold of."

He opens his diary and his face crumples. "Shit!"

"What's the matter?"

"I asked Gloria if I could have a meeting with her about the partnership position yesterday then forgot all about it."

Gloria Williams is the senior partner at Plumtree Lodge. If Ross is to stand any chance of being offered that partnership, he needs to keep in her good books.

"Can't you speak to her on Monday?"

"I'll have to, although it doesn't look very professional, does it? Arranging a meeting then not turning up."

It's not like Ross to forget something like that. He must be more stressed at work than I thought.

"Would it be the end of the world if you didn't get offered a partnership? I mean, there's plenty of time for all that, isn't there? And what's wrong with being a salaried GP?"

"Nothing really. Regular hours. None of the hassles of management." He laughs at the face I'm pulling. "Yeah, yeah, I can see what you're thinking. But I want more input into the running of the practice. Anyway, it's what I've always wanted at this stage of my career."

I stand up and put my arms round his waist, rest my head against his shoulder. I love the fact that he's so ambitious, so driven. Although a small, selfish part of me can't help wondering how much less of him I'll see if he becomes a partner. Having more responsibility and more money is all well and good, but that comes at a price. I dread to think how much his workload will increase if he ends up getting this partnership.

"Have you invited Gloria to the party?"

"Of course. I've invited all the partners and their other halves. I've even invited Smethers, my archrival." He chuckles, but I know he's only half joking. Andrew Smethers is his main competition for the partnership position. "You wait till you meet his wife. She's had so much work done on her face she looks like an anesthetized fish."

I laugh along with him, but, honestly, the closer we get to this bloody party, the more I'm dreading it. What are Ross's colleagues going to think when they meet me? The girlfriend who doesn't even have a job. I wish I'd never agreed to the idea in the first place.

"So how many from the surgery did you invite?"

"Everyone, of course."

I take a step back. "Everyone? Oh my God, Ross! How many is that?"

"Don't worry. They won't all come. I could hardly invite some and not others. News spreads faster than norovirus in that place."

His fingers stroke the back of my neck. "It's such a pity all your friends live so far away."

I nod. He makes it sound like there are loads of them, but after my parents and I moved to Dovercourt to make a fresh start, most of the girls at my new school had already formed their friendship groups. I made friends eventually, still see a few of them from time to time, still talk on the phone with them every now and again. But Callie's teaching English in Spain now and only comes back a few times a year, and Becca's based in Carlisle. I can hardly expect them to trek all the way to London for a housewarming party. I'm going to have to make some new friends. People who live round here. Like that girl I met at the open day. I should have taken her number, suggested we meet up.

"Lizzie? Are you okay?"

I stare at him in confusion. Why is he giving me that strange look?

"Sweetheart, I think you've just had a partial. You were staring past me."

I try not to look as crestfallen as I feel. I haven't had one of those in ages — at least, I don't *think* I have — and although they're relatively harmless, I still feel unnerved when they're pointed out to me.

He gives me a hug. "Don't look so worried, darling. It was only a tiny one."

"But what if I start getting more? What if the big ones come back, too?"

Ross steps back and assumes his "I'm a doctor so listen to me" face. "Worrying about the possibility of something happening is pointless. It's not as if you have any control over it, so you might as well *not* worry."

I roll my eyes. He can be maddeningly logical at times, and though I know what he says makes sense, it's not what I want to hear right now. I want him to put his arms round me and tell me that it won't come back. Not ever. Which is, of course, the one thing he *won't* say. Because he's a doctor, and no self-respecting doctor ever makes a promise they can't keep. Even to his fiancée. To be fair, I probably wouldn't believe him even if he *did* say that.

"That, if you don't mind me saying, is a typical male response."

He pretends to look upset. "Are you saying I'm a typical male? And there was me, thinking I was special."

I give him a playful push, but later, when he's spread his papers all over the dining-room table and I'm on my own again in the study, the anxiety returns. Maybe Ross *did* tell me he was going to be late the other night and I missed it because of a partial. I think I've underestimated how much stress this Elodie Stevens story has triggered, not to mention sorting through that wretched box and all the memories it's dredged up.

I'm worried about other things, too. Things I can't tell him because I can't put them into words but that seem to be gathering around me. Nameless, shapeless fears rising to the surface once more.

———————

"One day we'll have babies of our own," she said. "I've made a list of possible names."

She brushed an ant from her leg and flicked it across the patio.

"Did you know that an ant can lift twenty times its own body weight?" I said.

She rolled her eyes and I felt my cheeks redden. Why on earth was I talking about ants? If I wasn't careful, she'd find someone else to hang out with. I used to think that that bad thing we'd done would bind us together forever, but lately, I wasn't so sure.

I couldn't bear the thought of losing her.

12

It's the night of the housewarming party and the guests should be arriving any time now. The last three weeks have flown by. The spring weather has been glorious—it's been the tenth-warmest March on record. There haven't been any more of those strange phone calls, thank goodness, and the papers have at last moved on from the Elodie Stevens story. Plus, I've unpacked the last of the boxes *and* filled in the application form for Greenwich University. The only fly in the ointment is the nonappearance of my period.

I think of the impulse purchase I made in Boots yesterday, the pregnancy test that's still tucked at the bottom of my handbag. We had sex without a condom a few weeks ago and it's been playing on my mind, along with everything else. Ross withdrew in time, I'm sure he did, but still, I'm usually as regular as clockwork.

I don't want a baby. I mean, I *do*, one day. I'd *love* to be a mother. But not yet, not when my options are finally opening up. It's been wonderful these last two years. Not having any major seizures. Falling in love with Ross. Living a normal life at last. Something I never dared believe would happen.

I'm not pregnant, I can't be. I'm just a few days late, that's all.

Ross points the remote at the stereo in the living room and the mellow tones of John Legend singing "All of Me" float out of the speakers. We slow-dance, my head resting against his chest.

"The house looks incredible," he says. "I feel bad that you've had to do everything on your own. You've worked so hard."

"It does. You should. And I have," I say, enjoying the moment of closeness and gazing over his shoulder at the fairy lights strung around the mirror over the fireplace. I really panicked this morning when he had to go out on two emergency calls. But somehow, I've accomplished every task on my list, and most of the ones on his. It took me ages to get those lights looking right, and what with all the candles twinkling away, the living room now has the feel of a magical grotto. Housewarming. It's an apt name. The house does indeed feel warmer. Must be all those candles.

When the doorbell goes, we spring apart and into action—Ross to the front door and me into the kitchen to start cutting the bread. I feel awkward all of a sudden, wooden and unnatural, as if I've forgotten how to do something as simple as walk into my own kitchen. By the time Ross reappears with a well-dressed couple in their late thirties bearing wine and flowers, I've managed to drop one end of a baguette into the washing-up bowl. I whisk it out, hoping they haven't noticed.

"Darling, this is Andrew Smethers and his wife, Trina."

Wow. Ross was right about the cosmetic surgery, but it's been very well done. She looks amazing and nothing whatsoever like an "anesthetized fish." I make a note to tell him off for being so mean.

"Pleased to meet you," I say.

Trina Smethers leans forward and kisses me on both cheeks. It's much more of a city thing, all this kissing. I'm gradually getting used to it. Next to Trina, I feel big and awkward, although we're probably the same dress size. I brace myself for the small talk and the inevitable question about what I do for a living. What can I say that won't make me sound like a sad relic from the 1950s?

As it happens, I don't have to say anything because she gives me the loveliest smile, thanks me for inviting them, and steps aside so that her husband can take his turn at greeting me. I know Ross is a little wary of Andrew Smethers, what with them both vying for the same partnership position, but he seems really nice, and so does his wife.

The doorbell rings again. And so it begins. The voices, the laughter, the music. The popping of corks and the clinking of glasses. It's nowhere near as bad as I thought it would be. In fact, now that it's happening, I'm rather enjoying it. I thought I'd feel like a single guest at my own party, that it would remind me of all those dreadful school discos I used to go to, skulking in corners while everyone else had a good time, praying I wouldn't embarrass myself by having a seizure.

Ross is on his third beer already, and I'm sure he had a cigarette in the garden earlier, even though he's meant to have given up. For all his laid-back approach to the preparations, I can see how important it is to him that this party is a success. He beckons me over to where he's standing, with a rather funky-looking older woman with a purple streak in her gray hair.

"Lizzie, this is June, our highly efficient practice manager. Soon to be retiring, more's the pity."

I shake the hand June offers me. So there *are* still people in London who don't do the kissy-kissy thing. Thank heavens for that.

"Ross tells me you're applying to Greenwich University," she says. "I went there back in the early nineties when it was still Thames Poly. Made some of my best friends there." She gives a wistful smile. "Oh, to be a student again."

June introduces me to Lucy and Becky, the two receptionists, and for a moment I'm almost tempted to go for that job Ross was on about. If I do a part-time degree, maybe I could manage a couple of mornings a week at the surgery. It'll depend on the times of the lectures, of course.

"You look utterly gorgeous in that dress," Ross whispers in my ear. At last, he's starting to relax. I'm so glad I agreed to this party. Getting to know all his colleagues like this makes me feel part of his world. I don't even mind when his old medical-school chums turn up with enough alcohol to keep them going till next weekend. Their noisy exuberance and big, beery hugs make everyone relax and start laughing.

By ten thirty, even the rather staid Gloria Williams and her professorial-looking husband are flinging themselves around to Van Morrison's "Brown Eyed Girl" like a couple of loved-up hippies.

I'm surprised when the doorbell goes, because I thought anyone who was going to come would be here by now, and though it's fun and I'm having a good time, I'm really tired after all that anticipation and preparation. I've been rather hoping people might start drifting away in half an hour or so, and that it'll just be Ross's hardcore medical chums left and I'll be able to go up to bed and leave them to it.

"Don't panic, darling. It's probably just the police!" Ross laughs, squeezing past me to the front door. "Anyone want another drink, by the way?" he calls back into the room as he goes.

"I'd love some more red wine," Gloria says. She looks at me apologetically. "Poor Lizzie, you've only just sat down. I'll go and help myself, shall I?"

I leap to my feet. "No, don't worry. You stay here and enjoy yourself."

As I head back to the kitchen, I glance down the hall and see Ross helping someone off with their coat. If people are going to start arriving at this time of night, God only knows when it will end. Still, the party is a success. That's the main thing. Even if it takes us all of tomorrow to get the house back to normal.

Someone has left the back door ajar and the smell of cigarettes wafts in. I close it softly. Then I find a tray and put the open bottle of red wine and some more glasses onto it, just in case anyone else fancies one. Like *me*, for instance. Perhaps tonight I should take a risk and have a drink at my own party. Besides, one small glass of red won't do me any harm.

I lift the tray carefully and go back toward the living room. But as

I approach the front door I stop dead, breath frozen in my lungs. The tray arcs into the air, then crashes to the floor, reverberating like a cymbal. An explosion of glass and red wine sprays upward and outward, bursting onto the pale gray walls. A small cheer erupts from the living room. Then all external noise recedes.

Ross stares at me, his face twisted in confusion and shock. He steps toward me, the distant sound of glass crunching under his feet. Faces etched with concern cluster in the hallway. I'm aware of them on the periphery of my senses, but all my attention is focused on the woman standing before me, the woman unwinding a scarf from her neck.

I can't move. I can't speak. How can this be? How can Alice's sister be standing in my hallway?

13

THEN: BEFORE

THURSDAY, JULY 19, 2007

Mum comes into the kitchen with a basket full of dirty laundry.

"How lovely that the sun's shining on the first day of your school holidays," she says, beaming at me. "I think it's a sign, don't you? A sign that we're going to have the best summer ever." She plonks the basket on the floor in front of the washing machine. "Who was that you were phoning?"

"Alice. We're going on our walk."

There's a noticeable pause before Mum speaks again. "Why don't you ever ask Elizabeth Staunton over to play?" she says.

I give a long, dramatic sigh. Does she really think I still *play*?

"Because all she ever wants to do is talk about Justin Timberlake and, anyway, I prefer being with Alice. Just because you're friends with Elizabeth's mum doesn't mean I have to be friends with her daughter."

Mum opens the door of the washing machine and starts bundling the clothes inside. "No, of course it doesn't. But Elizabeth's a really nice girl, and surely you've got more shared interests with her than you have with Alice Dawson."

I don't like the way she says Alice's name, her surname in particular. The way she spits it out as if it's something unpleasant on her tongue.

"What, like being forced to practice the piano by our mums?"

She straightens up and gives me a pointed look. "Don't be silly, Lizzie. I don't *force* you to play the piano. I thought you liked it."

"I used to. Before all the theory exams."

"Elizabeth is very good at music theory. She could help you."

"Mu-um! I don't want Elizabeth Staunton to *help* me with my music theory, thank you very much. Anyway, what've you got against Alice? Isn't she posh enough for you, or is it because her mum and dad don't go to church?"

Dad chooses this very moment to come into the kitchen from the garden. "Lizzie! Don't talk to your mother like that! It's very rude."

"Well, I'm sick of being told who I can and can't be friends with."

Mum gives an exasperated sigh. "I'm not telling you you *can't* be friends with her. I just think you need to widen your circle, that's all."

Half an hour later, I'm still sulking about this conversation when I see Alice appear at the foot of our driveway. She's wearing her sister's denim jacket again, the one with the embroidered flowers on the sleeves. And there's something different about her hair. She's put it up. I'd like to put mine up like that, but it's not long enough. Mum likes me to keep it short because it's "easier to manage." Except it's not. It just sticks out at weird angles and looks stupid and ugly.

I grab the bottle of diluted orange squash I prepared earlier, plus the four flapjacks I've swiped from the cake box and wrapped in tinfoil.

"Bye, Mum, see you later."

"Bye, darling," she calls out from the kitchen. "Do be careful, won't you? Don't talk to any strangers."

Mum would be even more worried if she knew about The Walk and how isolated it is. She thinks we just wander down to the local park.

It takes us roughly a quarter of an hour to reach the turnoff that leads to Tippet Lane and the public footpath. Our favorite ponies are out in the field today and we stop to stroke their noses and feed them handfuls of long grass on our open hands. Alice seems quieter than normal. As if there's something on her mind. I don't like to ask her what it is in case it's something to do with her mum's depression. It usually is. Although she doesn't look sad exactly, just . . . mysterious.

I pass her a flapjack and tell her about Mum wanting me to spend more time with Elizabeth Staunton.

Alice pulls a face. "Isn't her dad a vicar or something?"

"No, he's a lay preacher."

Alice makes a little snorting noise. "Whatever that is."

"It's someone who occasionally leads the service but who isn't a formally ordained cleric."

Now Alice is giggling. "God, Lizzie, you sound like Mrs. Bentham."

I nudge her in the ribs with my elbow. "I do *not*."

Mrs. Bentham is our annoying religious studies teacher. She wears the most hideous open-toed sandals, the sort of thing my dad wears on the beach, and her breath always smells of garlic. But before long, I'm giggling, too, and for the next few minutes I impersonate Mrs. Bentham for Alice's amusement, even down to breathing out gusts of imaginary garlic breath in her face as I tell her off for being a disruptive influence.

"I bet that's why your mum wants you to spend more time with Churchy Staunton," Alice says. "Because she thinks I'm a *disruptive influence*."

She fiddles around with the bulldog clip at the back of her head. Strands of hair have escaped and are falling down her neck, but it looks nice. Sexy. I hope she doesn't start wearing it like that all the time.

"Catherine said it made me look grown-up, but she's done it a bit too tight. She's given me this jacket, too. Said I could keep it."

I try not to look bothered, but I am. I'd love a denim jacket like that. How come Alice gets all the good stuff? It isn't fair.

14

NOW

Gloria sweeps round my feet with the dustpan and brush, asking me to step aside for a minute. Two people are sponging wine off the wall. The faces peering round the living-room door withdraw and conversation resumes. Normality is being restored, except nothing about this situation is normal. Nothing about this situation is right.

Now Ross's hand is on my elbow and he's leading me gently into the study, away from the scene of destruction and the other guests. Away from the ghost in the hallway.

But the ghost follows us in.

Instinctively, I back away till I'm standing as far from her as possible, which isn't nearly far enough in this small square room. My bottom knocks into the unit where Ross keeps his vinyl collection, and that's where I stay, pressed up against the shelves. Her perfume reaches my nostrils. It smells of coconut. Maybe if she wasn't Catherine Dawson, I might be complimenting her on it, asking her what it is, but right now it's an affront to my senses. It repulses me.

Ross hovers between us. One minute he's fussing over me, checking I'm okay, the next he's apologizing to Catherine. Why is he apologizing to *her*? What the hell is going on? How does she know Ross?

"Lizzie? Lizzie Molyneux? Is it really you?" Her voice makes my scalp shrink. "You're Ross's girlfriend?"

Ross looks from me to Catherine and back to me again. "Is one of you going to tell me what's happening here? Do you two have some kind of history?"

I gulp. "You could say that." I'm amazed I can speak at all.

Ross stares at me, willing me to explain, but what can I say? Where would I begin?

"Lizzie was my little sister's best friend," Catherine says, lowering herself into the Ikea chair in the corner of the room, the one I use when Ross and I both need to sit in front of the Mac at the same time.

Ross raises his eyebrows as if to say, "Is that *it*?"

"Alice died," I say. There, the words are out. But now my tongue has stuck to the roof of my mouth. My knees begin to tremble.

Ross motions for me to sit down, nods at the leather chair, but I stay where I am, my back pressed to the unit, refusing to meet her eyes.

"Lizzie was with her when it happened," she says. I hold my breath as she looks down and twists a ring on her finger. "Alice was killed by a train. It was an accident," she says. "A tragic accident."

My chest heaves and air rushes into my lungs, almost choking me with its force. I try to compose the muscles in my face, try to keep them soft and light, but they tighten and contract. My jaw clamps tight like a vise. It's a wonder my teeth don't shatter in my gums.

Ross is staring at me, mouth open, his forehead creased in a frown. I watch his face as he takes it all in, absorbs the shock of it. He glances anxiously into the hallway and I know he's torn. Torn between staying here to find out what the hell is going on and returning to his guests—*our* guests—to check they're okay.

I think I see the exact moment when he makes a decision. "I'm going to leave the two of you to talk," he says. There's a reluctance in his tone, but still he moves toward the door. My eyes scream at him to stay. I can't be on my own with her. Why can't he see that? What's wrong with him? But he's already gone.

Every muscle in my body tenses as I wait for this apparition in front of me to dissolve and for the real Catherine Dawson to appear. The Catherine Dawson who stood outside my bedroom window in the middle of the night. And not just once either. She threw a stone only that first time, but I always knew when she was there, could feel her toxic aura radiating through the curtains. I told Mum and Dad in the end and she stopped shortly after. But the damage was already done. Whatever it was she'd whispered to Melissa and the others at Alice's funeral was enough to start the rumors when I went back to school.

She bows her head. "It took us a long while to come to terms with Alice's death." Her voice is low and flat. I watch her throat move as she swallows, my eyes traveling from the sharp blades of her collarbones to the blood-red beads that spill down the front of her black dress.

"I left home about a year after you and your parents moved away. Trained as a nurse. I only joined the practice a little while ago. I had no idea you were . . ."

Something inside me gives way. The new practice nurse. The one Ross keeps referring to. The one who went with him to visit a patient the other night, who ate chicken and chips with him while I waited at home, wondering where the hell he was. It's Catherine Dawson. What kind of freakish coincidence is this? What kind of headfuck?

Slowly, I move toward the leather chair and sit down, my hands gripping the armrests. It's the first time I've allowed my eyes to linger on her face since that first shock of recognition in the hall. Apart from a few lines around the mouth, she looks exactly the same as I remember her. Alice is there, too. In her eyes, her jawline, her coloring. Is this what she might have looked like, if she'd had the chance to grow up?

"I acted badly for a while," she says. "I'm sorry for that, Lizzie, but I was grieving. My little sister was dead and . . ." She takes a second to control her breath. "I just wanted to know how my baby sister died. *Why* she died. I couldn't accept the fact that we'd never know."

I swallow, nervously. None of this is real. It can't be. Catherine Dawson turning up at our party. Catherine Dawson working with Ross, eating takeaways with him. How is that possible?

"Lizzie? Are you all right?" Her voice is gentle, concerned. The sort of voice a counselor might use. But of course, she's a nurse now, a professional. It's been twelve years since Alice died.

The silence between us lengthens.

"I'm not trying to give you excuses," she says at last. "I'm just trying to explain what it was like." She's staring directly at me now, an imploring look in her eyes.

I turn away. I don't want to feel sorry for her, but somewhere in the back of my mind I know I'm recalibrating my emotional response, that, despite everything, a part of me is already trying to understand.

She stands up. "I'll leave. I'm ruining your party."

"No. Stay and have a drink with your colleagues."

I can't believe what I'm saying. But then, people change, don't they? Learn from their mistakes? Feel remorse? What do I know about losing a sister, what that does to a person? I know what losing a best friend is like, so how much worse must it have been for Catherine and her parents? What must it have been like in the Dawson home in the weeks and months following Alice's death? Besides, if I turf her out, what will Ross's colleagues think? He'll hate it if I cause a scene, especially in front of Gloria Williams.

I stand up, and so does she. For one dreadful second I think she's going to step forward and embrace me, but if that's what she contemplated doing, she quickly changes her mind and moves toward the door instead. She pauses at the threshold.

"Thank you," she whispers.

I watch her leave the room, unable to follow her, unable to move. My past has caught up with me, like I always knew it would. All this time I've been living on a fault line. Now, finally, something inside me cracks and shifts.

15

It's nearly one o'clock in the morning and the last of the guests left half an hour ago. In different circumstances, Ross's medical-school pals would probably still be here and I'd be tucked up in bed already, but they, like his colleagues, must have sensed the need to leave us to it.

The house that just five hours ago looked so pretty and inviting, so warm and glowing, is now littered with empty glasses and paper plates. I can barely look at the stained walls in the hallway, that lovely Mindful Gray now more like something out of a crime scene.

Ross is chewing the inside of his bottom lip. He takes a deep breath through his nostrils and leans forward in the armchair, arms crossed over his knees. He looks shattered.

"Lizzie, why didn't you *tell* me any of this?"

I'm curled up on the end of the sofa, my hands clasped round a mug of chamomile tea. A headache throbs at my left temple.

"I was going to tell you. It just never seemed to be the right time."

"It must have been horrendous, seeing that happen to your best friend."

"I *didn't* see it happen. By the time I came to, it was over. All I saw was . . ." I close my eyes till the image goes away.

Ross shakes his head. "I can't believe you've been dealing with all that trauma and I never even knew."

I take a sip of tea. "It was such a shock, seeing her sister in our house, seeing you chatting away with her in the hall." My words barely scratch the surface of how that felt, how it still feels. "She was so horrible to me after Alice died. She blamed me for her sister's death."

Ross comes over to me on the sofa and strokes my cheek with his finger. "Oh, sweetheart."

I want to tell him what it was like for me back then, but what can I say? Where can I start? And how can I tell him that it's not just Catherine's reappearance that's upset me, though God knows, that's bad enough, it's what she represents. The past and all the things I don't want to have to think about. The things I've deliberately *not* thought about, that I've packed away at the very furthest corners of my mind.

"Now don't take this the wrong way," he says, "because I'm not trying to make excuses for her behavior. I'm absolutely not. Scaring a thirteen-year-old girl late at night is a despicable thing to do, but . . ." He shakes his head. "Grief affects people in different ways. She'd just lost her sister."

"And I'd lost my best friend and was having to contend with rumors that it was me who'd killed her!"

He exhales through closed lips. "I'm presuming you had some kind of counseling to help you cope with all this?"

"Of course I did."

Angela Harris. I see her face before me, as if the last twelve years have been stripped away and I'm back in that bland, beige room with the picture of snow-tipped mountains on the wall and the box of tissues on the table between us. I watch her lips part as she readies herself to speak, hear her dispassionate voice asking me, once again, if there is anything else I'd like to tell her, anything at all that might be troubling me.

Ross sighs. "I think you should get some sleep and we'll talk again in the morning. It's late and we're both tired. I don't want you getting ill."

We both know what he means. Tiredness and stress: a dangerous combination as far as my epilepsy is concerned. He's never witnessed me having a full-blown seizure and, with any luck, he never will. He thinks he's seen me at my worst—puking into a toilet bowl when I had a stomach upset, drenched in sweat. He hasn't seen me at my worst. Nowhere near. But then, nor have I. That's the worst thing about this condition—other people witness my body doing things I'll never be able to see.

I watched a video someone had posted on YouTube once, and it confirmed all my fears. The thought of Ross seeing me thrashing about like a drowning fish, foaming at the mouth, wetting myself. I screw my eyes shut, but it's no good. The images won't go away. They line up like a series of disturbing black-and-white pictures in old medical textbooks.

"Come on," Ross says, helping me up from the sofa. "I'll bring you a glass of water."

I trudge upstairs, trying not to look at the ruined walls in our hallway. Some of the lining paper has torn where Ross has tried to sponge them clean. There's no way we're going to get rid of the stains. The whole thing will need repainting.

It must be getting on for 3 A.M. before he finally comes to bed. I've been awake the whole time, tossing and turning and getting myself all worked up. I knew something bad was going to happen. I sensed it, like the feeling I get before a seizure, when the world feels out of kilter and you can't put your finger on what's changed. It's like the universe has been sending me signs.

At first, I thought it was the news story about Elodie Stevens—similar cases always have an effect on me—but then there's that box Mum and Dad suddenly decided to bring over—why didn't they just leave it in the attic?—and the little train that appeared on the wall, and all those weird phone calls. And now, to top it all off, Catherine bloody Dawson has walked back into my life. There must be a reason for all this. It must *mean* something.

I hear Ross cleaning his teeth and peeing, then he climbs in next to me, his right arm encircling my body, his feet entwined with mine. I know if I told him what I was thinking, if I voiced my fears, he would try to placate me with statistical theories of improbability. He would tell me, gently and patiently, that these are all random events and that the universe is most unlikely to arrange itself purely on my behalf, and he would be right. But still . . .

Instinctively, I touch my stomach. Still no sign of my period. This business with Catherine has wiped it clean out of my mind.

I wait until Ross begins to snore before I slide carefully from his grasp and out of bed.

16

I tiptoe downstairs and rummage in the bottom of my bag. I need to get this pregnancy test done and find out one way or the other.

The light's been left on in the study, so I go in and sit on the leather swivel chair to read the instructions, trying my best to ignore the faint but lingering scent of coconut. Ross's Mac whirs into life. I must have accidentally leaned on the keyboard as I spread the leaflet out.

I stare at the screen, my eyes stuck fast to the headline of an all-too-familiar news article. So *this* is why he was so long coming to bed. He's been googling the accident.

NETWORK RAIL SAFETY UPGRADES TOO LATE FOR "OUR ALICE"

The distraught parents of 13-year-old Alice Dawson, killed by a train on an open crossing that traverses the Garleywood Public Footpath in Garleywood Tippet, have told of their heartbreak at losing their precious daughter.

"Alice's death has devastated our family," says Mick Dawson, Alice's father, owner of Dawson's Meats in Garleywood. "She was a beautiful, kind girl, popular with all her schoolfriends and loved by everyone who knew her. I don't know how our family will ever recover from this."

The exact circumstances of Alice's death are unknown. She was out walking with a friend, 13-year-old Lizzie Molyneux. The two girls were frequent users of the Garleywood Public Footpath and had used the crossing safely on numerous occasions. But at 11:25 on the morning of July 19, 2007, Alice was struck by a four-carriage train. The post-mortem revealed that she died on impact. Lizzie Molyneux was found by the train driver and guard on the side of the track, having suffered a seizure. Lizzie, an epileptic, has a history of severe tonic clonic seizures. She has no apparent recollection of her friend stepping onto the track. An inquest jury returned a verdict of accidental death. The Garleywood Public Footpath crossing is part of a planned series of safety upgrades, says Network Rail spokesman Bill Redditch. "Too late for our Alice," say the shocked community of Garleywood Tippet, many of whom are now calling for its immediate closure.

My eyes skim the article I last read twelve years ago and promised myself I'd never read again. I can't help being struck by the disparity between the description of Alice and the description of me. The thought of Ross sitting down here reading this on his own in the early hours of the morning fills me with sadness. Fills me with shame. I know the reporter was only quoting the words of her father, and of *course* Mick Dawson would have said those things, that Alice was beautiful and kind, popular with all her schoolfriends, loved by everyone who knew her. She was his precious little girl and he'd just lost her in the most devastating way imaginable.

But seeing her portrayed in this angelic light makes the references to me sound ugly and clinical: *an epileptic*; *severe tonic clonic seizures*. Maybe if we'd both been hit by the train and I'd survived but been injured, it might have been different. I'd be a victim, too, instead of just the "epileptic" friend who can't remember what happened.

Perhaps I'm being oversensitive and reading things into it that simply aren't there. Perhaps the phrase "no apparent recollection" does *not* imply a question mark hanging over my testimony. I know it's wrong of me to even *think* this way. After all, I survived. She didn't. What does it matter how I was described by a stupid reporter?

I torture myself by imagining the split second before it happened. Did Alice see the train bearing down on her? Did time slow down the way people say it does in moments of danger, her short life spreading before her in a tapestry of colors and emotions?

My scalp tingles as if Alice is shimmering over my shoulder. Reading about her own death. And though I know it's stupid, I can't help looking round. I don't want her to have suffered even a nanosecond of that torment and yet I can't help feeling she must have done. Why else do I keep seeing these pictures in my head? The terrible panic in her eyes. Her beautiful face contorted by a scream. What monstrous thing is my brain trying to reveal? And why now, after all this time?

I stand up and it feels like I've been sitting here for hours. My lower back is stiff, my legs almost numb. I pick up the leaflet for the predictor kit and turn away from the screen, force myself to read the words, to follow the instructions, try to shut everything else out and focus purely on them.

The extractor fan in the downstairs toilet is loud, and for a second I think that Ross will wake up and come down, but he won't. Of course he won't. Once Ross is asleep, he's dead to the world, especially when he's been drinking.

I start to wee, holding the end of the stick in the flow, then I balance it on top of the roll of toilet paper on the floor and rest my head in my hands, close my eyes and start to count. Sixty seconds. A hundred and twenty. A hundred and eighty.

I open my eyes and, even before I've picked it up, the two pink lines are clearly visible. The numbness in my legs has now spread to the rest of my body. It's affected my mind, too. I can't seem to think straight—there's just this eerie blankness. I carry the piece of plastic out into the hallway, holding it as if it's a delicate piece of glass or china, something that must be handled with the greatest of care. I take it into the kitchen and switch the main light on, the one I think is too bright, too clinical, but that right now is exactly what I need.

I rest the stick on the counter and stare at it for far too long. One of the lines is fainter than the other, but it's definitely there and, according to the instructions, that's a positive result.

A positive result. I take a few deep breaths. Maybe the way I've been feeling lately isn't about Alice at all. Maybe it's all been hormonal. In fact, now I come to think of it, that's a far more likely explanation than the universe having it in for me.

I pick up the stick and take it over to the little sofa by the window, try to focus on what this means. It's unplanned and scary and life-changing, but I can't deny this faint pulse of excitement that's getting stronger by the second. And maybe it's better this way. We could have waited years before deciding whether to try for a baby and then not been able to get pregnant. Or we could have worried ourselves sick about all the risks and ended up talking ourselves out of it altogether.

My scalp tingles again, just like it did when I was in the study. Except this time Alice isn't behind me, reading about her death, she's right beside me, watching me stare at the pink lines. My future. The one we used to talk about. The one Alice will never have.

17

THEN: AFTER

WEDNESDAY, AUGUST 1, 2007

"Tell me about the nightmare, Lizzie. The one you keep having."

Angela Harris's voice is low and soothing, but something about her worries me. I have the sense that she already knows what happens when I fall asleep, that she, too, can see the pictures in my head and that, somehow or other, she will make me speak about them. And then she won't believe that it's a dream. She'll think it's what really happened. And maybe it is. Maybe it really *is* what happened.

It's been less than two weeks since Alice died, and I don't want to talk to a counselor, but Mum and Dad said I have to. They said it's part of the "healing process." I've already spoken to a police psychologist. I've had enough of all these questions.

"Can you describe how the nightmare starts?"

She won't give up. I know that much.

"We've just gone through the kissing gate and we're heading for the gap in the hedge."

She gives an encouraging nod. I can't explain to her how strange the dream is. Because on the actual walk it used to take us ages to find the right gap. Even though we'd done it loads of times, that first part was always the trickiest, because the field was so huge and the hedge so long. It always looked different to how we remembered it the time before, depending on the length of time between each walk, the weather on the day, and what work the farmer had been doing in the field.

"What else can you remember?"

My chest flutters. Is she still talking about the dream? How do I know that all that stuff she said about confidentiality and me being able to say anything at all is true? How do I know she's not feeding everything I say straight back to the police? This could be some kind of trick, getting me to talk about my nightmare and then cleverly introducing new questions about the actual day. Because nobody seems to believe I can't remember anything. Even Mum and Dad keep asking me questions, and they *know* I can't remember what happens before a big seizure.

"The scarecrow is much nearer," I say.

She raises her left eyebrow. "Much nearer than . . . ?"

"Much nearer than it should be." I reach for a tissue and pretend to blow my nose. "Nearer than it is in real life," I add, to make her realize that we're still talking about the nightmare here and nothing else.

"Dreams are funny like that, aren't they?" she says. "Familiar but strange at the same time."

"Yes."

"How does the scarecrow make you feel, Lizzie?"

"Frightened. It looks like . . ."

My eyes skate away from Angela Harris's face and land on the painting behind her. The one of the snow-capped mountains.

"Alice always said it looked like a dead man on a stick."

My eyes are now glued to the painting. I don't like speaking of Alice in the past tense. At least in the dream, she's still alive.

"In the dream, it really *is* a dead man. But Alice doesn't believe me."

If I tell her the truth, that the scarecrow of my dreams looks like

Alice's corpse with all the smashed bits of her body stitched back to-gether, she'll think I'm some kind of psycho.

"Then what happens?"

"Then suddenly we're at the crossing and I'm waking up and I see . . ." I shut my eyes, then open them again. "Then I wake up and I'm screaming and Mum and Dad come in."

Angela Harris's eyes flick to the clock on the wall. She shifts posi-tion in her chair and closes her notepad with a decisive little snap, which I'm hoping is a signal that the session is about to end.

When I'm back in the car with Mum and we're driving home, I think about how the nightmare really ends, with the two of us fight-ing. Except it's me who's doing all the pushing and hitting. And then the train is bearing down on us and it's too late to get out of the way. But I never feel the impact. I always wake up in time.

18

NOW

It's Monday morning and the bus is rammed. I rub a little viewing circle in the steamed-up window. All the gorgeous spring weather we've been having has disappeared overnight and left in its place nothing but steady rainfall and a sky the color of wet slate.

The left knee of the woman sitting next to me presses painfully up against my leg. Packed in among all these bodies, I feel hemmed in. Trapped.

It's a good job I've registered at a different GP practice. I'd hate to bump into Ross today and see his concerned eyebrows shoot up. I'm not ready to tell him yet, not till I've processed the news myself. And now I know who else works there. . . .

I think of Ross in proximity to Catherine Dawson and my throat constricts. Seeing her in my home was like something long buried breaking up through layers of soil. A disturbing image flashes into my mind: skeletal fingers pushing clods of earth aside like bulb shoots reaching for the light. I screw my eyes tight shut and try to think of something else.

Half an hour later and Dr. Ahmed, a softly spoken woman who's probably in her early forties, comes into the waiting room and calls for me, hesitating slightly over my surname but making a passable attempt. I've been called a lot worse than Lizzie Molly-Noo. Luckily, I'll be a Murray when we get married. Lizzie Murray. That's much simpler. I even get to keep the same initials.

I follow her into her room and sit down. For some reason I can't tell her I think I'm pregnant, so I explain that I'm considering starting a family and ask her what advice she can give me regarding my epilepsy.

"Your AED dosage seems to be working well for you, if you're two years seizure free," she says, "and this medication isn't associated with birth defects, so there really shouldn't be too many problems. I'd like to do an EEG and an MRI scan first, though. Are you happy for me to do a referral?"

"Yes."

She taps away at her keyboard.

"We would keep you on your current medication, but since pregnancy itself causes a good deal of stress on the body—nausea, tiredness, et cetera—you'd need to monitor your health quite closely to avoid any triggers."

I try to swallow, but my mouth's too dry. Eventually, I manage to ask a question.

"Would my AEDs affect the baby's development?"

"Not these particular ones, although there's always a slight risk."

I nod. I know she has to tell me all this and, of course, I expected it.

"You don't have to rush to make any decisions. Why don't you go home and discuss it with your partner, then come back and see me when you're ready?"

"What would happen if I was already pregnant?" I ask her, and immediately feel like an irresponsible teenager.

Dr. Ahmed's dark almond-shaped eyes flicker. She rests her hands in her lap and asks if that's a possibility.

My voice, when it comes, is barely audible. "Yes."

"How late are you?"

I look somewhere beyond her right shoulder. "About a week, I think."

"Have you done a test yet?"

Now I really do feel like a fool. "Yes, but the second line was quite faint."

Dr. Ahmed smiles. "Shop-bought kits are very accurate these days. It's rare to get a false positive. I'll arrange for you to see the community midwife in the first instance."

She turns to her screen and starts tapping away at the keyboard. "Don't worry," she says. "Most women with epilepsy go on to have perfectly normal pregnancies and healthy babies."

That's right. I am a woman with epilepsy. Not an epileptic.

On the bus home, my bag stuffed with leaflets and with Dr. Ahmed's reassuring words still echoing in my ears, fear and excitement surge through me in equal measures. The timing stinks. All my plans about going to university will have to be put on hold, at least for a year or so, and God knows what Ross and my parents will say.

But the decision has been taken out of our hands now. And Dr. Ahmed says they'll monitor me really closely, that I'll be well taken care of.

I watch the same streets go by through the fogged windows, but now everything looks different, more vivid and meaningful. As if I'm seeing it with brand-new eyes.

19

Ross stares at me in astonishment.

"What do you mean, you're pregnant? Are you sure?"

"Of *course* I'm sure. I did one of those predictor tests."

His forehead creases into a frown. "But . . . but how could this happen?"

I raise my eyebrows. "And you a GP," I say, my voice light and teasing, my heart hammering in my chest. You'd think it would be easy having this conversation with the man you love, but it isn't. For some ludicrous reason, I feel like I've tricked him into something he doesn't want, even though he was the one who didn't wear a condom, who promised me he'd be careful.

He runs his hands through his hair. "Fucking hell."

My stomach plummets. Coming home on the bus today, I was scared, but happy. I'd convinced myself that this was a good thing. A good thing for *both* of us. But Ross doesn't want this baby. That much is clear.

Finally, he notices the expression on my face. "Oh, darling, I didn't mean . . ."

He comes round to my side of the bed and perches on the edge, takes my hands in his. "I was just thinking about what it all means, in terms of your meds and everything."

"It's okay, I've already discussed that with Dr. Ahmed."

He looks surprised. Hurt. "You've been to the doctor's already?"

"Yes, I wanted to be sure before telling you."

Only now I realize that that was a mistake. I should have told him straightaway. After all, we're in this together. At least, I thought we were.

"I thought you'd be pleased."

"Of *course* I'm pleased. Oh, Lizzie, sweetheart, I'm sorry. It's just that . . . I was so sure I'd pulled out in time." He laughs then. A short, incredulous laugh that gives me hope. "I just didn't expect this to happen so soon."

"You're not the only one who's surprised. It's come as a bit of a shock to me, too."

He gathers me up in his arms and squeezes me tight. He kisses the top of my head and that horrible dead feeling in my chest, the crushing disappointment of the last few minutes, disappears.

"Bloody hell, Lizzie," he murmurs into my hair. "When's it due?"

"Dr. Ahmed said the tenth of December."

"A baby," he says at last, his voice high with emotion. "We're going to have a baby."

I laugh through my tears. "I know! That's what I've been trying to tell you."

The first thing I see when I open the front door the next morning is a large bouquet of flowers and a pair of black-trousered legs sticking out from underneath. The bouquet moves to one side to reveal the chubby, pink-cheeked face of the delivery man.

"Someone's a lucky lady," he says. "Lizzie Molly-Nex? Is that you?"

"Yes," I say. "How lovely. Thank you."

I close the door and take the bouquet into the kitchen, beaming like an idiot. I've been wondering if he might do this.

I peel the little white envelope off the front of the cellophane and rip it open, staring at the words, confused.

To Lizzie,
So sorry I gave you a shock at your party. Thank you so much for letting me stay. Please forgive me. For everything.
Love, Catherine xx

I read the card again, still reeling with disappointment that they're not from Ross. Damn Catherine Dawson and her new personality. How dare she send flowers and thank-you notes! How dare she ask for forgiveness! Isn't it enough that I have to cope with the knowledge that she's working with my fiancé? Isn't it enough that she ruined our housewarming party?

Ross finds the flowers stuffed into the kitchen bin when he comes home from work. I never got round to putting them outside in the black wheelie bin, like I'd planned.

Later, when we're sitting side by side on the sofa, the TV blathering away, he broaches the subject, as I knew he would.

"You're probably going to bite my head off for saying this, but . . ." He gives me a worried glance. "Don't you think you're being a tad unreasonable?"

I don't say anything.

"I mean, it was *twelve* years ago. Can't you just forgive her and move on?"

"No. And I don't want her sending me any sodding flowers."

Ross sighs. "All this negativity isn't good for you, especially now you're pregnant. And I have to work with her, remember?"

My fingers clench into the palms of my hands. "I can't bring myself to be friendly with her."

"You don't *have* to be friendly with her. You just have to be civil. There's a difference."

He puts his arms round me and pulls me toward him.

"Have you any idea what it was like for me back then?" I say. "To have to listen to all those whispers behind my back? Whispers I'm certain she started."

Ross sighs again. "Kids can be cruel at that age," he says. "Vicious little bastards, some of them." He puts his hand on my tummy. "Ours will be perfect, of course."

I cover my face with my hands. "If it weren't for me starting that stupid argument—"

Shit. Shit! My words expand in the room, filling every available space. I can't believe I said that out loud. Nobody but me knows about the argument. Nobody.

"Hey," he says, grasping my shoulders and looking deep into my eyes. "You don't really blame yourself for Alice's death, do you? You mustn't do that, Lizzie. It wasn't your fault."

I swallow hard. He doesn't seem to have picked up on the argument thing, thank God.

"Of course not," I say. "But if I hadn't had a seizure, I could have stopped her crossing the line. I could have saved her life."

He squeezes me tight. "Have you considered speaking to someone?"

"You mean a therapist?"

He nods.

"I told you, I saw a therapist after Alice died. I can't keep raking over the past, Ross. It's too much."

"I don't mean about the past. I mean about the present. Talk to someone about how Catherine coming back makes you feel." He looks at me from under his eyebrows. "Maybe a counselor could help you work through your emotions," he says. "What if you need to confront your feelings about her if you're ever going to move forward?"

"You're sounding like a counselor yourself."

"Well, I am a GP."

"Hmm."

"Will you think about it?"

"Okay."

But I won't. I can't. Because it isn't just about Catherine Dawson. It's about me. And the thing in my head that won't go away. The thing I can't allow myself to think about.

I lean against Ross's chest and breathe in his clean, male scent. I don't want these pictures, but still they come, spooling out like a scary film I'm compelled to watch. It isn't true. It can't be. Everything I told the police and my parents and Angela Harris is true. I don't know what happened. I can't remember.

20

THEN: AFTER

WEDNESDAY, AUGUST 8, 2007

It's my second session with Angela Harris. Today, she is wearing brown velvet trousers and a green blouse. Her hair is tied back into a loose ponytail and she is writing something in her notebook with a scratchy pen—something about me.

I don't like that. Don't like the fact that she gets to write things down—things I've said, or things she thinks of when I tell her something—and I don't get to see them. I don't like the fact that she can keep secrets from me, but that I'm expected to tell her all of mine. It doesn't seem fair.

Alice had a secret she wasn't telling me, too.

Angela Harris uncrosses her legs, then recrosses them on the other side. She's wearing the sort of shoes I used to wear when I was about seven. Flat with a T-bar and a little pattern over the toes made with holes. "What else has been happening since we last spoke?" she says.

I worked out last week that she never asks me a question that I can answer with a yes or no, which is really annoying. I think she does it deliberately to make me say more than I want to. But she's slipped up with that last one, because although I can't answer it with a yes or no, I can say "nothing much" and she'll have to ask me something else.

"Nothing much," I say, trying not to sound rude. Because if you say "nothing much" in a certain way, it *can* sound a little bit rude.

"Nothing much of what?" she says, and my heart sinks. She's too good at this. She simply won't be beaten.

"Dad wanted us to go to the seaside, but we didn't go."

"Why was that, Lizzie?"

Why. Why. Why. Why. Why. It's one of her favorite words.

"Because Mum had a migraine and I didn't want to eat ice cream because it didn't seem right."

"Why didn't it seem right?"

"Because . . . because you eat ice cream on holiday and it doesn't feel much like a holiday anymore."

Angela Harris gives me a sad little smile. I try not to look at her face because I don't know whether she expects me to look at her eyes or not and it's hard to look at someone's face if you don't look at their eyes, so I look at her neck instead. She's got lines round her neck, just like Mum has.

She uncrosses her legs again and sits up a little straighter. She dips her head slightly to catch my eyes. I let her catch them, but only for a second.

"How do you think it would make you feel if you *did* go to the seaside and eat an ice cream?" she says.

I chew the inside of my bottom lip and try to think of what I should say. If I say it would make me feel guilty, she might ask me what I'm feeling guilty about. She might think I'm feeling guilty for a really bad reason. Like pushing Alice in front of that train. That's what she's trying to find out if I did, and so I have to be really careful. Because I didn't. I didn't do that, did I? My brain hurts from all the thinking.

"I don't know," I say.

Angela Harris smiles again, but it's not such a sad smile this time. It's more of a cross sort of smile. I don't think Angela Harris likes me much. I don't think I like *myself* very much.

21

NOW

For the past three weeks, I've been feeling sick all day, but I've had all the tests Dr. Ahmed arranged and been told everything is fine and that the sickness is normal—a good sign that the pregnancy is healthy. Evenings are the only time I feel remotely human, and tonight I've been well enough to eat a takeaway curry. Nothing too spicy, mind. A chicken korma and a plain naan. Ross has had his usual lamb madras.

I snuggle up to him on the sofa, determined not to ruin things by raising the subject of Catherine Dawson again. Since the party, we've had several more conversations where I've had to use all my self-control not to beg him to resign and find another practice.

The phone rings just as *Bake Off: The Professionals* is starting. I can tell from the tension in Ross's shoulders and the set of his mouth that it isn't good news.

"Thank you for letting me know," he says. "I'll come as soon as I can."

"What is it? What's happened?"

"That was the manager from the Beeches."

The Beeches is the nursing home where his father lives. "He hasn't . . . ?"

"No. But she says he's deteriorating. I'll book a flight for tomorrow." He sighs. "I can do the round trip in a day."

I stand up and start stacking the foil containers inside each other, clearing the mess on the coffee table. "I'll come with you. Let's see if we can book the tickets now."

Ross gently prizes the containers out of my hands. "I should think flying to Aberdeen and back in one day is the very last thing you need to be doing right now."

"But I *want* to. We could tell him about the baby. I know we agreed to keep it to ourselves for a while, but what if your dad doesn't . . ."

Ross does a bitter little laugh. "I doubt it'll even register with him. Honestly, Lizzie, you're better off staying at home. You've built him up in your mind as this poor, tragic figure, but the reality couldn't be more different. That's why I've never taken you to see him. The difference between my dad and yours couldn't be greater." He shakes his head, sadly. "The truth is, and I hate to admit this, but I'm ashamed of him."

I rest my hand on his sleeve. "I know you blame him for your mother's death."

He's never actually admitted this, but I've guessed as much from some of the things he's said in the past about the stress his dad's behavior caused her.

"I don't blame him for her death. But I've spent most of my life wishing he'd died instead of her." He looks straight at me then. "I've shocked you now, haven't I?"

"No. I understand." At least, I'm trying to.

"Then you'll understand that I need to go alone. I need to make my peace with him before he dies. I'll go online and see if I can book an early flight."

———

The next morning, Ross is gone before I wake up. I open my eyes and heave myself up onto my left elbow. I put my glasses on and look at the clock radio. Nine forty-three! I *never* sleep this late.

I crawl out of bed, mouth clamped shut, and stumble to the toilet, hang over it, limp as a rag doll, my skin all clammy. Within seconds, last night's curry makes another appearance.

Round about midday I rally a little and go through into the kitchen to make some toast. Ross rings while I'm waiting for it to pop out of the toaster.

"You looked so peaceful this morning I couldn't bring myself to wake you," he says.

"I wish you had. I'm late taking my meds now."

As soon as the words are out, I regret them. I don't want him thinking of me as someone who needs to be looked after, someone who has to be reminded to take her tablets. I'm his fiancée, not his patient.

"Shit! I didn't think."

"It's not your fault. Even if I *had* taken them on time, I'd have probably brought them up by now."

"Why don't you go for a walk in the park? That'll make you feel better."

He's right. Some fresh air will do me good. He was right about not dragging me to Aberdeen as well. There's no way I'd have coped with flying today.

"Where are you now? Are you at the Beeches yet?"

"No, I'm in a cab leaving Dyce. The plane was delayed. I'll text you later."

After we've said goodbye I eat my toast with a banana. Each mouthful I swallow and keep down feels like a small victory.

It's sunny outside but there's still a chilly breeze. I zip up my waterproof jacket and stride to the end of the street and the entrance to Maryon Wilson Park. It surprises me sometimes how much green space this part of London has. I won't have far to go to take my baby for a walk.

Ribbons of hair flutter round my face as I pass through the gate. The park seems to be full of mothers and pushchairs today, or am I just more tuned in to noticing them now?

Dr. Ahmed has been very reassuring, and Ross has told me I'll be better looked after than most pregnant women, but I'm still really scared. Getting through the pregnancy and labor is frightening enough, but what happens *after* the baby is born? I'd hate for something bad to happen if I start having seizures again.

By now, I've walked round the park twice. The combination of air and exercise has worked its magic on my head and the nausea is at last easing off. But I have to keep walking till all these worrying thoughts get blown away. There's not much a good brisk walk can't make better, that's what my dad always says. I set off for the gate on the far side of the park and soon I'm crossing the road for the houses on the other side.

Gone are the Victorian and Edwardian terraces that make up most of the dwellings where Ross and I live. Here it's mainly 1930s housing with stucco or pebble-dashed walls and big front gardens. They remind me of the house I grew up in, before we moved to Dovercourt. I was one of the few children at my school who lived beyond the limits of the sprawling Garleywood Tippet housing estate.

I'm almost at Plumtree Lodge now. It's a modern two-story building with white stucco walls and an elaborately curved roof. The locals call it the Wedding Cake. I wonder how long you have to live in a place to call yourself a local?

The pressure in my bladder is starting to build. It's going to take at least twenty minutes to walk home, and I'll be really uncomfortable by then. Perhaps I could nip in to the surgery and use their toilet. I don't want to, but if I'm quick, I could be in and out before anyone notices me, and they're bound to, after the party. One thing's for sure, I won't be applying for that part-time job, no matter how convenient it might be. Not with Catherine working there.

22

I'm heading back to the main entrance when I hear someone call my name. It's Gloria Williams, the senior partner. She's come out of her consulting room and is walking toward me.

"How's Ross's father?" she says.

"Not sure yet. His plane was delayed."

"Oh dear," she says. "Well, give him my love when you speak to him. It must be so hard with his father living all the way up there."

"Yes, yes, it is."

I've just spotted Catherine talking to one of the receptionists. I need to get away before she sees me, but it would be rude to cut Gloria off and, anyway, it's too late. Catherine is waving and coming over, looking every inch the efficient nurse in her navy uniform with her dark, glossy hair swept up into a bun. Once again, I see Alice in her face.

"Hi, Lizzie. We were all so sorry to hear about Ross's dad," she says. "Sounds like he's in a bad way."

Gloria touches me gently on the arm. "I'd better dash," she says. "Thank you again for that wonderful party at your house."

"I got your message," Catherine says, as soon as Gloria has gone.

I gawp at her. What does she mean? What message?

Her forehead creases in a puzzled frown. "About the flowers? I'm so glad you liked them."

Right. The flowers. The ones I shoved in the kitchen bin. Ross must have taken it upon himself to thank her for them on my behalf. Cheers, Ross.

"Oh, right, yeah."

"Lizzie, are you okay? Only you look a bit peaky."

"I'm fine."

"Lizzie, I know this whole situation is awkward. . . ."

Oh no, she's going to say something nice. Something sensible. Something I can't ignore. "But is there any possibility we can call a truce? For Ross's sake. It must be terribly difficult for him, caught in the middle, so to speak."

I glance at her face for the briefest of seconds. Just long enough to see the worry lines etched in her forehead and round her mouth. Perhaps it *is* unfair of me to carry on like this, refusing to accept an apology. I mean, what harm can it do to be civil? I'm better than this and, besides, it won't do to let Catherine Dawson take the moral high ground.

"Well, it was a long time ago."

Reluctantly, I hold out my right hand, and Catherine clasps it with both of hers, pumping it up and down. It's hard to believe that this softly spoken, reasonable person asking for my forgiveness and sending me bouquets of flowers is the same hateful young woman who was so mean to me as a child. I know I should say something nice, but she needs to get the message that we're never going to be friends.

"I've wanted to say sorry for so long," she says, still holding my hand, tears welling up in her eyes. She seems so genuine and, infuriatingly, my eyes fill up, too.

"Alice was my best friend," I say, my voice little more than a whisper. "I still miss her."

"Of *course* you do. You two were so close." Her eyes lock onto mine, but there's nothing scary about them now. Quite the opposite. They're full of sadness and compassion. "So very close." She blinks and looks away. "I miss her, too. Every single day."

She reaches into the pocket of her tunic and draws out a business card. She looks awkward as she passes it to me. Embarrassed.

"Just in case you ever fancy a coffee or something," she says.

I don't want her bloody card, but refusing it seems pointlessly childish, so in the end I take it.

For a few strange seconds, I sense her teetering on the edge of something, just like before, at the party, as if she might actually hug me. I take a step toward the exit.

"It's been really nice bumping into you again, Lizzie," she says.

I mumble a reply and step out into the fresh air, gasping a great lungful of it as I walk away and don't look back.

———————————

She wanted to practice kissing, she said. So that when the time came and she had a boyfriend, she'd know exactly what to do.

Time had passed and we were older now. Teenagers at last. Thirteen is an odd age. Some days you feel almost grown-up. Other days, you're still very much a child. Building dens in the woods. Fishing for tiddlers with nets and jam jars. Stuffing your face with so many strawberries you feel sick.

"Proper French-kissing," she said. "With tongues."

My cheeks burned. Surely she didn't mean to practice with me? And yet, now that the words were out there, I knew it would happen. Because it was always like that. Her coming up with the plans and me falling in with them. What else could I do? She was the only friend I had.

First, we pushed a chair against her bedroom door. Then we sat on the edge of her bed. My armpits were wet with nervous sweat. My mouth was dry. I wanted it to be over as quickly as possible because we still had an hour's worth of homework to do and it was pressing on my conscience. But as soon as our lips parted and the tip of her tongue found the tip of mine, I never wanted it to stop.

I wanted to practice forever.

23

THEN: BEFORE

FRIDAY, MAY 25, 2007

It's Friday evening at last and Alice and I are getting ready for the youth-club disco. Next week is half-term, thank God. Mum calls it the Whitsun week.

Alice takes hold of the strawberry lip gloss and leans toward the speckled mirror in her bedroom. She slides the rollerball from side to side across her mouth. I suppose it's only fair that she gets to use it first, seeing as it's hers.

Then she presses her middle finger in the blue eyeshadow palette and smears it over her eyelids, blending it into the creases and dabbing another layer on the outer corners.

"Do you see how I'm blending it in?" she says, as if she's some kind of makeup guru and I'm her student. Alice is my best friend ever, but sometimes she's really, *really* annoying.

I pick up the discarded lip gloss and put some on my own lips. I don't like the sickly sweet smell in my nostrils, or the sticky feel of it, but if Alice is using it, I want to as well.

Alice looks perfect. She's wearing a pair of white capri pants, a pink cropped T-shirt, and her sister's denim jacket with embroidered flowers on the sleeve. I can't believe Catherine's letting her wear it. I'm wearing capri pants, too, but mine don't look as good as Alice's. They're black and baggier in the leg and my white calves look too fat. I was so happy when I tried them on in Topshop, but as soon as I got them home, I knew they were a mistake. I should have worn my jeans. Too late now.

Catherine is standing in the hallway when we go downstairs. She makes a little adjustment to Alice's hair and tells her she looks *fab*. Then she makes her promise to be home by nine thirty at the latest and not to take any shortcuts. Much as I'd have liked an older sister, I wouldn't want one as bossy as Catherine. I don't know how Alice can stand it, but Alice just rolls her eyes and opens the front door.

Catherine taps me on the shoulder as I'm about to follow Alice outside. "New trousers, Lizzie?" she says.

I look at her in surprise. She hardly ever says a word to me. She normally looks down her nose at me, as if I'm something the cat's dragged in.

"Yes, I bought them from Topshop."

Catherine smiles and I wonder if she's finally decided to stop being such a bitch. "Well, as long as you've kept the receipt, I'm sure you'll be able to change them for a pair that actually fits."

So, that'll be a no, then.

When we arrive, it's already filling up. Dave Farley and some of the other boys are standing in huddles on the edge of the hall, swigging Coke from cans and messing around on their phones. One of the youth-club leaders is busy pulling down the blackout blinds against the evening sun and there's a line of girls waiting to put their requests in to the DJ—Melissa and Bethany and a cluster of other girls in crop tops and denim miniskirts, or black leggings so thin they look like tights. Melissa and Bethany are moving their bodies and sticking out their bottoms in time to Rihanna's "Umbrella." They've straightened their fringes and curled the ends of their hair.

Bethany waves at us and I wave back. Then I realize my mistake.

She isn't waving at *us*, she's waving at Alice. Of course she is. My cheeks go red, but hopefully no one has noticed because the blackout blinds are fully down now and . . . oh no, someone's trained lights on a giant mirror ball suspended from the ceiling. Everyone cheers as the multicolored pattern starts raining down the walls. I stare at the floor, unable to catch my breath. I won't be able to stay now. Flashing or moving lights of any kind give me seizures.

Alice touches me on the shoulder and, before I can stop her, she's marching off to speak to the young guy adjusting the position of the spotlights. I head for the exit, eyes down, a rising feeling in my gut. But just as I reach the double doors that lead into the corridor, the spotlights are turned off and everyone groans in disappointment. I turn round and edge my way back into the hall. It won't be long before word gets out that they've turned them off because of me.

Someone switches on a couple of stationary lights dotted about the place, but it's not as pretty as the mirror ball. Nowhere near. I know Alice did it for me, because she doesn't want me to have a seizure, but I wish she hadn't. I'd rather have gone home. But then she'd have had to leave, too. She's loyal like that. I'd have felt guilty then. Even guiltier than I do now, for ruining the light show for everyone else.

When I'm standing in the queue to buy a drink—7Up for Alice and apple juice for me—the girl in front of me is complaining to her friend about the mirror ball. I don't know for sure whether she's saying it because she knows I'm right behind her and can hear every word, but I'm pretty sure she is. I want to grab her stupid high ponytail and jerk her head right back and tell her not to be such a selfish cow, but I just stand there, waiting my turn, pretending I can't hear. Swaying along to Nelly Furtado.

Sally Peters and Heather Langton are talking to Alice when I get back with the drinks.

"Hi, Lizzie. I love your new trousers," Sally says. I know she's only being nice because they look awful—Catherine's left me in no doubt about that—but at least she isn't being sarcastic. She isn't saying it how Melissa or Bethany would say it. How they probably *will* say it at some point during the evening.

A couple of times, I notice Dave Farley glance over in our direction. I think he's looking at Alice. I mean, it's hard to tell exactly who he's looking at in this dim light, but it definitely won't be me, and it certainly won't be Heather. Later, though, when Snow Patrol comes on—I never remember the names of the tracks, but it's that lovely slow one—he crosses the dance floor and heads straight for me. Straight for *me*.

Oh. My. God. He's going to ask me to dance. He's smiling at me. Not at Alice or Sally. Not at Melissa or Bethany or any of the others, but at *me*. I haven't made a mistake this time. My mouth goes completely dry. It's really happening. In front of everyone. I try to look cool and unbothered, but I'm so gobsmacked and happy I can't stop my mouth from spreading into a smile. This is it. He's almost here and everyone's looking. Alice's mouth has opened slightly. She can't believe it either. Everyone's going to see Dave Farley ask *me* to dance.

But then he swerves away from me at the very last second and holds his hand out to Alice instead. Oh no. My whole body freezes in embarrassment and my stupid smile is fixed on my face like someone's drawn it on. This is awful. This is the worst thing that could have happened.

Somehow or other, I manage to keep my head high, to make it seem like I'm not in the least bit bothered, that I wasn't actually expecting him to ask me at all. I watch Alice out of the corner of my eye. She won't dance with him. I know she won't. She'll want to, but she won't. Not after what he's just done. We're best friends. We stick up for each other. She'll say no and then *he'll* be the one who's humiliated. He'll have to walk back across the dance floor all on his own, to the jeering laughter of his mates. No slow dance for you, Dave FuckFace Farley.

Except Alice doesn't shake her head and brush him off. She hands her little clutch bag to Heather Langton and follows him onto the dance floor. I shuffle closer to Sally and Heather, cheeks burning, and pretend to be interested in their conversation, pretend not to care about what's just happened.

I can't believe Alice is dancing with him. How *could* she?

Later, when we're on the way home and it's just the two of us, I tell Alice exactly what I think of her.

"How *could* you?" I shout. "How could you dance with him after what he did to me? Don't you care about my feelings at all?"

"Of *course* I care about your feelings. But . . . but *God*, Lizzie! You *know* how much I fancy Dave. And anyway, I don't think he did it on purpose. I think maybe he *was* going to ask you to dance and then he changed his mind at the last minute. Maybe he was worried you'd say no and embarrass him."

"Embarrass *him*? You're having a laugh, aren't you? You know exactly what he did and you still danced with him, knowing how I'd be feeling. You're so fucking selfish, Alice Dawson. I hate you!"

I turn on my heels and storm off in the other direction. "In fact," I shout back at the top of my voice, "I wish you were *dead*!"

24

NOW

Ross texts just as I'm ladling some soup into a bowl. I'm not really hungry but I have to eat something. All I've had today is a tiny square of toast and a banana.

With Dad now. He's lost so much weight I barely recognize him. I'll say one thing for him tho—he's a fighter. Xxx

He's sent a photo, too. A selfie of the two of them. He's right. His dad looks really ill.

Before I have a chance to reply, another one comes through. You were right. Maybe you should have come too. Next time, yes? Love you loads. Xxx

Next time. If his dad lasts, that is.

I text him straight back. I'm always right. You should know that by now! Love you too. Xxx

I dunk a piece of bread into my soup and force it down, relieved that I'm *not* sitting in a nursing home in Aberdeen feeling as queasy as this. According to the pregnancy websites I've been poring over, the nausea can last for twelve to fifteen *weeks*. For some poor women it continues for the entire pregnancy.

I'd love to phone Mum and ask her what it was like for her when she was carrying me, but then I'd have to tell her I'm pregnant and Ross and I have decided to wait till I'm at least twelve weeks before we break the news. I don't want them worrying. And they will. Of course they will. It's what they do. It's what they've always done.

Eventually, I give up and tip the soup down the sink. I wander into the living room and put the TV on, but there's nothing worth watching. I turn it off again and go back into the hall. The sunlight makes the stained glass in the front door cast colorful patterns on the wall, but all I can see is the red-wine stain. Ross has had another go at trying to remove it with bleach and water and it's definitely faded. But the whole wall will have to be repainted. If I weren't feeling so bad, I'd go and buy some paint right now. Get it done as soon as possible. At least then I wouldn't have to look at it every day. Wouldn't have to be reminded of that awful moment when I first saw Catherine Dawson in my house, saw Ross helping her remove her coat, chatting away to her.

I wander into the study and sit in front of Ross's Mac. I wonder if he's been looking for more information on Alice's death. He's bound to be curious. I would be, if the tables were turned.

I click on the Safari icon and check the latest items on his browsing history. Oh. He's been looking at reports on the Epilepsy Research website, specifically ones that focus on pregnancy and childbirth. My breath catches at the back of my throat and any resentment I've been harboring for him saying thank you to Catherine for the flowers disappears. He might be a GP, but he's never been a dad-in-waiting before. He needs reassurance just as much as I do.

Suddenly, the urge to talk to Mum is overwhelming. I don't care what we decided. She's my mother and I need to speak to her.

"Lizzie, I can't believe you didn't tell us straightaway."

"I wanted to, believe me. But we thought it best to wait until . . ."

"You'd decided what to do."

"What do you mean? Mum, surely you don't think we'd . . ."

They've put me on loudspeaker again. Dad's saying something in the background, but I can't make it out.

"Sorry, darling, I shouldn't finish your sentences. Bad habit of mine."

I take a deep breath and exhale slowly. I can't believe she'd even *think* such a thing. She of all people. "Mum, we never even considered . . ."

"Of *course* not, darling, I didn't mean anything by it. I don't even know why I said it. It's *wonderful* news. Here, your dad wants a word."

"Congratulations, Pumpkin. You must be thrilled."

I can't help hearing a thread of anxiety run through his upbeat words, or maybe it's just a projection of my own. "We are. It was a real surprise."

"These things often are. . . ."

Mum grabs the phone again. "What does your doctor say? Will you have to come off your AEDs?"

"I'm fine, Mum. You mustn't worry."

"It's just that they've been working so well for you."

Why does she always have to state the obvious? Dad's talking in the background again, only now I can hear every word. "Sue, don't start quizzing her on all that. I'm sure Ross is keeping an eye on things. He is a GP, after all."

Mum's laugh comes trilling down the line. I'm not fooled by it for one second. She's frightened for me. All the excitement I wanted to share with her fizzles out in my throat. I should never have told them over the phone. It was a stupid idea. Stupid. What was I thinking?

Because it's not just her worrying about my epilepsy, it's all the baggage surrounding her own experience of being pregnant. She almost miscarried when she was carrying me. Tripped over a child who darted in front of her on the street and had to be on bed rest for weeks on end. It's a miracle I was born at all. No wonder she's anxious.

I take a deep breath. I was going to bite the bullet and tell them

LESLEY KARA

about Catherine Dawson as well, but they're already freaking out over the pregnancy. I need to let them deal with that first before throwing them another curveball.

"You are pleased for me, aren't you, Mum?"

"Of *course* I'm pleased. I'm delighted. We both are, aren't we, Nigel? When are you coming to stay for a weekend? We can't wait to see you."

"Soon. I promise. It's just that Ross is always so tired at the weekends. He works such long hours."

"I suppose you'll be bringing the wedding forward now."

"Erm, I don't think so."

There's a noticeable pause. "But surely if you're going to have a baby . . ."

I press my lips together. I might have known she'd bring this up. Ever since Ross and I got engaged, she's been asking us about our plans. The thing is, having a baby makes it even more likely we'll hold off for longer. I don't want to walk down the aisle with a big belly sticking out the front of my dress. How's that going to look in the photos?

Dad says something in the background and Mum says, "Okay, okay."

"I'm being told to stop interfering," she says.

Dad always knows when to step in.

After we've said goodbye, my mind keeps playing back the early part of our conversation. I imagine them in their sitting room, analyzing the risks. Or rather, Mum will be analyzing the risks and Dad will be telling her not to, but doing it all the same.

Is Ross worrying, too? He's made a good show of reassuring me so far, but is it all just a ploy to keep me calm? I cast my mind back to when I first told him, that fleeting expression of panic on his face. Had a termination crossed his mind, too? Should it have crossed mine?

If ever I needed one of my girlfriends to confide in, it's now. But the truth is, ever since I met Ross I've been drifting apart from them, not making an effort to see them. I shouldn't have let things slide, but that's exactly what I have done.

Catherine's card flashes into my mind. I remember the worry lines on her forehead when she asked if we could call a truce, the way she clasped my hand, could barely bring herself to let it go. There were tears in her eyes. Tears in mine. She's a nurse practitioner. She must have loads of experience with pregnant women. She'll know something about epilepsy, too. But no, it's unthinkable. Reaching some kind of understanding about the past is one thing. Becoming friends is quite another.

An odd sensation washes through me. A sense that something inside my head has shifted, almost as if I'm revisiting a familiar old memory. My knees buckle. Oh God, I know what this is.

25

A slab of light bathes my right cheek. I squint and try to turn my head, but the effort involved is too much. There's an abrasive sensation on the left side of my face. I try to lift my head but only manage to raise it a few inches. I'm lying on the floor between the sofa and the coffee table. I clamber onto my knees and touch my left cheek. It's sore from where it's been pressed onto the carpet.

Tears come then, coursing silently, hotly, down my cheeks.

It's happened again. After all this time.

I heave myself up onto the sofa and slump back against the cushions. Somewhere, a long way away, a phone rings. Why doesn't anybody answer it? I force my eyelids open. The slab of light has now gone. The room is chilly. I ought to get up and go to the toilet, put a jumper on. If only I could swing my legs over the edge of the sofa, but they're blocks of lead.

A wave of nausea surges up to my chest. I clamp my hand over my mouth and curl up on my side in a tight little ball till an overwhelming tiredness swallows me up and drags me back down into darkness.

"Lizzie?" Ross's voice wakes me. "Lizzie, how long have you been lying here?"

I try to speak, but my mouth isn't working.

"Shit. You must have had a seizure," he says. His voice sounds as if it's coming from a great distance, but he's right here beside me. I can feel his warm hands on my arms, my face. "I'm going to go and get a blanket. You're really cold."

A jolt of panic courses through me as I remember. "The baby!"

Ross kisses my forehead. "The baby will be fine."

But when he returns with the blanket, I can see he's as scared as I am, though he's trying his best to hide it.

He tucks the blanket around me, then puts one hand on my forehead and takes my pulse with the other. "It's okay, darling. You know this sleepiness is normal after seizures. And you don't appear to have injured yourself. Even so, I'm going to take you straight to A & E. Just to be on the safe side."

I struggle to sit up, but the effort involved is too much and I flop back down again. Ross perches on the edge of the sofa and strokes my forehead.

"Did you throw up this morning?" he asks.

"Yes."

He sighs, heavily. "I could kick myself for not anticipating this. I think what's been happening is that your body hasn't been fully absorbing your medication."

He kisses the tip of my nose. "I'm going to carry you out to the car, okay?"

"Can't I just go to my doctor's in the morning? We'll be hanging around for ages and you've got to be at work tomorrow."

He scoops me up in his arms. "This is important, Lizzie," he says. "Right now, you're the only patient in the world I care about."

I balk at the word "patient," but I'm too tired and groggy to object and, besides, he's worried. He's putting on a good show of being relaxed and matter-of-fact about all this, but when I steal a glance at him from the passenger seat, his face is taut and pale.

———

By the time we get back from the hospital, it's half past three in the morning. I can barely keep my eyes open and my limbs feel weighted. Ross lowers me onto the bed and helps me take my clothes and shoes off, covers me tenderly with the duvet. Then he strips off and falls into bed next to me. Poor Ross. All that traveling in one day, and then hanging around in A & E for hours on end while I had blood tests and scans. But at least I've been thoroughly checked over.

I turn my head to speak to Ross, but he's already sound asleep at my side. I rest my hand on the small of his back. I didn't even ask him about his father.

I stare at the ceiling. Having a major seizure after all this time is a huge wake-up call. But just because it's happened once doesn't necessarily mean it will happen again. I just have to be more careful from now on. More vigilant when it comes to keeping my meds down.

Every couple of minutes the headlights from passing cars shine through a gap in the curtains and pattern the wall. I count the seconds between cars, notice small variations in the quality of light and the size and shape of the patterns. Anything to stop my mind dwelling on the terrible feeling of dread that sits in the pit of my stomach like a stone. The feeling that won't be assuaged by rational thought.

The following weeks pass in a tedious blur of nausea and tiredness. I've been eating salty crackers to stop myself from throwing up and I'm making a real effort to stay calm, but I can't help feeling resentful that what's meant to be a happy and exciting time has been overshadowed by my re-immersion into the world of hospital appointments and medical tests. Something I thought was a thing of the past.

"You'd still have to go to hospital, even if you didn't have epilepsy," Ross says one evening when I try to explain how it makes me feel. We've been measuring the spare room for curtains. The spare room that *was* going to be my study, but which is now going to be turned into a nursery.

"You should hear Catherine on the medicalization of pregnancy and childbirth," he says. "It's her—"

He stops when he sees my face and realizes what he's just said.

Tension crackles between us like static. "It's her *what*?" My voice is cold, hard.

"It's her pet peeve," he says at last.

A flush of anger suffuses my face. "How come you're so familiar with her *pet peeves*?"

He gives me an exasperated look, as if I'm the one who's in the wrong, and maybe I am, but it's too late now. I'm all wound up.

"Because I *work* with her, Lizzie. Colleagues talk to each other. Surely you can't expect me to ignore her?"

"No, of course not. But I don't expect you to bring her into our private conversations."

The silence between us lengthens. Solidifies.

"I'm sorry," he says at last. "I'll try not to mention her again."

"Thank you."

He tries to hug me, but something I've forgotten until this very second, what with the seizure and all the hospital tests and the nausea, arrives in my head and sets me off again. I wriggle free from his arms.

"You thanked her, didn't you? For those flowers."

He looks bewildered. "How do you know that?"

"I popped in to the surgery to use the toilet, the day you flew to Aberdeen. I bumped into her. I told you I didn't want her sending me flowers. Now you've just encouraged her."

I sound childish and petulant, I know I do, but now that I've started, I can't help it. He shouldn't have thanked her for them. They weren't for him, they were for me. And I didn't want them.

He sighs. "I thought it was the polite thing to do. I felt awkward, not saying anything."

"I see, so her feelings are more important to you than mine. Well, at least I know where I stand."

"Oh, for God's sake, Lizzie! Don't be ridiculous!"

He flings the metal tape measure on the floor so that it bounces up and hits the skirting board. Then he leaves the room without saying another word. He's never lost his temper with me before. Never.

I lean back against the wall and slide down till I'm in a crouching position, my head in my hands. This should be a happy time for us: a new house and a baby on the way. It should be exciting—the beginning of our life together. Instead it feels spoiled already. Catherine might be a nicer person now, but she's still managed to fuck everything up.

26

THEN: AFTER

TUESDAY, SEPTEMBER 11, 2007

There's going to be a special school service for Alice. Mr. Davis made an announcement about it this morning, and Mrs. Peacock has just given us letters to take home. I can't peel my eyes away from the heading, underlined and in bold: **The Alice Dawson Memorial Service**. There's going to be a plaque, too, and a tree planted in her honor.

It all seems so unreal. I keep expecting—hoping—to wake up and discover that it's all been a bad dream, that it never really happened and that instead of the empty seat next to me, Alice is still sitting there, her ink-stained fingers fiddling with her pen or rearranging the contents of her pencil case. She was really looking forward to Mrs. Peacock being our form teacher. "Mrs. Peacock is cool," she used to say, mainly because of the small tattoo of an anchor on her left inner wrist. Alice was mad for tattoos. Couldn't wait till she was old enough to have one of her own. She would have done, too.

"Whenever I feel worried or anxious about anything," Mrs. Peacock explained to us last year in her music class, before we knew that she'd be our next form teacher, "I look at my anchor and feel safe and grounded."

I take out one of my Berol coloring pens—the black one—and draw a little anchor on my own inner wrist right now, but no matter how many times I look at it, I don't feel in the least bit safe and grounded. I feel dangerously loose and adrift. Cut off from everyone around me.

Melissa Davenport is staring at me from the other side of the classroom. "Miss?" she calls out. "I think Lizzie's trying to slit her wrists."

Someone, somewhere, whispers the words "guilty conscience."

Mrs. Peacock stands up and peers across the classroom. "Don't be silly, Melissa. Lizzie, what are you doing?"

"Nothing, Miss. Just doodling."

"She's giving herself a tattoo," says a voice from behind me. Bethany Charles. One of Melissa's inner circle.

"Okay, that's enough," Mrs. Peacock says. "Time to put your things away, girls. And remember to give those letters to your parents when you get home." The bell goes a second later.

As I'm walking out of the classroom, Mrs. Peacock taps me softly on the shoulder. "Lizzie, can we have a quick word?"

I hope she's not going to ask to look at my wrist, because it'll be embarrassing—I'm not very good at drawing and my anchor looks more like a wonky arrow—but she doesn't. She gestures for me to sit on the spare chair at her desk and then she sits down in her own chair, adjusting it slightly so that we're facing each other. I can see her knees sticking out from under her skirt.

"How's it going?" she says, and I don't know whether it's the question itself or the kind, gentle way she says it, but my eyes start burning with unshed tears and I know I'm not going to be able to stop them coming out without wiping my eyes with my fingers, and then she'll know I'm crying. But if I don't, she'll know anyway. And now she does. Because here they come. Big, fat, treacherous tears rolling down my cheeks.

"If things get too much for you, Lizzie, you know you can always come and talk to me."

I nod, unable to look at her face for fear I'll break down completely.

"It can't be easy for you. . . ." She points to the letter about the remembrance service and the memory tree. "Mrs. French said you didn't go to your counseling session yesterday."

"I already see a counselor."

"I know you do. But I think it's important you have someone here at school you can discuss things with, too. She's been helping some of the other girls work through their feelings about Alice. If it's not working out with Mrs. French, you'll come and tell me, yes? We can look at other options."

"It's fine. I had a headache, that's all. I wanted to go home."

"I understand that. But maybe you could let her know next time, yes? Or let me know so that I can get a message to her."

"Okay." I sniff. "Sorry."

Mrs. Peacock nods and lays three fingers on my forearm. "I'll have a word with Melissa if you'd like."

"No!" My head shoots up. "It'll only make things worse. I'd rather you didn't."

Mrs. Peacock presses her lips together and exhales through her nostrils. I get the feeling she'd like to say more, but is having to hold it back.

Sally Peters is waiting for me outside the classroom when I come out. She's been nice to me since we started back at school, although not quite nice enough to sit next to me in class. She's told me she can't stop sitting next to Heather Langton or it wouldn't be fair on Heather. Although, apparently, it's fine if it's unfair on *me*.

"Don't take any notice of Melissa," Sally says as we walk across the playground. "She's a right cow."

"Where's Heather?"

"Chess club."

Ah, so that's why she's walking home with me. But hey, beggars can't be choosers. At least I won't have to face the school gates alone, where Melissa and Co. are bound to be hanging around with the boys. Maybe Sally will ask me back to hers. She lives in the next street along from Riley Road, where Alice lives. Where Alice *lived*.

A horrible empty feeling comes over me and, for a minute or so, I think I'm going to be sick. Alice and I went to Sally's house last year, sat in her bedroom with her and Heather and painted each other's nails. Another time we played catch outside Sally's house on a summer evening, a whole group of us standing on both sides of the street, chucking a big inflatable ball back and forth and shrieking with laughter. That kind of thing would *never* happen where I live. For a start, Birchwood Avenue is a much busier road and, even if it wasn't, people there don't let their children play outside.

I know we're lucky to have a big house and garden, but sometimes I wonder if I'd have been happier living on the estate instead of being stuck out at the edge of town, a long bus ride from school. Maybe then I'd have fitted in and made more friends, wouldn't have been so reliant on Alice.

But Mum and Dad have never liked the estate. They've always said how rough it is, and how it's gone downhill since the seventies, when it was first built. They were really upset when I failed my eleven plus and didn't get into the grammar, and since the next-best school was two bus rides and a ten-minute walk away, I ended up here, with all the kids from the estate.

If only I'd passed that stupid test, I'd never have met Alice. She'd still be alive today.

27

NOW

"Love is like wood," Mum says when I tell her that Ross and I had an argument yesterday. "It expands and contracts depending on the weather. You have to allow for some shrinkage every now and again."

She's always coming out with little sayings like this. She's right, though. I've been expecting Ross and me to carry on as though nothing has changed, as though the "loved-up phase" we've been enjoying since we met would last forever.

"You've been through some pretty major life changes recently," Mum says. "It's a new relationship, remember. You're still getting to know each other, learning how to adapt to each other's moods. You have to work at these things, darling. They don't just happen."

I haven't told her *why* we rowed. Who we were rowing about. Not yet. I'm working my way up to it. Maybe Ross is right and I do need to speak to a counselor. Someone to help me sift through this maelstrom of emotions and find a way through. It won't be like it was before, with Angela Harris. But can I really face being questioned about the past?

We chat for a few more minutes before saying goodbye. The phone rings almost as soon as I've put it down.

"Mum? What did you forget?"

But it's a stranger's voice in my ear. A woman with an Australian accent.

"Hello. May I speak to Lizzie Molyneux, please?" Whoever she is, she's actually managed to pronounce my name correctly.

Maybe it's someone from the community midwife team.

"Speaking."

"This is Ruby Orchard. You won't know me, but I'd very much like to speak to you about something." She has that rising inflection at the end of each sentence. "I'm not trying to sell you anything, I promise. I just need five minutes of your time."

"How can I help you?" She's lying about not trying to sell me anything. It's the cold caller's favorite line. Ross would have hung up by now, but I always feel a little sorry for them. It must be a soul-destroying way to earn a living.

"I'm writing a piece about Elodie Stevens, the poor girl that got killed by a train? I understand your friend, Alice—"

I slam the receiver down in fury. A bloody reporter. How the hell did they find me? I know it's impossible to have zero online presence—there are news articles with my name in, for a start—but I don't do social media. Never have. I've been on a couple of epilepsy chat forums in the past, but always under a pseudonym. I've been so careful never to give away any private details.

It rings again straightaway. I let it go to answerphone and listen, fists clenched at my side, heart racing.

"Miss Molyneux, I think we might have got cut off there. I'm doing a piece on the debate that's going on about Network Rail's program of level-crossing closures."

Her voice fills the room, a torrent of words battering my ears.

"Not everyone agrees with the closures. They think it causes more problems in rural communities. Prevents access and forces people to

use dangerous roads instead. I'm keen to get a range of different opinions. I've already spoken to a representative of the Dawson family and
I was wondering whether—"

The message ends abruptly. The recording time has reached its
limit and so have I. I rush to the downstairs toilet, lift the lid, and
throw up.

28

I tell Ross about the phone call as soon as he comes home. We've made up after our argument yesterday, but things have been a little subdued between us, so I'm glad of the need to talk to him directly about something else. Giving him a problem to solve is just what I need to get him back onside. Besides, it's Friday night. I don't want this atmosphere hanging over us all weekend.

Ross looks furious on my behalf. "Don't feel pressured into talking to this reporter if she rings back. Put the phone down on her."

"I just can't understand how she's tracked me down. And why now, after all these years?"

"Because of this other girl who's died, I suppose. It's got them sniffing around for similar stories in the past. As for tracking you down, you know what reporters are like. They have their ways."

"I can't help wondering who . . ." I bite my lip and stare out of the window. Now that the thought has occurred to me, I realize we're probably going to end up rowing yet again.

"What?"

"I can't help wondering who this representative of the Dawson family is. The one she said she'd already spoken to."

Ross shifts in his chair. He looks about as uncomfortable as I feel. We've landed straight back into the same dodgy territory that had us rowing before, but it's too late now. I have to say what's on my mind.

"I can't imagine Sheena or Mick Dawson would want to get involved with reporters. They must have been besieged by them when Alice died. We certainly were, although Mum and Dad did a pretty good job of keeping me away from all that." I look him squarely in the face. "What if it's Catherine she's spoken to? What if it's Catherine who's given her our number?"

Ross closes his eyes. When he opens them a few seconds later, he looks tired and more than a little wary.

"Would you like me to ask her on Monday? Because you know I'll have to talk to her to do that."

I force myself not to react. "No. I'll ask her myself."

In the end, we have a quiet, cozy weekend, and for that I'm grateful. Ross finds several websites that compare the size of a developing fetus to different types of fruit and vegetables. At just under twelve weeks, our baby is currently the size of a plum, or a lime, or a small peach, depending on which website you look at. We look at them all. We also make plans to visit my parents in two weeks' time, by which time Peach Murray will be the size of a large lemon. We don't mention Catherine Dawson once.

But when Monday comes around and Ross has driven off to work, I retrieve her card from my coat pocket and compose a short text message. Just because Ruby Orchard didn't phone back over the weekend doesn't mean she won't try again, and I'm determined to find out if it was Catherine who put her on to me.

I need to speak to you about something. Tell me a good time to call. As an afterthought, I add my name.

Her response comes almost immediately.

I'm free now. Let me call you?

Okay, I text back, heart thumping.

The sudden ringtone on my mobile makes me jump, even though I'm expecting it. This is all happening so much faster than I'd anticipated. Why didn't I wait till later in the day, when I'd composed myself more?

"Hello?" My voice sounds high and nervous.

"Lizzie," she says. "I'm so glad you messaged me. I didn't think you ever would."

I clear my throat. "Nor did I, but . . . I've had a phone call I need to talk to you about."

"Go on."

I pause, unsure how to continue. It would be better to have this conversation face-to-face, so I can see her expression when I tell her. That way I'll know if she's telling the truth.

"I was wondering if . . ."

What? What am I wondering? If she'll come round for a coffee and a chat? No, the thought of her in this house again fills me with dread.

"Would you like to meet somewhere?" she says. "There's a café in Charlton Park. Do you know it? I could be there in half an hour?"

"You're not at work?"

"No, it's one of my study days."

"Okay. I'll see you at the café in thirty minutes."

The café is full when I arrive. It's a quirky little place with pictures of Henry VIII and other notables on the outside. Inside, it's set up like a quaint tea shop. Small tables and odd chairs squeezed into a rectangular space that can't be more than eight by four meters. There's a noise of chatter and the clattering of teacups, the hiss from the coffee machine. Catherine isn't here yet and, unless someone vacates a table, we won't be able to sit inside, which is probably just as well, because the smell of bacon is turning my stomach.

I hang around near the doorway, unwilling to settle at one of the outside tables even though there are blankets thoughtfully folded over the back of each chair. It might be less than a month till summer, but there's a cold wind blowing today. Maybe we won't have a coffee. It might be better to walk round the park instead.

I feel a tap on my shoulder and spin round.

"Hi, have you been waiting long?" she says. She's wearing a navy coat that hangs open over jeans and a white jumper. The tip of her nose is pink.

"No, I've just arrived. There aren't any free tables inside."

"Let's sit here, then," she says, and I find myself agreeing, even though I've just convinced myself that walking would be preferable.

"What will you have?" she says. "My treat." She tucks a strand of hair behind her ear.

"An Americano, please. Decaf."

She nods and smiles. "Wise choice. I should switch to that, but I'm a terrible grump without my shot of morning caffeine."

She goes inside to get them and I sit down at one of the round metal tables, spreading a pale blue check blanket over my knees and feeling faintly ridiculous. Why on earth am I doing this? It's crazy.

Then I think of Ruby Orchard's phone call, her proposed article on railway-crossing deaths, and I know I have to find out if it's Catherine she's spoken to, and what she might have said.

Five minutes later, when Catherine is sitting opposite me, her elbows planted on the table, her long, slender fingers cradling her mug of coffee in front of her chin, I finally pluck up the courage to broach the topic.

"I had a phone call on Friday. From a reporter."

Catherine lowers her mug and places it carefully on the table. It might just be the chill in the air, but I could swear that her cheeks are getting redder.

"Did you give her my number?" The directness of my question takes us both by surprise.

"No! Absolutely not. I would never—"

"Only I don't understand how a reporter has found me after all this time. It seems rather a coincidence."

"Lizzie, you have to believe me, I didn't give her your number. I didn't even know what it was until this morning, when you texted me."

"She rang the landline."

"Was it someone called Ruby Orchard?"

"Yes."

"She found me, too. It's because of this latest tragedy. Elodie Stevens."

"I know."

Catherine sighs. "I wasn't going to speak to her, not after all the press intrusion we had before. That kind of thing puts you off reporters for life—they're like vultures, some of them—but, well, Ruby sounded different. It's a serious piece she's putting together. I . . . I agreed to meet her."

She takes a sip of her coffee. "I only intended to stay for one drink, but we really hit it off. It was only the next morning that I realized they're all like that, aren't they? Friendly. Chatty. It's an art, getting a complete stranger to open up to you and drop their defenses." She gives a rueful laugh. "I should have known better than to meet her in a wine bar. It had been a long day at work and, well, you know how it is."

"So you told her you'd met up with me again."

Now there's no mistaking the color in her face and neck.

"It came out in conversation, yes, that you were the girlfriend of one of my colleagues." *Fiancée*, I silently correct her. "I'm sorry, Lizzie. It was a stupid mistake to make. I guess a snippet like that's all they need to ferret someone out. But honestly, I don't think you've got anything to worry about. As I said, it's an interesting piece she's planning. Not at all sensationalist. The way I see it, if her article helps to get the remaining open crossings closed or at the very least improves their safety, it'll be a good thing, won't it? So no other child will suffer the same fate as Alice and Elodie and all the others who've needlessly lost their lives in the past."

"When you put it like that . . ." I say. But I know I'll never speak to Ruby Orchard. I won't speak to any reporter.

29

We wait till Catherine has left the house. Then we kneel on Alice's bed, which is positioned under the window in her room, and, with our elbows on the sill, we watch as she walks up the street in her denim shorts and high heels, her tiny shoulder bag bouncing against her hip bone.

I'm glad Alice and I have made up after our horrible row the night of the disco. We've both said sorry and we're almost back to normal, although I don't think either of us is ever going to forget about it.

"Where's she going?" I ask.

"She's meeting her boyfriend for lunch in Nando's."

"What's he like?"

"Dunno. Never met him."

"What's he called?"

Alice shrugs. "Every time Dad or I ask her, she gets all cross and tells us to mind our own business."

"Is that fake tan on her legs?"

"She's had one of those professional sprays at the beauty salon."

"Hope he's worth it."

Alice giggles. "Not if he's taking her to Nando's, he isn't."

"Do you think they have sex?"

Alice peers down the street. Catherine has now disappeared from sight. "Let's go and look in her room and see if we can find any evidence."

"What, you mean like check her sheets?"

Alice rolls her eyes. "No, of *course* not. She never brings him here. I mean *contraceptives*."

We've just learned about contraceptives in Sex and Relationships at school.

It gives me an uncomfortable feeling, being in Catherine Dawson's bedroom. If she changes her mind for some reason and comes back to the house and catches us in here, she'll go ballistic. I'll never forget that time she slapped Alice round the face. Such a vicious slap, too. Alice's cheek was red for ages afterward. She tried to be brave and pretend it didn't hurt, but it must have really stung. I'm sure if Alice had been on her own, Catherine wouldn't have reacted half so badly. It was the fact that she'd sprayed the perfume onto *my* wrist that made her so angry. Why does she hate me so much?

Alice is already kneeling in front of her sister's bedside cabinet and looking in the top drawer. I peer, nervously, over her shoulder. It's really messy in there. Candy wrappers and lip-balm sticks; empty boxes of paracetamol; hair grips and scrunchies; emery boards and throat sweets. At least she won't notice that the contents of the drawer have been disturbed.

At last, Alice pulls out a rectangular blister pack of white pills with days of the week printed under each one and little arrows indicating which order to take them in.

"Are these what I think they are?" she says, a note of glee in her voice.

I count the pills. "Twenty-one. Yes. She's on the pill."

"I wonder where they do it."

"Perhaps he's got a car."

Alice giggles again. "We ought to follow her. See where they go."

She puts the pills back in the drawer and shuts it. "*Shall* we? We could spy on them in Nando's."

"But what if she sees us?"

"She won't. Come on, it'll be fun."

We pull on our trainers and leave the house. If we were at mine, I'd have had to tell Mum and Dad where we were going—they'd want to know. But things are different at Alice's house. Alice's dad is dismantling a car engine in the back garden and doesn't seem the slightest bit bothered what we do, and her mum is in bed again. Last week she was up and about and chatting to the neighbor. Last week was a *good week*. That's what Alice told me earlier, in that matter-of-fact way she has when she talks about her mum's illness. Last week was a good week and this week isn't. I hope I never suffer from depression.

We walk to the high street. It doesn't take long from Riley Road. Catherine must be there by now.

"I don't see how this is going to work," I say. "If we look through the window, she'll see us, won't she?"

"God, Lizzie, you're such a worrier. We're not *going* to look through the window. We're going to watch from somewhere we can see the entrance and wait till they come out. Then we'll follow them."

"But they might be in there ages."

Alice gives one of her long sighs. "You'd make a terrible detective. You have to be patient on a stakeout."

She pulls out a big packet of American Hard Gums that she's somehow managed to stuff into the pocket of her jeans. She must have swiped it from the goody cupboard on her way out—the one that's always stuffed full of sweets and chocolate biscuits and packets of crisps. The sorts of things my mum and dad never buy.

We sit on the wide stone steps outside the town hall, the packet of Hard Gums between us. We watch. We wait. We chew.

Every time someone goes in or comes out of Nando's, we sit up a little straighter. The sun is warm on our bare legs—Alice's are browner than mine, which is annoying, but then she has a different skin tone to me, more olive-colored, so she tans easily. With my pale freckled skin, I have to be careful I don't burn. I tried one of those self-tanning lotions once. Big mistake. I looked orange and streaky for weeks.

The gums taste good and for a while it's fun. But it soon gets boring, having to look in one direction the whole time, and I've eaten too many gums and my teeth feel all sticky. I'm thirsty, too.

All of a sudden, Alice grabs me by the arm. "There they are! Look! They're heading for the bridge. Let's go!"

We follow them from a distance. Now, this *is* exciting. I feel like I'm a character in a film. A private eye. The man is tall and slim. He's wearing board shorts and a T-shirt and he's got a navy baseball cap on the wrong way round. His arm is loose around Catherine's waist and she's leaning up against him as they walk. Her shorts are cut so high you can actually see her bum cheeks. Every so often the man's hand slips away from her waist and down toward the back of her shorts. One time he does this, he grabs a handful of her right bum cheek and gives it a squeeze. Catherine doesn't even flinch. She just lets him.

We've crossed over the bridge now and are heading for the subway that goes under the dual carriageway.

"They're definitely going to do it," Alice says, her eyes glued to her sister's bottom.

We follow them down into the underpass, waiting till they're almost at the end of the tunnel before we set off after them. When we see which exit they've taken we speed up.

Out in the sunlight again, it isn't immediately clear where they've gone, and for a few seconds we think we've lost them. But then I spot them in the car park, climbing into a blue car.

"Shit," Alice says. "That's the end of that, then. They're just going to drive off, aren't they?"

Except the car doesn't go anywhere. We climb over the low wall that separates the car park from the pavement and creep as close as we dare, keeping low so that we're hidden by the other parked cars.

"Hang on," I say. "Where's she gone? I can only see him in there now. She must have got out."

Alice peeps round the white van we're now hiding behind. "No, she's still in there."

"But why can't we—"

Alice looks at me and inserts her index finger into her mouth, starts sucking it and pushing it in and out.

I clap my hands to my mouth and collapse in a fit of giggles.

"Look at his face, Lizzie. Look at his *face!*"

I squint to get a better view. It's hard to see much from this distance but I can just make out that he's extended his head back onto the headrest so that his chin is sticking up in the air.

Alice retrieves the packet of Hard Gums from her pocket. There are only two left now so we have one each.

We watch. We wait. We chew.

"How long do you think it takes to give someone a blow job?" I ask, my mouth still full of Hard Gum.

Alice smirks. "Depends how good you are. They like it more if you swallow."

The last of the Hard Gum slips down my throat. I slide my eyes to the side to look at Alice's face. How come she knows all this stuff and I don't? I think of the way Dave Farley's hands rested in the small of her back when he danced with her. How close together they were. No, she can't have done. She would have told me, wouldn't she? That nasty feeling I get when I think of Alice having a boyfriend makes me clench my jaw.

Suddenly, her expression changes and I look back at the car. The man in the back-to-front baseball cap has started convulsing in the driver's seat. I stare at him, transfixed. What on earth . . . ?

Alice nudges me in the ribs with her elbow. "Think you've got your answer, Lizzie. I make that just under five minutes."

30

NOW

"This is meant to be the finest example of Jacobean domestic architecture in the country," Catherine says. She's reading from her phone. "And now they've got a pizza restaurant in the minstrels' gallery."

She laughs, and for one startling moment it's as though Alice has come back as a fully grown woman. I never realized before how alike the two of them were. Their voices, their laughs, their mannerisms. She has the same high cheekbones as well. The same olive-colored skin and dark, glossy hair.

I'm not quite sure how it happened, because agreeing to meet for a coffee was only ever intended as a means to quiz her about that reporter, but instead of going straight home as soon as we'd finished, I've somehow allowed myself to be led round the park and entertained by her, as if we're old friends. Now we're standing in front of Charlton House. I stare at the imposing red-brick building, trying to work out what's going on here.

A gust of wind blows my hair over my eyes and I reach into my pocket for a scrunchie, gather my wayward curls into a ponytail.

"You look so different now," Catherine says. "Long hair suits you."

I spy on her from the corner of my eye. The old Catherine would probably have followed this up with something horrible like "Especially when it covers your face." But this new, nicer Catherine lets the compliment hang in the air and I find myself thanking her.

"Do you ever think of the old days, in Riley Road?" she asks.

The mention of Riley Road does something weird to my insides.

"I think of them all the time," she says. "I almost went back to see our old house a few years ago."

"Oh, so your parents moved, then?"

"Yes, they live in a little village in North Devon now. Moving to the countryside was good for them. Especially Mum."

I take a deep breath. Even though I know that Sheena Dawson suffered from depression well before Alice died, her younger daughter's tragic death must have catapulted her into the darkest place for the longest of times and I can't help feeling guilty about that. Because I could never give her what she needed. I could never tell her what happened.

"They must be very proud of you, being a nurse."

She nods. "They are."

"You used to work as a secretary, didn't you? What made you go into nursing?" I keep my voice as casual as I can, aware that my heart is beating faster. Surely she must realize that it's the last career I would ever have imagined her pursuing.

She sighs. "I suppose it was because of Mum. Her depression forced me to take responsibility for things from a very young age. I had to help Dad look after her. And when Alice came along, I looked after her, too. Dad worked long hours at the shop and Mum wasn't up to much at all after the birth."

A crow swoops across the sky and lands on one of the chimney pots of Charlton House. A few seconds later, it's joined by two more. The three of them screech at one another and Catherine and I both look up at the same time.

I steal a glance at her from the corner of my eye. It wasn't exactly the happiest household even *before* Alice died. If Sheena Dawson wasn't lying in her bed in a welter of depression for weeks on end, she was distant and uptight, more concerned with cleaning the house from top to bottom and despairing over the state of their garden than with the emotional well-being of her two daughters.

"It must be nice to have a vocation," I say, trying to steer the conversation back onto safer ground. "I've never really worked out what it is I want to do with my life."

"Why do you think that is?" she says.

"I've no idea. Perhaps I've let my seizures hold me back. Or rather, the fear of them."

Catherine doesn't respond. It was the wrong thing to say. The only seizure I can think of right now is the one I had at the railway crossing. She must be thinking the exact same thing. How *could* I have been so thoughtless?

But suddenly, she's leaning in toward me, eyes wide. "You shouldn't let *anything* hold you back," she says. "When you work out what it is you need to do, you have to go for it, one hundred percent."

"I *was* going to apply to do an English degree at Greenwich University."

"So what's stopping you?"

I open my mouth, then close it again. The urge to tell her about the pregnancy clamors at the back of my throat. Something stops me, though. Some instinct it might hit a nerve.

"Not sure, really. Maybe I just need to settle here first."

"Lizzie," she says, standing still all of a sudden. "Would it be all right if we did this again sometime? I mean, you probably don't want to and I wouldn't blame you at all if you'd rather not, it's just that, I don't have many friends here yet and . . ." She shakes her head and starts walking again. "Sorry, it's a stupid idea. I didn't mean to put you on the spot like that. Forget I ever said anything."

"No, it's okay, really. I . . . I think I'd like that, too."

"I must say, I'm surprised," Ross says, when I tell him that evening of my walk with Catherine.

He's just shed his clothes into the laundry box and is standing on the landing, completely starkers. I'm still getting used to this part of living together. I wish I was as unselfconscious about my body as he is of his.

He walks into the bathroom and starts running the shower. "Surprised in a good way," he adds. "It's not healthy to hold on to grudges."

He's not the only one who's surprised.

"It's hard to explain," I tell him, so I don't even try. After everything Catherine put me through as a child, becoming friends with her seems crazy. But there's a connection between us I can't deny and, somehow, despite everything, it feels like it's meant to happen.

He steps into the cubicle and reaches for the shower gel. My eyes travel down his body as he starts to lather it. He catches me watching him and grins, crooks his forefinger to beckon me in. A minute later, I'm standing in there, too, pressed up against him, water streaming off our soapy bodies as he kisses my neck. It's the first time we've made love in weeks. Now that my nausea is finally on its way out, things are getting back to normal at last.

All thoughts of Catherine disappear into the steam.

31

I stand on my parents' doorstep and press the bell. It seems strange not being able to let myself in with a key. I've still got one in my handbag, but I'd never use it. In fact, I must remember to give it back to them. This isn't my home anymore; I'm a visitor now. But as soon as Dad opens the door and I step inside, the years fall away. Whatever changes they make to the decor, whatever new pieces of furniture they buy, the familiar smell of my childhood always greets me.

"Hello, Pumpkin," Dad says, taking a step back to look at me. "You're putting on a bit of weight, love."

"Very funny."

He gives me a big hug. Then Ross appears behind us with the bags and I move aside to let him clasp Dad's hand and do their jolly shoulder-slapping thing.

Mum's now at the foot of the stairs. "You look wonderful, darling."

"She always was a good liar," I say to Ross, and Mum pretends to look cross.

"You *do* look wonderful," she says. "Just a little pale, that's all. Which is only to be expected."

"Did Mum tell you what's happening this afternoon?" Dad asks.

"Yes, and it's fine."

"It seems so rude to disappear almost as soon as you've arrived," Mum says. "Especially when I've been on at you to come down for ages. But we'll only be gone an hour and a half. If there was any way we could have got out of it, we would have done."

"Stop worrying, we'll be fine."

"You could even come with us if you wanted?"

I put my head on one side. "Hmm. Looking after Liz Metcalfe's lighting shop for an hour and a half or lying on your sofa watching telly and eating cakes? What to do, what to do . . ."

I look at Ross and he joins in the game, pretends to be weighing up the options.

"Do you know what?" he says. "I think we'll leave you to it."

"Right, then," Mum says. "Let's sit down and catch up. Lunch will be ready in about an hour. More than enough time for Dad to bore you with the plans for our week in New York."

Mum and Dad have just left the house for their shop-minding stint. I go upstairs to unpack our things in the spare room, leaving Ross dozing in front of the TV. Out of habit, I wander into my old bedroom and sit on the end of the single bed. As I gaze out at the North Sea, with the dock cranes in the distance, I feel myself soften and relax like I did the first time we moved here, when all the stress and tension I'd been holding in my body since the accident began its slow retreat, as though the tide was washing it away.

Dad always says that living by the sea is good for the soul. He would walk with me sometimes, in those early days, just the two of us, out on the sand in the early mornings, collecting driftwood and shells. We didn't go in for long conversations. Occasionally we chatted about this and that, a TV program we'd both watched, or a book one or the other of us had read, but most of the time we walked in companionable silence. I really miss those walks.

I stand up and go over to the tall chest of drawers where my clothes used to be. It's being in this room again that's bringing it all back, making me think of things I haven't thought about for ages. The drawers are now full of Mum's craft supplies: balls of wool and knitting needles; patterns and magazines; sewing tins and button boxes. I examine the rest of the room and take in all the small changes that have been made since I left: different pictures on the wall; a diary and pen on the desk; a vase of dried flowers.

I open the window and sit in the wicker chair where once I discarded the clothes I couldn't be bothered to put away, which Mum used to tell me off about. I smile. Now here I am, about to enter a whole new phase of life by becoming a mother myself, while Mum's leaving that phase behind and focusing on herself again. She's even volunteering at the local hospice. She hasn't worked since before I was born. And now she and Dad are starting to do things they've always wanted to do. Like visiting New York. It makes me realize how liberated they must feel now that I'm so much better and have left home, how my epilepsy limited *all* of our lives.

It's then that I remember the pink shoebox. The one full of memories from when I was a baby. First lock of hair, first pair of bootees. As a young child, I'd loved it when Mum showed me these things. It made me feel special.

I open each of the drawers in the tall chest, wondering if perhaps I might find it in one of them. It seems a likely place to keep it, but it isn't here. I'll have to ask her about it later.

But as I drift back into the spare room to start unpacking our bits and pieces, I remember where I saw it last. At the bottom of Mum's wardrobe. I drop Ross's spare T-shirt on the bed and rush off to see if it's still there.

As my fingers touch the brass doorknob of their closed bedroom door, I hesitate. That same feeling of excitement and trepidation I had as a child whenever I trespassed over this threshold takes hold of me once more. I push open the door, hearing the familiar shushing sound as it moves across the thick pile of the carpet. Back then, I was bored and nosy. I knew it was wrong to look at their things when they weren't there to grant permission. But it's different now. Mum won't mind me getting the baby box out. Especially now that I'm pregnant.

The wardrobe is an art deco mahogany armoire. Solid and imposing with an internal mirror. I used to think it was ugly and old-fashioned. Now I think it's beautiful.

My eyes travel along the rail of Mum's clothes and I notice that she has swapped her mismatched hangers for those satin-padded ones. She has arranged her shoes at the bottom, all paired up neatly on lining paper, and for a second or two I think she must have put the baby box somewhere else, but then I see it, tucked into the corner right at the back with a pair of old sandals on top of it.

I draw it out and kneel down on the carpet. The first thing I see when I take the lid off is the little pink book that lists all my vaccinations and developmental milestones. The section I loved the most as a child was the one that recorded things like when I first smiled and how old I was when I first used a spoon.

I turn the pages and read the sentences in Mum's lovely neat handwriting. Then I pick up a pair of tiny bootees and marvel at how my feet must once have fitted inside. Knowing Mum's love of knitting, she'll probably already be planning which bootees she's going to make for *my* baby.

Next to catch my eye is the ring box containing my first lock of hair. I open it up and stroke the pale, gingery-blond curl, so delicate and fine. There's a teething ring, too, a tiny white hat with a little bobble on top, and a big wodge of congratulation cards.

I start reading them, although I've no idea who most of these people are. As a child, I was only interested in the pictures on the front. Mum used to read out some of the messages to me. This one is a "congratulations on your bump" card. It's a line drawing of a heavily pregnant woman. I open it up. "Dear Sue," it says, in large, scruffy handwriting at the top on the left.

Just then, a car pulls up outside. I drop the card onto the floor and go to the window. Mum won't mind me looking in this box, I'm sure she won't, it's all about me as a baby, after all, but perhaps I should have asked before going through her wardrobe. In fact, I *know* I should have.

It's not my parents, though. It's the neighbor's car. Even so, they'll be back soon and I don't want them to find me in their bedroom. I'll put the box back where it was and ask Mum about it later. We'll go through it together.

But when I pick up the card from the carpet, I can't help noticing the name of the person who sent it. The scrawled sign-off at the bottom right of the card says "Loads of love, Sheena."

Sheena. I've only ever known one Sheena, and that was Alice's mum. But Alice and I didn't become friends until we started secondary school. We'd never even met before then. Whoever sent Mum this card must be another Sheena. Strange, though; it's not exactly a common name.

Curious, I begin to read the message that's written inside.

Dear Sue,

    Congratulations on your pregnancy! Mick and I are thrilled for you both, we really are!

Unease trickles slowly down my spine. Mick and I? Does that mean . . . ? It must be Mick and Sheena Dawson. Alice's parents. But that's impossible. They didn't know each other then. I read on, my heart in my mouth.

    You've been trying for so long, I bet you can hardly believe it! And Sue, you're never going to believe this either, but we're having another baby, too! So we'll both have our babies at more or less the same time! Isn't that fantastic? Catherine is over the moon. She can't wait to be a big sister!

                      Loads of love,

                          Sheena xxx

I stare at the card, blood rushing in my ears. I read it again, letting each sentence unfold in my head. This doesn't make sense. Why would Sheena Dawson have written to Mum, congratulating her on her pregnancy? This makes it sound like they were best friends. Besides, the Sheena that wrote this sounds so full of life. All those exclamation marks! All that happiness. Alice's mum was never like that. The Sheena Dawson I remember was a quiet, joyless woman, a woman prone to long episodes of debilitating depression.

I read the words one more time and rock back on my heels. *Mick and I are thrilled for you both.* Why haven't Mum and Dad told me any of this? Why didn't Alice's mum tell *her*?

I clasp my hands together in front of my chin. I think of how my parents, especially Mum, tried to discourage our friendship. All those tight-lipped comments about an "unsuitable family." Not to mention the awkwardness I so often felt at Alice's house, as if I wasn't really welcome.

I check the other cards, the ones people have sent to congratulate my actual arrival, rather than just the pregnancy itself, and skim the greetings in each one, but the Dawsons didn't send another one.

Something peculiar happens inside my stomach. A flipping sensation that's got nothing to do with the baby. It's far too early for me to be able to feel any movements. "Catherine is over the moon. She can't wait to be a big sister."

I hug my arms across my chest. Catherine was nine years old when Alice was born. Old enough to know who her mum was friends with. My mind races as I tuck the card back in its envelope and put it back with the others. I put the lid on the box and return it to the back of Mum's wardrobe, carefully placing the sandals on top. Everything exactly as it was before.

Except it isn't. Everything is in a different place now. For whatever reason, Mum has lied to me. Dad, too. Lying by omission.

32

Ross looks confused, as well he might. I've just woken him from his doze on the sofa and I'm talking nineteen to the dozen.

"Whoa," he says, muting the TV. "Slow down and start again."

"I've found a card to Mum in my baby box. It's from Alice's mum. From before Alice and I were even born."

He gives me a blank look. "And this is important *because*?"

"This is important because they didn't know each other back then."

He frowns. "Well, clearly they *did*."

"So why don't I know about it? Why have they never told me?" I pace to the window. "If Mum used to be friends with Alice's mum, why didn't she say anything when Alice and I became friends? Why didn't Alice's mum say anything to *her*?"

"I dunno. Maybe they didn't think it was important. Lizzie, should you even be looking through your mum's things?"

"I wasn't looking through her things. I was looking in my baby box. I looked in it loads of times when I was little. Anyway, you're completely missing the point here. They were good friends when they were both pregnant, with me and Alice. Something must have happened or they wouldn't have been so against Alice and me being friends."

Ross scratches his head. "You've never told me they were against your friendship."

I sigh. I'm expecting too much of him, I realize that now. How is he supposed to know these things if I've never told him?

"Well, they were, and I could never work out why. Neither of us could. All this time I thought they didn't approve of Alice's family because they weren't churchgoers or 'not the right sort of people,' or something stupid like that."

Ross blows air through his closed mouth so that his cheeks billow out. "We can't know everything about our parents' past lives."

Just then, I hear the sound of a key in the front door. "They're back," I whisper. "What am I going to do?"

"Hello!" Dad calls from the hallway. "Only one customer the whole time. It's a wonder Liz Metcalfe makes a living out of that shop."

Ross throws me a warning look. He shakes his head and mouths the word "nothing."

I don't know how I manage to act normally, but somehow I do. Ross is right. I can't just confront them about this. I can't put them on the spot by asking them outright. What I can do, though, at some point over the weekend, is ask Mum if we can look at my baby box together and then maybe, just maybe, I can casually open the envelope and read the card out. Far better for the conversation to evolve naturally. It's sneaky, I know, but no less sneaky than keeping me in the dark all these years.

The right moment happens a couple of hours later. Dad and Ross are having a whiskey together in the back room and talking about rugby. Mum and I are watching an old film, or rather, we're half watching it while Mum knits and I flick through old copies of her magazines. If it weren't for the contents of that card still rampaging through my mind, it would be the perfect lazy afternoon.

"I was thinking, do you still have my old baby box?" I'm aware of the tremor in my voice, how awkward I sound, but Mum doesn't seem to notice.

"Of course I still have it," she says. "It's one of my most treasured possessions."

"Can I have a look at it? It's ages since I've been through it."

Mum places her knitting on the cushion beside her and springs to her feet, smiling. "Good idea. I'll go and fetch it, shall I? I'm getting fed up with this silly film, aren't you?"

My heart beats faster while I wait for her to return. She's taking a long while. I hope I put the box back the right way or she'll know straightaway that I've already had a look.

Finally, she comes back into the room and puts the pink box on the coffee table between us, lifts the lid, and pulls out the same pair of bootees I marveled at earlier.

"Oh, Lizzie, look at these! I remember your tiny pink feet in my hands. How they used to curl and uncurl. Your nails were soft as paper."

For several minutes we ooh and aah over the bootees and the little hat and the teething ring, me acting as if it's the first time I've seen them in years. I lift out the wodge of baby cards and open each one in turn, reading out the messages while Mum lies back in her arm-chair and smiles, or makes little comments about the senders.

"Jenny's husband died a few years ago. Did I tell you?

"Goodness me, Sheila Haynes. I haven't seen her in a while. I think she moved to Wales.

"Amy Carter's daughter is on a gap year in Thailand. The poor woman's going out of her mind with worry."

When I get to the last one, my chest tightens and I know for a fact what I've known for the past few minutes. The card from the Daw-sons is no longer here. Mum must have taken it out.

———————————

It wasn't just the kissing, although that's how it started. It was other things, too. We couldn't stop ourselves.

"It isn't wrong," she told me. "You know that, right?" And I did. I did know that. But somehow it felt wrong. Just like that first dare had felt wrong.

But as time went by, we forgot all about it. It was just me and her. The two of us. Behind the closed door of her bedroom with the chair pushed against it and the curtains pulled tight.

It was just us, and what we did.

The rest of the time, at home with our families, at school, it was like it wasn't happening. We talked about other people we fancied, other lives we would live. As if what happened behind that closed door was completely separate. A world in itself. Another dimension.

Sometimes, when we weren't in that room, I wondered whether that world existed at all, or whether it was all one of my more elaborate daydreams. But at other times, it was more real than anything else I had ever experienced.

It was the only world that mattered.

33

It's Monday morning and Ross has just driven to work. We didn't get back from Mum and Dad's till late last night. We talked about my discovery for almost the entire journey home. Ross thinks I need to let it go.

Ross reminds me of my dad sometimes, not wanting to go too deep into the whys and wherefores, preferring to let sleeping dogs lie. Perhaps it's true, what psychologists say, that women are invariably attracted to men who are versions of their fathers. He thinks my parents have a right to keep aspects of their past lives to themselves, and though I agree with him in principle, I can't let it go. I can't. My curiosity has been fired up and I need answers.

I have to ring Mum. And I have to do it now.

"Mum, did you hear what I said?" My voice has started to tremble.

The silence on the other end of the phone is glacial.

"Yes," she says at last.

"I know I should have asked you first, but it isn't as if I haven't looked in there before."

She still hasn't answered my question, so I try again. "Why haven't you ever told me that you and Sheena Dawson used to be friends?"

She takes a deep breath and exhales. "Because there was nothing to tell. We used to know each other for a little while, but we didn't keep in touch."

"But, when Alice and I became friends, why didn't you—"

"Oh, Lizzie, if a friendship doesn't last, there's usually a good reason for that. You can't just pick things up where you left off."

"But surely you'd have made at least some effort to—"

"Look, we should have told you we knew the Dawsons as soon as you and Alice became friends. I realize that now. But at the time, there didn't seem much point. We didn't want to renew their acquaintance and we were pretty certain they wouldn't want to renew ours. Too much water under the bridge. Besides, we had no idea how close the two of you were going to become."

"What sort of water?"

"Lizzie, it was a long time ago! Your dad and I had started going to church. The Dawsons weren't really our sort of people. I mean, we'd known them for ages, but we were growing apart. Sheena had all sorts of problems, always blowing hot and cold. It wasn't her fault—she was ill. Catherine virtually had to bring herself up. She was only nine, but she was always roaming around the estate with a load of kids, playing out late. A bunch of noisy little urchins, your dad used to call them. And she was very . . . *precocious.* I often used to see her hanging around with the boys."

Mum sighs. "I tried to speak to Sheena about it once and it didn't go well. She went mad. Accused me of being a stuck-up busybody. Besides, she'd got close to the woman living next door to her by then. Our friendship was on its last legs."

"But, when Alice died, surely you could have—"

"Could have what? Said how sorry we were, how devastated? We did. Of *course* we did. We sent a card. We sent flowers. We went to the funeral. What more could we have done?"

"It's just weird that you've never told me. I'm not a little girl anymore, Mum."

"Oh, darling, I know you're not." She releases another small, tight sigh. "In hindsight, we should have told you. But don't you see, Lizzie? The longer you keep a secret from someone, the harder it is to tell them the truth."

I swallow hard. I know that what she's saying is true. I've never told Mum and Dad about my nightmares. I mean, they knew I had them, but not what they were about. I could hardly tell them that, could I? And who knows when or if I'd ever have told Ross about what happened to Alice if Catherine hadn't materialized in our lives when she did? I'm going to have to tell Mum about that, too. If I'm expecting her to be open with me, I have to do the same.

"There's something I need to tell you," I say. "Catherine Dawson is a nurse at Ross's surgery."

There is a shocked silence.

"You can't be serious!"

"I am. Imagine how I felt when she turned up at our housewarming party."

"But Lizzie, that was ages ago. Why are you only telling us this now?"

I'm about to say "That's a bit rich, coming from you," but I bite my tongue. The last thing I want us to do is fall out.

"She's different now, Mum."

There's a pause as she takes this in. "Lizzie, surely you can't have forgotten how badly she behaved after Alice died?"

"Of course I haven't forgotten," I say. "But that was twelve years ago. She knows it was wrong of her and she's apologized."

"Ross works with her, you say?"

"Yes, she's one of the practice nurses at Plumtree Lodge."

"I thought she was a secretary."

"She was. But then she trained as a nurse."

"I presume this means you've told Ross about Alice? I mean, there's no reason why you shouldn't have. You are *engaged*, after all.

It's just that . . . we both kind of assumed that you hadn't, that you wanted to draw a line under all that."

"I don't think it's particularly healthy to keep secrets from someone you love. Do you?" The words are out before I can think better of them.

I hold my breath, scared I've gone too far.

"Do you see her socially?"

"We've met since the party, yes."

"I'm not sure about this, Lizzie. I really don't think it's a good idea to get mixed up with the Dawsons again."

I can just picture the lines of concern etching Mum's face, the way she'll be tightening her mouth so that her chin looks all puckered.

"Has she said anything about . . . her parents? Do they still live in the same house?" Her voice is stretched with tension.

"No. They moved to Devon."

I hear her sigh again. It sounds like relief. "Listen," she says. "I've got to go. I'll phone you later."

"Later" turns out to be less than fifteen minutes.

"Lizzie, I've been speaking to your dad."

I guessed as much the second she hung up. It's so unlike Mum to finish a call first. She must have been desperate to fill him in.

"He's very concerned at this . . . this growing *friendship* between you and Catherine. He thinks—*we* think—that you should rein it back a little. Keep your distance."

"But you've always taught me to be forgiving. Isn't that the Christian thing to do?"

It's a cheap shot, I know it is, throwing her own homilies back in her face, but if it's so important to her, and Dad, that I don't get involved with the Dawsons again, then they need to be honest with me about why.

Suddenly, Dad's on the phone and I realize I've been on loudspeaker all this time. I should have guessed.

"Lizzie, your mum's not feeling very well. This has been very upsetting for her. I want you to think about what it was like before we moved to Dovercourt. What a dreadful time you had. What a dreadful time we *all* had."

I perch on the edge of the sofa. It's like I'm a young girl again, listening to one of his lectures when I'd done something wrong.

"I'm sure Catherine *does* feel sorry for her actions," he says. "And I realize it must be difficult, her working alongside Ross. But believe me, it's never a good idea to revisit the past. We're not saying don't forgive her, of course we're not. We're just saying don't get too close. Join some clubs. Go to an evening class. You'll soon make new friends."

Oh my God. It's like history repeating itself. My parents advising me not to get too friendly with Alice. To widen my circle. What the hell is it they're not telling me?

34

The phone conversation with my parents has left me numb. I feel as though a protective layer of skin has been stripped away, leaving me exposed and vulnerable. There's definitely more to this than they're letting on.

I sink down onto the sofa. It must have been a real wrench for them to sell their beloved home and start all over again somewhere else. Why didn't they have meetings with the school and tackle the bullying head-on? Or transfer me to another school? Why didn't they make more of an effort to talk to Sheena and Mick about Catherine's behavior and the problems it was causing? It's almost as if they were too scared to even approach them about it.

Unless they felt guilty. Guilt by association. With me. My chest tightens. Is it possible that my own parents think I might have been lying? Heat stains my cheeks at the thought.

I go into the messages on my phone and see the one Catherine sent after our meeting in the park the other week. Despite what I said about wanting to see her again, I've been purposely ignoring her message up till now. I'd made up my mind that enough was enough. I'd accepted her apology and cleared the air. Anything more was out of the question, no matter how nice she now seems.

But things are different now and Catherine's the only person, apart from my parents, who might be able to help me get to the bottom of all this. I need answers. Answers that Mum and Dad, for whatever reason, aren't giving me.

I send her a text. Can we talk?

She rings me straightaway.

"Lizzie?"

"Something's come up," I say.

"Is it that reporter again? You don't have to talk to her, you know. It's entirely your decision."

"This isn't about the reporter. I've not heard from her again."

"So what is it?" she says.

I hesitate. "It's . . . well, it's a bit delicate, actually. I think I'd rather talk face-to-face. When's your next day off?"

"Wednesday."

My heart sinks. I'm impatient for answers now. Still, I don't suppose a couple of days will make much difference.

"I'll be at Greenwich on Wednesday morning," she says. "Why don't we meet somewhere for lunch or a late coffee?"

When Wednesday comes around, it's gray and damp. So much for flaming June. Catherine and I are sitting on a leather sofa, sipping cappuccinos in the Waterstones café.

I clear my throat. "I saw my parents at the weekend."

She widens her eyes. "How are they?"

"They're fine, but . . . look, can I ask you something?" I watch her face closely for her reaction. "Do you know if our parents ever met? I mean, before Alice and I did."

She puts her coffee down. "What makes you ask that?" she says.

"It was something I found. A card. From your mum to mine — well, from your parents to my parents, but it's always the woman who writes the cards, isn't it? She was congratulating my mum on her pregnancy. And *she* was pregnant, too, with Alice. She sounded so happy, so excited."

Catherine nods, slowly. "Yes. Our mothers were best friends." Hearing her confirm it makes my head swim.

"Were you ever going to tell me?"

She looks embarrassed. "Possibly. Probably. If we saw more of each other, which I hoped we would. I thought you might even know by now, to be honest."

"They must have stopped being friends at some point after the card was sent and before I was born," I say. "Because there's no congratulations card from them for my birth. Only on the pregnancy itself, and they would have sent another card when I was born if they were still friends, wouldn't they?"

"That's right," Catherine says. "They'd fallen out by then. And then, of course, your parents moved away."

"Moved away?"

"Yes, to wherever it was you grew up. Beechwood Avenue, wasn't it?"

"*Birchwood* Avenue." Our eyes meet briefly. Catherine looks away first. I'm surprised she doesn't remember. She stood outside my window in the middle of the night enough times after Alice died. But there's no point dwelling on that. Not now.

"So, did your mum and dad use to live near them in Bishop Street, then?" I ask her.

"Bishop Street? No, what makes you think that?"

"Because that's where my parents lived before they had me."

Catherine looks puzzled. "No, they lived on the estate, in Riley Road. They were neighbors."

Something inside me falls away. "My parents used to live in Riley Road? Are you sure?"

"Yes. They lived a few houses down from us. I remember our mums sitting on the canvas swing chair in our garden, drinking tea. They used to know each other from school."

I stare at her, open-mouthed. This can't be true. Why would my parents lie about where they used to live? They wouldn't, surely.

And yet they lied about not knowing the Dawsons.

"But they've always told me that before I was born, they lived in Bishop Street."

Catherine smiles. "That's a whole lot nicer than Riley Road, isn't it? I can see why they might have wanted to *edit* things a little."

"But they're not like that!"

As soon as the words are out, I realize how hollow they sound.

It all begins to fall into place. I used to think that uncomfortable feeling I had in the presence of Alice's mum was because she was so depressed, but it must have been more than that. She didn't like me because she didn't like my mother. And then her daughter died and I was the one with her when it happened. No wonder we weren't invited to Alice's wake.

"And she never told you what it was that made them fall out?"

Catherine screws up her face and looks into the middle distance. "I have a vague memory of hearing Mum talk about it once with the woman next door. Something about your mum being jealous, I think, but I can't remember any of the details."

I'm aware that I'm frowning. It's the notion of my mother being jealous of Sheena Dawson. It doesn't seem possible, and yet, how well do any of us really know our parents, the people they were before they had us? I think of my own jealousy and how it used to rage inside me. An unstoppable force. Things I try not to dwell on start pricking away at the back of my mind. Seeing Alice dance with Dave Farley after he'd humiliated me in front of everyone. The torrent of anger that erupted out of me as soon as the two of us were alone.

"I was only nine," Catherine says. "To be honest, I didn't take much notice of Mum's friends. I was too busy playing with the other kids on the estate."

Catherine's face clouds over and she stares out of the window. "All that had to stop when Alice was born," she says. "I mean, I didn't *mind* looking after her. Of course I didn't. I *loved* having a baby sister, but well, Mum was so depressed, she could hardly look after herself, let alone a baby, and Dad was always so busy in the shop."

"So was it postnatal depression?" I ask her.

Catherine shrugs. "That's what they said at the time. It started off feeling like I was just helping Mum out while she wasn't well, but she never seemed to get any better and so I kind of took Alice over completely. Did everything for her. Every hour I wasn't at school I was playing with her, feeding her, changing her nappies. It was almost as if . . . almost as if she were mine."

She takes a sip of her cappuccino and I can see that there are tears in her eyes.

"She was a beautiful baby. I remember the way her tiny hands used to grip the bottle. And that blissed-out, drunk look on her face when she'd had her fill. Her milky burps when I rubbed her little back."

I look away, my throat almost closing up. When I look back, Catherine is stirring another sugar into her cappuccino. There are tear tracks on her cheeks. The two of us sit in silence for a little while, each absorbed in our thoughts and memories.

"Sorry," she says. "You were asking about your mum."

"Please don't apologize. I shouldn't have started quizzing you. As you say, you were only a child. I'd be hard-pressed to remember much about my mum's friends when I was that age."

"But I *do* want to apologize about my behavior later on," she says.

I look down at my lap. "It's okay. You already have."

"I know, but I want you to understand what it was like for me back then. After spending most of my childhood and teenage years looking after Mum and Alice and keeping everything ticking over while Dad was at work, I'd finally got a life of my own. Alice was about to start secondary school and Mum was almost back to her old self. I was going out to work as a secretary, enjoying a social life, making plans to leave home. Then you and Alice became friends and Mum got ill again. I'm not saying that was your fault, Lizzie, but in my head I associated the start of your friendship with Mum's depression coming back. And then when Alice died . . . well, you can imagine . . ."

Her face lengthens in sorrow. I stare at my knees, the familiar undertow of guilt tugging my mind back to that fateful day.

"It's why I was so mean to you," she says.

My throat is too clogged with emotion to speak. To my shame, I've never once considered what it must have been like for Catherine, how much of her childhood and young adult years were eroded by the burden of caring for her mother and her sister.

"It's always troubled me how I treated you before. But now I feel like I've been given a second chance to put things right," she says. "After all, whatever happened between our mothers, once upon a time they were best friends. And you were best friends with Alice, so maybe . . . maybe there's a chance that *we* could be friends, too."

Her phone rings then and I'm glad of the distraction as she checks who it is and gestures "sorry" at me while she takes the call. It's all been getting a bit intense and I'm glad of the time to gather my thoughts.

"Sorry about that," she says, when she finishes the brief conversation. "I wouldn't normally have answered it, but it was June from the surgery and since I've just asked her the most humongous favor, I could hardly ignore her."

She gathers up her things and reaches for her jacket. "I'm going to have to go, I'm afraid. June's kindly offered me her sofa to crash on so I said I'd pop round and discuss it with her."

"Where are you living now, then?"

"In a flat in Woolwich, but the lease ends at the end of the month and the landlord won't extend it. He wants to renovate the house." She puts on her jacket. "About time, if you ask me. Tight bastard'll probably turn the living room into another bedroom and hike the rent up as soon as he's done."

She drains her cup of coffee. "It's fine, though. I've found a nice new place in Deptford. The only trouble is, the current tenant can't move out until two weeks after I need to move in." She smiles. "So it looks like I'll be sleeping with Madame Bovary and the Queen of Sheba."

I give her a questioning look.

"June's Persian Blues," she explains, laughing. "I'm going to be picking cat hairs off me for weeks."

"Two weeks is a long time to have to sleep on a sofa," I say.

She grimaces. "It's even longer if you're allergic to cats." Then, when she sees my face she says, "I'll be *fine*. As long as I remember to pick up some antihistamines."

I think of our spare room. Maybe I should offer it to her. After all, it's only for two weeks, and it would prove to Ross that I'm making an effort, that I'm moving forward and not holding on to grudges. And besides, I like her company. For some reason, Mum and Dad don't want me to revisit the past. They don't want me to get close to her, but they didn't want me to get close to Alice either. And how can I trust them when they've been lying to me all my life? Maybe if I get to know Catherine better, I'll find out why.

———————

It was a dysfunctional relationship from the very start. I realize that now. As a child, I never questioned the psychology of it. Why would I? She was everything to me. My emotional crutch. My confidante. My savior. So when I realized she needed me, too, of course I agreed to help her. How could I not? That's how this whole thing started.

That woman had ruined everything. Turned her mother into a shadow. A wraith. If we could do something—anything—to make her suffer like poor Sheena was suffering, then that would right the wrong that had been done to her. Sheena would get well again and be happy, and then Catherine would be happy. Everything would revert to how it was.

At the time, it was exciting. A game of dare, but one that had motive and justification. I do believe we convinced ourselves that we were on some kind of moral crusade. Children can be so judgmental, can't they?

I can still hear her cry as she toppled forward, the dull thud of her body as it landed on the pavement. But I didn't look back. I kept running and running and running till I made it to the park and could

*disappear into the clump of trees by the playground and catch my
breath.*

*Catherine was there, waiting for me, her eyes shining with admira-
tion. "You did it, Ross! You actually did it!"*

*But it was all for nothing. Apart from the shock and a few bumps
and bruises, Sue Molyneux was fine. She had to spend a few weeks on
bed rest, but she didn't lose the baby.*

Afterward, Catherine said I didn't bowl into her hard enough.

PART TWO

There must have been a moment, at the beginning, where we could have said—no. But somehow we missed it.
—Tom Stoppard, *Rosencrantz and Guildenstern Are Dead*

After Alice died and the Molyneuxs moved away, Catherine talked about finding them so many times. She'd never really forgiven me for messing up the first time. Because if things had gone according to plan, Lizzie Molyneux would never have been born and Alice might still be alive. It was a fantasy of hers—an obsession—and I went along with it because it kept her happy.

And because I was obsessed, too. With Catherine. I never thought for one moment that it would actually happen. As the years passed and we got on with our lives, the less we spoke of them. It seemed unlikely that we'd ever see or hear of the Molyneuxs again. I can't tell you what a relief that was.

Sometimes, late at night when I couldn't sleep, I remembered the words Catherine had written on that card, how we watched as the flame consumed each and every stroke of the pen. In my mind's eye, I see her slender fingers close over the pile of gray ash in the palm of her left hand and I'm following her out of her bedroom and down the stairs all over again, across the yellowing lawn to the rough piece of dirt at the very end of the garden. Behind the swing chair.

Since I qualified as a doctor, Catherine and I had been drifting apart, and I didn't know how I felt about that. Part of me was relieved. I knew deep down that it wasn't a healthy relationship, never had been. She represented the side of me I wanted to forget. But I couldn't help feeling abandoned, too. She had this knack of making me feel like the little boy I once was. A sad, lost, angry little boy, craving love and attention. So when she phoned up out of the blue and wanted to catch up, I felt excited at the prospect of seeing her again.

She'd got her nursing qualification now, and she seemed different. More settled. I won't lie—I couldn't wait to hold her. To fuck her. She was the drug I couldn't kick. I'd had other girlfriends over the years, but no one quite like Catherine. There'd never been anyone like Catherine.

I'd been making plans to visit a university pal at his parents' bungalow on the east coast. They'd recently passed away within a couple of months of each other, and I said I'd go up and spend a few days with him, help him sort out their stuff. I wasn't particularly looking forward to it, to be honest, but he was a friend and I didn't like to say no. When I told Catherine where I was going, she invited herself along, too. The trip suddenly held more appeal. Catherine's presence would, I thought, make the whole thing so much more bearable.

I should have realized straightaway that she had an ulterior motive. Should have guessed she'd never truly given up looking for the Molyneuxs. When she suggested the trip to Dovercourt, I'd assumed she just wanted to walk on the beach, but when we got there, she was more interested in the houses facing the sea than the sea itself. It wasn't until we caught sight of Nigel Molyneux deadheading roses in a front garden that she finally came clean with me. Told me she'd been doing some sleuthing on the internet and that, voilà, her tenacity had finally paid off. Her face was jubilant.

I knew in that moment that it would all start up again, that it had never really stopped. And I knew, with a sinking sense of inevitability, that whatever she wanted me to do, I'd do it.

Like that first, dreadful dare.

But we were children then. This time, it was different.

35

I pat and smooth the pillows on the spare bed, hoping I won't regret my generous impulse. Ross was a bit taken aback when I told him I'd offered Catherine our spare room. Almost angry. I know it was rash of me and that I should have spoken to him first, but after everything he's said about me needing to move on from the past and how I ought to make more of an effort to be civil to her, I thought he'd be fine about it. In any case, it's only for two weeks and it seems daft, her having to squeeze all her things into June's one-bedroom flat and share a sofa with two long-haired cats, when we're lucky enough to have this place all to ourselves.

I open the little wardrobe and count the hangers. I don't expect Mum and Dad will be too pleased when I tell them. *If* I tell them. I haven't made up my mind whether I will or not yet. It'll be hard for them to understand how different Catherine is now. How much she's changed. Besides, I'm still reeling from the revelation that not only did they used to know the Dawsons, they lived on the same estate, the same *street*. What else haven't they told me?

I've always thought of my parents as allies, as *friends*. The two people who have my best interests at heart, whom I can turn to when I need help and support, or just want to talk things through. Maybe I feel this even more because of my epilepsy and the things we've gone through together. But the fact that they've lied to me all these years has changed how I feel about them. I still love them, of course I do, but something has shifted between us now.

I feel a slight flicker in my tummy. Is this what I think it is? Is it the baby moving? Fluttering its tiny limbs like the wings of a butterfly? I know it's the most natural thing in the world, but it's such a weird sensation. Instinctively, I cradle my belly with my hands and wait for it to happen again. When it does, it makes me giggle. It feels so alien.

This time next week, it'll be my mid-pregnancy scan. I was pretty out of it during my first scan because they did it the night I had the seizure, so I'm really looking forward to this one. Ross has booked the morning off work to come with me. I can't wait for us to get our first proper sight of her. Or him. Although I'm convinced it's a girl. Sometimes you just know these things, don't you? It's intuition.

Catherine arrives about an hour after Ross gets home. He's been on edge ever since he walked through the door and I'm beginning to realize my mistake. Home is Ross's sanctuary after the stresses and strains of his working day. He likes to shower as soon as he gets in—to wash away the "stink of the day," as he calls it. I think what he really means is the stink of the patients. He likes to change into something loose and comfortable. A pair of tracksuit bottoms or lounge pants and T-shirt. He's obviously not pleased about having to share his personal space with a colleague, about her seeing him off-duty. It's blurred the line he likes to draw between work and home. But it's too late now. I've offered and she's accepted. He'll just have to put up with it.

By the time Catherine has emptied out her car, all the space between the front door and the stairs is taken up with bags, cases, and boxes. I had no idea she'd have quite so much stuff.

"Right," Ross says, grabbing hold of a purple hard-shell suitcase covered in stickers. "Let's get this lot upstairs before one of us trips over."

He looks, and sounds, distinctly pissed off and, though I understand why, I wish he'd be a little nicer. Poor Catherine looks embarrassed. Maybe she's regretting it, too.

She takes a bag in each hand and follows him upstairs. By the
time I've got hold of a few more items and am on my way up with
them, she's already deposited her first load and is coming back down
for more.

"Let me do this, please, Lizzie. I don't want to put you guys out
any more than I already have. I'm feeling bad about imposing on you
like this."

"You're not imposing on us at all. Is she, Ross?"

"Of course not," he says, but his voice is clipped and he doesn't
smile when he says it.

Later, when Catherine is moving around upstairs in her room and
Ross and I are in the kitchen, I tackle him about it.

"Can't you at least *try* to be a little friendlier?" I say, taking the la-
sagna I made earlier out of the oven. "It can't be easy for her, having
to move in with us like this, playing the gooseberry in another couple's life."

"That's just it," he says under his breath. "She didn't *have* to move
in with us, did she? She could have stayed with June, like she'd
planned."

"She's allergic to cats," I tell him.

Catherine suddenly appears in the doorway. Neither of us heard
her come downstairs. I hope to God she didn't hear our conversation.

"You made me jump," I say, and she laughs.

"Sorry. At work they call me the Ninja Nurse."

She takes the cutlery I pass over to her and sets it out on the table.
"It's so kind of you to make me supper, Lizzie," she says. "I really
didn't expect it."

"Well, I thought, seeing as it's your first night . . ."

She smiles. "Thank you." She flashes an awkward glance at Ross.
"I promise that, most of the time, you won't even know I'm here."

Oh no. She must have heard us talking just now.

Ross helps himself to a beer, takes a long, greedy pull at it as soon as he's cracked it open. I don't expect him to offer me one, because he knows I won't drink it, but surely he's going to offer Catherine one. He must see how rude it will seem if he doesn't.

I give him a pointed look and, finally, he gets the message.

"Thanks," she says, taking the bottle Ross has just opened and handed to her. "If you're sure you don't mind. I don't want to deprive a tired, thirsty doctor of his last beer."

I laugh. "You won't, don't worry. He's got a whole box of them in there."

"You not having one, Lizzie?" she says, arching her eyebrows.

"No, I don't drink much, to be honest. Never have, and . . ." I give Ross a sidelong glance and a little smile. "I guess there's no point hiding it anymore?"

Ross opens his mouth as if he's going to say something, then closes it again. I suppose I've already given the game away now.

Catherine's about to bring the bottle of beer to her lips, but pauses midway. Her eyes widen. She looks from me to Ross and back to me again, her lips parting in surprise.

"You're not . . . ?"

I nod, beaming. "We are. We're having a baby."

Catherine places her bottle on the counter and steps forward to give me a hug. "Congratulations, Lizzie! That's *fantastic* news."

She looks at Ross from under her eyebrows. "You kept that one under your hat, didn't you, Dr. Murray!"

Ross looks like a rabbit in headlights and I immediately regret blurting it out like that. But I refuse to spend my whole time worrying about his reaction to things. Besides, what difference does it make *when* we break the news? His colleagues are bound to find out sooner or later.

"It was a bit of a surprise to us, too," he says. I wish he'd look a bit happier about it.

After supper, Catherine insists on loading the dishwasher while Ross and I sit on the sofa and watch a bit of telly.

I look at him sideways. He's staring at the screen, seemingly engrossed, but somehow I sense that he's not really watching it at all. He becomes aware of my gaze and gives me a quick glance.

"I didn't realize you were going to tell her tonight," he says. He sounds tense, as if I've done the wrong thing.

"Nor did I, but it's okay, isn't it? You don't mind, do you?"

"No," he says. "Although it's going to be a nightmare at work once this gets round. Everyone popping in to slap me on the back and make daft comments."

I give his arm an affectionate squeeze. "At least you'll get it over with." I kiss him on the cheek. "I'm sorry I didn't give you more warning. And I'm sorry I didn't talk to you before offering her a room. I'm too impulsive, aren't I?"

"No, you're not. We're just very different types of people, that's all," he says, squeezing my hand. "It's what makes us work."

I snuggle into him. "Do you think she'll come in here and watch telly with us?"

"I hope not," he says.

I can't help laughing at his hangdog face. "Two weeks will fly by, you'll see."

36

By the time I wake up, Ross has already left for work. I wish he wouldn't do that, just go off without waking me.

Sunlight oozes in through a crack in the curtains and I find myself staring at a massive gray cobweb I've never noticed before. It swathes the corner of the ceiling above the wardrobe and has started to inch its way along the coving. I'll have to try and get rid of it with a broom.

From somewhere in the house comes a faint murmuring. Ross must have forgotten to turn the TV off. I get up and make my way downstairs. My head feels fuzzy this morning. Ross was tossing and turning half the night and so I didn't sleep particularly well either. He said he felt uncomfortable, knowing that Catherine was on the other side of our bedroom wall. He didn't even want to make love, which is most definitely a first. Ross *always* wants to make love.

As I reach the bottom step and turn, a shape materializes at the end of the hall. For one heart-stopping moment, I think it's an intruder. But it's only Catherine. I thought she'd have left for work by now.

"Morning," she says, in a cheerful singsong voice. "Didn't mean to scare you." She laughs, prettily. "Told you I was a ninja."

She's carrying her breakfast into the living room. "Hope you don't mind, but I've helped myself to cornflakes and coffee. I'll buy my own food from now on, though. I don't expect you to feed me as well as give me a roof over my head."

"Of course I don't mind. And you're very welcome to eat with us in the evenings if you want to."

She shakes her head. "I couldn't. Last night was great, but I don't always know what I'm going to be doing in the evenings and I don't want to put you out."

She settles herself onto the sofa, the bowl of cereal in her lap. I'd have probably sat up at the table if I were in her position—a guest in someone else's house—but I don't really mind. I like eating on the sofa, too. Always have done. Mum used to tut about finding crumbs down the sides of the cushions.

"Alice used to love eating her breakfast in front of the telly," she says wistfully.

It still feels a bit awkward talking about Alice. Then again, Alice is the thread that connects us, so it's hardly surprising. And Catherine obviously feels comfortable talking about her.

"Her favorite cereal was Rice Krispies," she says. "I used to tell her off for sticking her hand straight into the box and pulling out a handful to eat dry. Not that she ever took any notice."

She does a sad little laugh. Then she gives me a quizzical look. "If you don't mind me saying so, Lizzie, you look a bit tired this morning. Why don't you sit down and let me make you a cup of tea and some toast?"

I shake my head, but she's having none of it.

"Look, you and Ross have been kind enough to let me stay. The very least I can do is bring you a cup of tea now and again."

My shoulders soften. "I do feel rather grim this morning."

Catherine tilts her head and looks at me from under her eyebrows in much the same way my mum does when she's about to give me some advice. "You must listen to your body, Lizzie. It's telling you to take it easy."

"Well, if you insist."

"I do. Now, what do you want on your toast? Butter and jam? Marmalade? Poached egg?"

I smile. "Butter and jam will be fine. No work today, then?"

She puts her bowl of cereal onto the coffee table and gets up. "I've arranged to go in later this morning. I've been racing around all week. It's nice to take things easy for once."

By the time I've drunk my tea and eaten some toast, I'm feeling miles better.

"So how many weeks pregnant *are* you?" Catherine says. Her face is happy, animated.

"Almost eighteen," I tell her. "I've got another scan next week."

"Eighteen weeks already! Wow! You hardly show at all. I take it Ross will be going with you?"

I laugh. "He'd better!" I tuck my legs under my bottom. "Yeah, he's booked the time off from work already."

"I remember when Mum got pregnant with Alice, how excited I was. I kept looking at the black-and-white photo she brought back from the hospital and convincing myself the baby was waving."

"Do they still tell you what sex the baby is?"

"Depends on the sonographer, I think. They tend not to, unless you ask them directly. Do you want to know, then?"

"I think I already *do* know. I mean, obviously I don't know for sure, but I have a strong feeling I'm going to have a girl."

For some stupid reason my cheeks go red. It's that survivor's guilt thing I still carry around. The knowledge that I'm doing things Alice can't. Catherine must have noticed because she gives me a sad little smile. "Do you ever wonder what Alice would be like, if she was still here?"

"All the time," I say, determined not to cry but coming perilously close. "I think . . . I think she'd look a lot like you."

Catherine looks pleased at this. She jumps up all of a sudden. "Wait here, I've got something to give you. I meant to do it last night, but what with your *announcement* . . ."

She runs upstairs and when she comes down again, she has a small photo album with her. She leafs through it and holds it out toward me.

"Do you remember this?" she says.

I stare at the glossy photo and am instantly transported to that summer's day in the garden at Riley Road. The day Mick Dawson took photos of us with his digital camera. In this one, Alice and I are eating lollipops, both of us doing silly poses, huge grins plastered all over our faces.

"You can keep it if you want," she says. "I've got doubles of them."

"I'd love it, thank you. I only have one of her." But then I remember. It was the one on the front of the Order of Service for her funeral. The card I tore up into little pieces. I shouldn't have done that. I don't even know why I did. It seems wrong. Almost sacrilegious.

"If we'd been young now, we'd have probably been obsessed with taking selfies, wouldn't we?" I say, hoping she won't notice the guilty blush that's just crept into my face. "I'd have had loads of photos of the two of us."

"True," Catherine says.

She takes the album back and eases the photo out of the plastic wallet. Her fingers remind me so much of Alice's: long and slender with neatly filed nails. She turns a few pages and extracts another photo. Then she hands them both over and I see that the second one is of Alice and me sitting on the swing chair, deep in conversation. It makes my heart lurch seeing the two of us there, so young and innocent. So blissfully unaware of what was to come.

Sheena Dawson is also in the photo—the back of her, anyway. It must have been one of her good days, because she's chatting to the neighbor over the fence and wearing a pretty summer dress.

"Look at the two of you," Catherine says. "Thick as thieves." She chuckles indulgently. "Remember that time the two of you bunked off your geography field trip?"

I hold my breath, unsure how to respond. I had no idea she even knew about that. Alice must have told her. Or maybe she overheard the two of us plotting.

I nod and smile, hoping it's a passing comment and that she won't say anything more about it. Because if she knows the details, if she knows *how* we bunked off, what it was we did in order to get away with it, then that might explain why she doubted my story about what happened the day Alice died. But Alice would never have told her what we did. It was our secret.

"Are you sure I can keep them?" I ask her.

Catherine nods. "Of course. Look at Mum in this picture. She looks so well and happy. So young."

I breathe a sigh of relief that she's changed the subject. She probably thinks we just skived off.

37

THEN: BEFORE

SUNDAY, JULY 1, 2007

The sun is hot on our bare legs and the soles of our feet are filthy where we've been running around on the dry, dusty grass in Alice's garden. I promised Mum I'd be home by five o'clock at the latest, because I've got to have a bath and hair wash and get my stuff ready for the boring geography trip tomorrow. A visit to a sewage-treatment works. Yippee.

Except I won't be going on the trip, and nor will Alice. We have a plan.

"This *has* to work, Lizzie," Alice says. "There's *no way* I'm going to spend the day looking at rivers of poo. It's *gross*. I don't care how interesting Mr. Rutherford says it is."

"Fancy having to eat your lunch in a place like that," I say. "It's going to be really hot tomorrow, too. Can you imagine the smell?"

Alice pretends to gag into her hand.

"Right, let's go over it one more time," she says. "Because if we end up on that coach to Shitsville, I might have to slit my throat."

We put our heads together and take it in turns to whisper exactly what we're going to do, from the second I get off my bus, right up until the moment Alice gives me the sign. If we stick to the plan, we'll be able to spend most of the day lounging around in the garden and listening to music.

But as I'm walking home, I start having second thoughts. I've never pretended to have a seizure before. Why would I? It's wrong, so very wrong. And it's the worst feeling in the world, lying on the ground with a crowd of faces peering down at me as if I'm some kind of freak. It's embarrassing. Humiliating. It's like being stripped bare in public. Why would I put myself through that on purpose?

Because I've promised Alice I'll do it. That's why. Because I *still* feel bad about what happened after the disco and that awful, awful thing I said. This is my chance to really make it up to her. If I lose her friendship, I lose everything. And anyway, I don't want to go on that smelly geography field trip any more than she does.

Mum does her usual fussing around the next morning.

"Don't wander too far from the teachers and parents, will you?" she says. "And remember to drink plenty of water to keep yourself hydrated. Oh, and make sure you put your factor fifty on."

I roll my eyes behind her back.

"I wish I'd offered to help," she says.

I send a silent prayer of thanks to old Mrs. Samuels down the road. She and her hospital appointment are the reason Mum isn't going to be one of the parent helpers today.

She hands me my packed lunch and watches me stuff it into my rucksack. Then she kisses me goodbye and the feeling of unease that's been fluttering away inside my belly ever since I woke up swells and swells till I think I'm going to be sick. Suddenly, the prospect of a day out at a sewage plant doesn't seem quite as bad as what Alice and I have planned, but I can't wriggle out of it now. Alice will be cross and I don't think I can bear it if we start arguing again.

Sometimes, I wonder whether it's only a matter of time before Alice drifts away from me and starts hanging around with Melissa and Bethany instead. I've seen her gaze over at them in the classroom from time to time, as if she wishes she were sitting with them, a proper, paid-up member of the cool girls' gang.

My bus is packed when it pulls up, and I squeeze down the middle and cling on to the pole near the doors. A boy near me is eating Cheesy Wotsits and what with the smell of them and the coating of orange dust on his mouth and fingers, which, for some reason, I can't stop looking at, even though I don't want to, and the continual stopping and starting of the bus, it's a wonder I don't throw up.

At last, it's time to get off and, as planned, Alice is there at the bus stop, waiting for me.

"All set for the trip?" she says, a mischievous gleam in her eyes. It's all right for her. She's not the one who has to make a fool of herself.

I nod. The closer we get to school, the more nervous I get. My armpits are already wet with sweat and I'm embarrassed about the spreading stains on my school blouse. I want to get this over with as fast as possible.

We slow down till the big group of chattering Year Sevens overtakes us, and that's when Alice gives me the sign we've agreed on. She pauses to retie her shoelace and I start to stagger around for a bit, pretend to fall over, which is a lot harder than I ever imagined. I should have practiced more in my bedroom. I did try, but I didn't want Mum and Dad to hear me crashing around and come rushing in to see if I was all right.

Now I'm lying on the pavement, jerking my limbs, doing exactly what Alice did when she showed me what I looked like when I'm having a seizure, because, of course, I've never actually seen it. I feel stupid and self-conscious. I'm not doing it right. It must be obvious to anyone watching that this isn't real. I can't believe I'm actually going through with it, but I'm doing it now, so I can't stop.

I'm aware of some of the Year Sevens turning round and edging closer, hear their comments. "Look at that girl on the pavement!" "OMG, she's having a fit." "What the fuck's she doing?" "'S epilepsy, innit." "Yeah, she's in my sister's class. She's always doing it."

Alice kneels down beside me and places my head, tenderly and carefully, in her lap.

"Can you get a message to Mr. Rutherford?" she says to one of the Year Sevens. "He'll be outside the gate by the coach. Tell him Lizzie Molyneux's had a seizure on the way to school and that Alice Dawson's looking after her till her mum gets home."

Two women on the other side of the street come rushing over, but Alice reassures them. "It's okay," she says. "My friend has epilepsy. There's no need for an ambulance. She'll come round in a minute and I'll take her home. This happens all the time."

"Are you sure?" one of them says. "Maybe we ought to call one just in case."

I open my eyes and blink rapidly, as if I've started to wake up. I went on a St. Johns Ambulance casualty simulation camp once and was told my "coming round after fainting" performance was one of the best they'd ever seen. I pull out all the stops to re-create it now. The last thing I need is an ambulance. If I'm taken to hospital, they'll know I've been pretending. There must be ways they can tell if someone's had a seizure or not. I'll be in the most awful trouble.

"Hello, Lizzie," Alice says. "You've had a little seizure, but you're fine now. Just rest here for a while."

I must say, she's playing her part to perfection. I must be, too, if the look on these women's faces is anything to go by.

"Can I phone your parents?" asks one of them. I shake my head.

"I'm fine now, honestly." I sit up, slowly and gingerly. "I just need to go home and rest. Alice will take me."

Alice helps me to my feet and grabs hold of my rucksack.

"Come on, Lizzie. Let's get you home to your mum."

"You will tell Mr. Rutherford, won't you?" she calls back to the Year Seven girl, who nods and races off toward the school with her friends.

Alice links her arm in mine and the two of us walk slowly back the way we've come, crossing the road to catch the next bus home. We don't say a word about what's just happened till we get off at the stop at the bottom of my road. Then, at last, we collapse in a fit of shocked giggles.

We did it! We actually did it. Now all I've got to worry about is pretending to be tired and forgetful when Mum gets home from taking Mrs. Samuels to the hospital, and with any luck that should be ages yet, because she said she's going to take her to lunch afterward, and when Mum and Mrs. Samuels get together they can chat for hours on end.

A bit like me and Alice.

38

NOW

It's Monday morning—the day of my scan—and Ross and I are about to leave for the hospital when his phone rings. I know straightaway that it's work and that something urgent has come up. I can see it in the sudden droop of his shoulders, hear it in the resigned tone of his voice.

"I'm so sorry, Lizzie," he says when he's finished the call. "One of my terminally ill patients is close to death. I've got to attend."

I try hard not to let my disappointment show, because I know it can't be helped and of course he must go, but I've been so looking forward to this scan and I really wanted Ross to be there with me. He's been unusually quiet and out of sorts since Catherine moved in, even though she's kept out of our way as much as possible. Apart from a couple of evenings where she's sat and watched the telly with us, and the odd encounter over breakfast, most of the time she's either been out or studying up in her room.

Ross grabs his bag and jacket from the study and heads for the door. "I'll text you as soon as I'm done and, if you're still at the hospital, I'll pick you up. Okay?" He looks at his watch. "You'd better phone for a cab to take you there. It'll take too long if you go on the bus."

It's only when the front door has closed behind him that I release the sigh I've been holding inside. I know he's only being a good GP and that I should be proud of him for rushing off to be at the side of one of his patients, but I can't help thinking that he didn't try hard enough to see if anyone else could go in his place. I also can't help thinking that he doesn't seem as disappointed about this as I am, but then I'm probably just imagining that. Ross doesn't show his emotions as easily as I do. It doesn't mean he doesn't have them.

"Lizzie? What's wrong?" Catherine is coming downstairs and is staring at me quizzically. She's still in her dressing gown, because it's her day off today. Her skin is flushed from the shower and her hair is still damp.

I wipe a stray tear from the corner of my eye and pull myself together. "It's fine, honestly. Ross has got to attend a dying patient so he can't take me for my scan. It's not the end of the world."

"Oh, but that's so disappointing for you both," she says. "The mid-pregnancy scan is a real milestone. You can't possibly go on your own. Why don't I take you?"

I hesitate. If Ross can't be there, I'm not sure I want anyone else. She's right, though. It *is* a milestone. Why doesn't Ross realize that? Although, of course, he was there when I had the first one, the night he took me to A & E. Not that I can remember much about it—I was so wiped out.

"Let me drive you there, at the very least," she says.

Then again, it might be good to have her there. If they find anything they're worried about, will they tell me if I'm on my own? I doubt they would. And I so need the reassurance this scan can give me.

Fifteen minutes later, we're outside on the street. The sky is a whitish gray, but the air is warm and humid. Climbing into Catherine's little red Peugeot is like stepping into a greenhouse. Hot and stuffy. Airless.

Before I can sit down, she has to scoop up a nursing journal, a pair of sunglasses, some lip salve, and an old baseball cap and toss them onto the already cluttered backseat. I've never seen so much junk in one car.

"Sorry about the mess in here," she says, brushing what look like crisp crumbs off the seat and into the footwell. "One of these days I might actually clean it up."

"Ross would have a fit if he saw this," I say, grinning. "He treats his car like the inside of a temple."

Catherine smiles and puts the car into gear. She opens the windows as we drive off and a welcome breeze wafts in.

"The gel might feel a little cold at first," the sonographer says.

The lighting in the ultrasound room is low and the screen is angled away from me at the moment. The sonographer needs to concentrate and take all the necessary measurements first. I scrutinize her face for any signs of concern: a narrowing of the eyes, a flicker of dismay distorting her features. But whatever she can see on that screen, she's giving none of it away.

I glance at Catherine, who has, I now notice, shifted her chair farther back so that she can get a better glimpse of the screen. Now I'm scanning *her* face, too, my chest tight with anxiety, but she's wearing the exact same expressionless mask as the sonographer. The one all health professionals seem to adopt.

"Okay, all the measurements are fine. Exactly what we would expect at this stage." I breathe a huge sigh of relief. "Bladder and kidneys working well," she says. "And there's a very healthy heartbeat. Do you want to have a look now?"

The sonographer turns the screen toward me and, at first, I can't make anything out. Gradually, as my eyes become accustomed to the gray speckled blobs floating against a black background, I see the unmistakable evidence of a baby. Not that I need to see it. I only have to look at my expanding waistline or sense the tiny shifts and flutters of movement that I've been feeling more and more this last week to know that a little person is growing inside me.

"Can you see the baby's spine?" Catherine says, leaning forward excitedly. "Some people say it looks like a delicate string of pearls. Look, it's pointing right toward the scanner."

I follow the direction of her finger with my eyes.

"And the stomach looks nice and full." She points to a small black bubble that has just come into view as the baby twists into a different position.

The sonographer glances at her when she says this, and Catherine tells her that she's a nurse. I wondered if she would.

"No malformations, you'll be pleased to hear," the sonographer says, adjusting the screen again so that only she can see it.

I look at Catherine, suddenly aware that the person I most want to have beside me right now to hear this good news and to celebrate this moment isn't here. Catherine notices the slight wobble in my lower lip because she reaches out and squeezes my wrist.

Back in Catherine's car, I can barely peel my eyes away from the grainy photograph in my hand.

"I thought you might ask her if she could tell what sex it was," Catherine says, as she reverses out of the parking space and drives toward the exit.

"I didn't like to. Why? You didn't see anything, did you?"

She shakes her head. "You can't always tell, and as soon as I mentioned I was a nurse she tilted the screen away. Did you notice?"

Catherine slows down to let a woman with a pram cut in front of the car. "Anyway, I think you're probably right about it being a girl. I certainly didn't see anything that looked remotely like a penis."

I laugh. "I could just about recognize the head and the arms, to be honest."

It feels good to be laughing with her like this. I'm so glad she came with me.

"Shall we stop off for a celebratory coffee and cake somewhere?" she says. "My treat. And you can tell me what names you both like."

"Give me the chance to talk to her, Ross," she'd pleaded. "It'll be the perfect opportunity for the two of us to really bond."

Christ knows what she'd have done if I hadn't agreed. When she rang my phone and impersonated Lucy on reception, I almost grew a pair and said, "Sorry, but I really can't miss Lizzie's scan. You'll have to ask Andrew Smethers if he can go in my place."

But I'd have paid for it later. I always did.

It used to be worth it because of what came after. Let's just say, Catherine's requirements in bed were far from vanilla-flavored and I enjoyed the temporary illusion of being the one in control.

But things were running away with me now. It was like I'd stepped onto a moving walkway and the only way off was to keep going until I reached the end.

The trouble was, I no longer knew what the end looked like.

39

"Poppy Murray," Catherine says, savoring the name I've just suggested. It's one of the ones I've been considering for the last few weeks. "That sounds nice. I like it."

We're sitting on the same leather sofa in the bookshop café where we sat before. Only this time, we've got a selection of baby-name books spread out on the low table in front of us.

"So do I. But what if she grows up to be an engineer or an accountant? Ross thinks her name won't sound sensible enough."

"Hmm. He may be right. 'Poppy' definitely veers toward the whimsical." She picks up one of the books and turns to the index. "What about Evie? That's a pretty name. And she can always call herself Eve if she turns out to be the serious, earnest sort."

I take a sip of coffee and give the name some thought. When I look up, Catherine is staring into the middle distance, almost as if she's gone into some kind of trance. Perhaps she's getting fed up with all this baby talk, although it was her idea to get the books off the shelf in the first place.

"Catherine? Are you all right?"

She smiles, brightly, as if a switch has just flicked on in her brain and she's back in the moment. "I was remembering how I helped my parents choose Alice's name," she says. "They were arguing about it, like they argued about everything in those days." A shadow passes across her face. "And then I held up the book I was reading. It was *Alice in Wonderland*."

A hard lump gathers at the back of my throat. I'd never heard Alice's parents arguing, although of course, by the time the two of us became friends, it was eleven years *after* the scene Catherine has just described. Perhaps they'd sorted out their differences by then, or learned to live with them. Or perhaps there *had* been tension, and I'd put it down to Alice's mum's depression. I expect I was too wrapped up in my own little world to take much notice of other people's parents.

Another memory surfaces. Alice's mum had just been admitted to hospital and Alice was telling me how some of the patients had bandages on their arms and rocked backward and forward, how others wandered around talking to themselves and shouting things out. She said they kept the main doors of the unit locked and that it was scary. I'd wanted to go with her, to see for myself what it was like. But Catherine must have been eavesdropping, for suddenly she was in the room with us, her face pinched with anger. "No," she'd said. "Only family are allowed to visit."

A chill passes through me as I remember the venom in her voice. I look across the table at this new, gentler Catherine, thumbing through one of the books on her lap, and the chill recedes. It must have been a dreadful time for the Dawson family, and especially for Catherine. Having to put her own plans on hold to look after her little sister yet again. And there's so much stigma attached to mental illness, even more so back then. She wouldn't have wanted me seeing her mother in that place. No wonder she felt so bitter. She was just trying to protect her family. I'm sure I'd have been the same if it had been one of my parents.

"Freya is an interesting name," she says, absentmindedly flicking through the pages.

I make a vague, noncommittal sort of noise in the back of my throat. Poppy is still my favorite.

"Older names seem to be coming back now, don't they? What were your grandmothers called?"

I pull a face. "I'm not calling her Marjory or Daphne, thank you very much."

Catherine laughs. "No, maybe not. Mine was called Dorothy. I'm guessing that's not in the running either." Her face softens. "Alice and I used to call her Nanny Dot."

A thought has just occurred to me. If my instincts are right, and this baby really is a girl, maybe I should call her Alice as a way of honoring her memory. Does Catherine think so, too? Is that why she brought up the story about *Alice in Wonderland*? Is that why she's so keen to help me choose a name?

I take a sip of coffee and pretend to read the blurb on the back of one of the books. The urge to say Alice's name out loud, to hear the soft, whispering sound of it, is overwhelming. I press my lips together. It's one thing to name a child after a grandparent or an older relative, but to name them after someone who died in such terrible circumstances, and at such a young age—no, I couldn't. I shiver. It makes me uneasy just thinking about it.

"Perhaps you need to wait till she's born before you decide," Catherine says.

I put the book down. "Yes." I feel a sudden urge to confide in her about my fears surrounding the birth. And, more important, what happens afterward, when Ross has gone back to work and I'm on my own in the house with a newborn baby.

I've been thinking about that a lot lately, but every time I've tried talking to him about it he says what he always says when I worry about something that hasn't happened yet—that there's no point getting all worked up about something I have no control over and that I need to relax and take things one day at a time.

I never imagined I'd be thinking this, but I bet Catherine will be able to put my mind at rest. After all, she's a nurse now and, though she isn't a mother herself, she knows what it's like to look after a new-born. While the scan has reassured me that the baby is safe and well for now, there are so many other questions troubling me. Like, how will my body cope with sleepless nights and the stress of being a new mother? What if I start having seizures again? And what if I have one when I'm alone with the baby and drop her? It's my biggest fear.

Seeing the baby wriggling around on the monitor this morning, wonderful though it was, has brought all my anxieties to the surface.

"Lizzie?" Catherine says. "What's wrong?"

And so I tell her. I let all my worries and fears come tumbling out. By the time I've finished, my voice is wobbly with emotion. "And even if I don't have a major seizure, I know I still have partials from time to time. I only lose consciousness for a few seconds, but anything could happen in that time, couldn't it? It only takes a few seconds for something bad to happen."

I stare at my knees. It only takes a few seconds for someone to die. The image of a denim sleeve caught up in a bush flashes into my mind and I have to concentrate really hard to make it go away. Sometimes the image is so real it's as though it's right here in front of me.

Catherine does her best to ease my fears. She doesn't tell me anything I don't already know, or haven't read for myself on the internet, but somehow it helps, hearing her say the words out loud.

"You need to develop coping strategies," she says, and for the next ten minutes, she goes over all the things I need to do to keep myself and my baby safe. Setting the alarm on my phone to remind me to take my tablets; sleeping when the baby sleeps; making sure I've got lots of quick and easy meals in the house, so I don't get hungry or have to spend too much time preparing something to eat; setting up a nappy-changing place both upstairs and downstairs, so I don't have to use the stairs if the baby needs changing; sitting on the floor with my back supported when feeding her, so if the worst happens and I do have a seizure, she won't have far to fall; using a car seat to carry her around the house and up and down the stairs; and, of course, making sure someone phones me at regular intervals throughout the day, to check that I'm okay, preferably someone with a key. Like Ross, or a friend or neighbor.

Not for the first time, I can't help feeling resentful that epilepsy still features so largely in my life, that I'll never be free of it. It's like a specter, waiting in the shadows. The fear of its sudden ambush never entirely goes away.

Catherine starts arranging the books into a pile on the table. I move to help her, but she's already scooped them up and is out of her seat.

"I'll put these back on the shelves," she says.

Her face looks different somehow, sadder, more thoughtful, and I immediately feel guilty. At least I'm alive, sitting here on a warm summer's morning, drinking coffee. I have a loving fiancé and in less than five months' time, I'm going to have a baby. Alice never got the chance to do any of these things. That's what Catherine must be thinking right now. She could even be a little broody herself. Thirty-five is a difficult age for a woman without a partner.

Either way, I need to stop feeling sorry for myself and count my blessings.

40

THEN: AFTER

THURSDAY, SEPTEMBER 27, 2007

It's the day of Alice's memorial service. When the bell goes at the end of the afternoon, we all troop into the hall instead of going home. I've been on tenterhooks all day. I just want it to be over. The funeral was bad enough. I don't really see why we need to go through it all again, but Mrs. Peacock says that it's a chance for everyone at school to say a proper goodbye—all the children and teachers who couldn't go to the funeral but who nevertheless want to pay their respects.

Music is playing softly as our class take their seats. I'm half expecting to see the white coffin on the stage, although of course it's not there. The coffin has been buried. Alice has been buried. There is a large picture of her, though. It's propped up on a chair and it makes it seem like she's still here. Still watching us all. Watching me. I don't want to look at her face, her happy, smiling eyes, but I can't tear my gaze away. It's as if she's looking directly at me.

White helium balloons with Alice's name on them have been tied to the back of the chair with long white ribbons. Every time one of the doors to the hall opens and air wafts in, they bob about and I can't decide whether balloons are a good thing or not. It's almost like it's her birthday, but then, as Mr. Davis says when he starts speaking, we're not just here to mourn the loss of Alice, but to celebrate her life. So maybe the balloons are okay, after all.

Parents—those who wanted to attend—are sitting on either side of the hall with the teachers, mine included. Mum gives me a sad little smile every time I catch her eye. Mr. and Mrs. Dawson are sitting in the middle of a much shorter row of chairs that have been arranged in a semicircle right at the front. Catherine is sitting next to her mum, and a woman I recognize from the funeral is sitting next to her dad. I think it's a cousin. The outer two chairs are where Mrs. Peacock and Miss Nandy, our form teacher from last year, are sitting. Catherine is talking quietly to her mum, who hasn't yet lifted her head toward the stage. Maybe she can't bear looking at the photo either.

I shrink back behind the head of the girl in front of me. The last thing I want is for Catherine to turn round and stare at me, like she did at the funeral. Like she did outside my bedroom window.

Mr. Davis talks of Alice's contribution to the school community. Her place in the netball team. Her love of art. He holds up a painting Alice did last year—a self-portrait. I remember her doing it. Remember comparing it to my own dismal effort. It doesn't look much like her, in my opinion, but it's well drawn. You can see she had talent.

Alice's mum blows her nose, loudly, and her dad clears his throat. I'm glad I can't see their faces and I realize now why they've sat them there. It's so people can't gawp at them when they cry.

Melissa Davenport and Bethany Charles are sitting in the row in front of me, a little to the right. They've both started to snivel into tissues. More girls start to cry. From our class, and from other Year Nine classes, too. I should be crying, but for some reason I can't. It's not that I'm not sad. It's not that I'm not hurting still inside, because I am. I don't know why the tears don't come, but even when I hold my eyes open for as long as I can without blinking, it's no good.

I take a tissue out of my pocket and dab my dry eyes, sniff loudly. If I don't cry, people will wonder why.

Now Miss Nandy is climbing the steps up to the stage. Mr. Davis stands aside so that she can take her place in front of the microphone. Miss Nandy tells us what a lovely, kind girl Alice Dawson was, and how it was a pleasure to be her form teacher. Then she reads "Remember" by Christina Rossetti, followed by an Inuit proverb about stars being openings in heaven where the love of our lost ones shines through to let us know they're happy.

Her voice starts to break on the last line and it's this that finally makes me cry. The sound of Miss Nandy struggling to hold it together, to finish her sentence. The tears flow freely now, but with them come sobs, embarrassing, noisy sobs that make everyone turn to look at me, including Catherine Dawson. But I don't care. I don't care anymore. Alice is dead and it's all my fault.

It's all my fault.

41

NOW

Today is Ross's birthday and I want to put his cards and presents on the table, so that they're ready and waiting when he comes down for breakfast. I'm really looking forward to his reaction when he sees what I've bought him.

As I make my way downstairs, the house is still and quiet, only the sound of Ross's deep, regular breathing interspersed with the odd snore can be heard. Catherine's door is shut, but there's no sound coming from behind it. She didn't get back till late last night and, though I've enjoyed her company and am grateful for the reassurance she's given me about the baby, I was glad that Ross and I had the house to ourselves.

Ross seemed a lot happier, too. He hasn't been himself since she arrived. Still, she'll be moving into her new flat on Sunday.

I retrieve his cards and presents from the cupboard where I've stashed them away and arrange them on the dining table. Being an only child with one parent dead and another in a nursing home, he doesn't get many cards, but a few have arrived in the post over the last few days, including one from my parents, who right now should be en route to Heathrow for their long-awaited week in New York.

By the time Ross appears, fully dressed and ready for the day ahead—he doesn't come down in his lounge pants anymore, I've noticed, not since Catherine has moved in—I've made myself a mug of decaf and am sitting with it by the window, watching the antics of the pigeons in the garden.

"Happy birthday, you," I say, getting up to give him a hug. "What would you like? Scrambled eggs on toast? Bacon sandwich?"

"Hey, I haven't seen you up at this time for weeks."

"Yeah, well," I say, patting my tummy. "I'm going to have to get used to early mornings once this one's arrived."

"Early mornings and sleepless nights." He smiles, but there's something wistful about it, as if he can't quite believe it's going to happen. "Can't wait."

He opens my card first. I've made one of those personalized black-and-white ones of a young couple gazing at each other lovingly and drinking champagne. The caption reads: "Ross and Lizzie spent the evening kissing and cuddling on the sofa." Then, underneath in brackets: "Clearly, their internet connection must have been down."

Mum and Dad have sent one of a cartoon doctor trying to listen to someone's feet with a stethoscope. There are a few more on a similar theme. Ross laughs and draws the first of my gifts toward him. He looks delighted when he pulls the paper off. It's a vinyl record—Bruce Springsteen & The E Street Band. A 2017 Record Store Day exclusive I bought off eBay a couple of weeks ago.

"I love it," he says, turning the sleeve over and reading the back. "But how did you know I wanted it? I don't remember telling you."

I tap the side of my nose and assume a mysterious expression. "I heard you mention it the night of the housewarming party, when you were talking to one of your old mates."

I nudge the other present toward him. "Go on, open this one now."

He makes a show of feeling it through the paper. Then he tears it open and draws out the framed photo of his mother, which I've had enlarged. He stares at it for a long time and I can see how surprised he is, how pleased. He gives me one of his bear hugs.

"Thank you. I've been meaning to get that framed for ages."

"I know you have. That's why I did it."

Catherine appears in the doorway in her blue toweling bathrobe just as we're in the middle of a kiss. Ross pulls away quickly and busies himself tidying up the discarded wrapping paper and envelopes. Honestly, I know he feels awkward having her stay with us like this, but I wish he wasn't quite so uptight about it. We are allowed to be affectionate with each other in our own house, aren't we?

"Hey, what's all this?" she says. "You should have told me it was your birthday, Ross. I would have got you a card."

He jams his hands into his trouser pockets and does a tight little smile.

She comes farther into the room. "I've got some bad news, I'm afraid," she says.

Ross and I both stare at her, expectantly.

"The landlord of my new flat contacted me last night." She twists her mouth into an awkward shape. "I might not be able to move out on Sunday after all. There's been a slight delay with the other tenant. I'll know exactly how long we're talking about later today, but hopefully it's only a matter of a few more days."

Ross looks furious and, though I can't deny I'm disappointed, too—I was looking forward to us getting back to normal—I'm taken aback by his rudeness.

"Of *course* you can stay. It's no problem at all, is it, Ross?"

At last, he takes heed of the look in my eyes and softens a little.

"Yeah, it's fine," he says.

Catherine clasps her hands together at her chest in a gesture of thanks. "I'm so sorry to impose on you like this. I really am. Are you *sure* it's all right?" She's looking directly at Ross now.

He shrugs. "Yeah, whatever." I wince at his choice of words. He can be so insensitive sometimes.

"So," Catherine says. "What are you two *lovebirds* doing to celebrate tonight, then?"

Ross screws up the wrapping paper and stuffs it into the recycling bin. The muscles in his face tighten. "We're going out."

I give him a sharp look. What the hell is wrong with him?

"Anywhere nice?" she says. I can't understand why she's persevering with him when he's clearly in a mood. Why doesn't she just ask me, or drop the subject altogether? It's almost as if . . . almost as if she's *enjoying* his discomfort. As if she's deliberately goading him.

She walks to the fridge and removes the carton of orange juice, pours herself a large glass. I feel a twist of irritation in my stomach. I've told her to help herself to whatever she needs, and I meant it, but there's something not quite right about her today. An air of entitlement that grates on me. What's that old saying? Guests, like fish, start to smell after three days, and it's been almost a fortnight now.

"You'll have to ask Lizzie," Ross snaps. "It's a surprise."

———————

It was a mistake from the start: the whole fucking charade. Catherine made it seem so easy, though.

"Get close to her," she'd said. "I mean, really close. Make her open up and tell you the truth. She pushed Alice in front of that train, Ross. I know she did. She told Alice she wished she was dead. Alice was in tears when she came back from that disco. Then the sly bitch pretended to have a seizure so the two of them could bunk off a school trip. If she could pretend once, she could pretend twice. And if she won't talk, go ahead and break her heart anyway. Why should she get to be happy?"

God, how she hated her.

She gave me instructions right from the start. How to approach her in the café that first time. What to say. What to do. Somehow, she'd known exactly what Lizzie would need to see or hear in order to fall in love with me. Although, I like to think I might have managed at least some of that on my own.

I found it interesting, the things Catherine tolerated and the things she didn't. She was surprisingly cool about the sex. Made me tell her *all about it. It turned her on. And when Catherine got turned on, I did, too.*

When she first suggested that I ask Lizzie to move in with me, I said, "No way." It seemed like a step too far, but Catherine had a way of bending me to her will. She'd molded me into a creature of her own making, and I'd let her. I was stupid to get involved. Stupid and weak. Because the truth was, I no longer cared whether Lizzie did push Alice. Kids do all sorts of bad stuff. I know that more than anyone.

The original plan was to encourage her to apply for a job at the surgery so that Catherine could "meet" her there. When that didn't work, the plan evolved. It was always evolving. We'd have a house-warming party instead. Catherine would do what she needed to do and I'd split up with Lizzie when she was done. Lizzie could have gone back home to Mummy and Daddy, her heart well and truly broken. A nice big notch in Catherine's belt.

But then I messed up again. I messed up big-time. Getting Lizzie pregnant was never part of the plan. Nor was her finding that fucking congratulations card. Why on earth did Sue keep it all these years? As some kind of memento? At least Catherine can't blame me for that. Not wearing a condom, though, that was entirely my bad.

Or was it? Was it really? Maybe it was just a fantasy. Mr. and Mrs. Normal and their baby. No games. No danger. No risk.

No, it was unthinkable. And yet . . .

And yet.

42

I watch from the window as first Catherine, then Ross, climb into their respective cars. Catherine drives off almost immediately, but Ross is still trying to maneuver out of an impossibly tight parking space. The man from number 14 with the pimped-up Mazda has hemmed him in again. I can see Ross cursing to himself. Eventually, he pulls away and I exhale, slowly. It's nice to have the house to myself at last, especially after the tension between Ross and Catherine just now. What the hell was all that about? Has something happened between them at work, some misunderstanding?

Upstairs, I notice that, for once, Catherine has left her door ajar. Up till now, I've resisted being nosy but, for some reason, today I push the door open a little wider and step inside. After all, it's not actually *her* room, is it? I have a perfect right to enter it when she's not here. What if I were to need a spare coat hanger from the wardrobe, for instance?

Except of course, I don't. I have no reason to be standing here in the doorway looking at how Catherine has settled in other than pure curiosity and maybe a smattering of annoyance that her stay here might end up being longer than two weeks.

The room smells of her. Or rather, the coconut oil she likes to use. I can see that she's made some attempt to organize things, but lots of her stuff is still in boxes and bags on the floor. To be fair, there's nowhere else for it to go.

The duvet has been hastily pulled into place, a corner of the rumpled bottom sheet still visible at the end of the bed, and a flimsy pair of bed shorts and camisole top have been flung onto her pillow. I'm glad she always wears that blue toweling robe of hers, the one that's hanging from the hook on the back of the door. I'd hate for Ross to see her in this getup.

A memory flashes into my mind. Alice and I following her to Nando's one sunny Saturday. The denim shorts she'd made herself cut so high that half her bum was hanging out.

I give the rest of the room a quick scan. Catherine has arranged her books on the floor against the wall. Most of them are nursing textbooks, but there are also a few psychological thrillers, a couple of old foreign-language phrase books, and an illustrated children's Bible. I'm surprised she has something like this. She doesn't strike me as particularly religious.

I pick it up. I used to have one a bit like this. There's a picture of the three wise men arriving at Jerusalem on its dog-eared jacket and the pages have that thin, silky feeling. The illustrations remind me of those Hollywood epics from the 1950s and '60s that I used to watch with Dad. On the inside cover, an inscription reads: "Xmas 1994. To Catherine, with love from Nanny Dot."

Nineteen ninety-four. My year of birth. Alice's, too.

Nanny Dot. She mentioned her the other day, didn't she, when we had coffee together after my scan?

I snap the Bible shut and put it back where I found it. Ever since I'd met up with Catherine again, she's gone out of her way to help me and be kind to me, and here I am, snooping around in her private things. I'm so nosy, I should be ashamed of myself.

I'm on the verge of leaving when I catch sight of the little art book that used to live on a shelf in the Dawsons' living room. Memories of Alice and me flicking through the pictures come flooding back, and I can't resist having a quick look before I go. I perch on the end of the bed while I leaf through its well-thumbed pages.

I stop at Balthus's *Girl with Cat,* remembering how Alice and I used to call it the Pedophile's Pic. I look at the girl in the picture. Her hands are clasped behind her head as she sprawls, suggestively, on a chair, one leg bent on a stool in front of her, the other on the floor, her inner thighs and white underwear on display. Something about the expression on her face reminds me a little of Catherine this morning when she looked at Ross, and of what she might have looked like as a young girl.

What was it Mum told me on the phone? That she and Dad disapproved of how Catherine used to hang around with boys on the estate. "She was very . . . *precocious.*" Those were Mum's words. Is that why her Nanny Dot bought her a Bible? I wonder. Because she thought her granddaughter needed some spiritual guidance?

A horrible thought comes into my head. Maybe there's more to Ross's uptight behavior than simple awkwardness at sharing his home with a colleague. A cold feeling washes through me and I can't believe I haven't even considered it before, or maybe I have, subconsciously at least. Maybe he fancies her. That would certainly account for his awkwardness whenever she's around and his reaction when I told him I'd offered her a room. Of *course* he wouldn't want her living with us if he was having an affair with her, or planning on one.

Now that I come to think of it, wasn't he always bringing her up in conversation before the party? The new practice nurse this, the new practice nurse that. And it was Catherine who accompanied him on that home visit I didn't know about till he came home late. Catherine who ate chicken and chips with him. Where did they eat it? I wonder. In his car? No, Ross would never allow someone to eat a takeaway in his beloved car.

My mind returns to the night of the housewarming party. Was

there a familiarity between the two of them, an intimacy with each other, that somehow I missed? I think of when the doorbell rang and he went off to answer it, force myself to replay what I *actually* saw. He kissed her in greeting, I'm sure of it—but then, he'd kissed all his female colleagues as they arrived. A little peck on the cheek. Nothing strange in that. He'd helped her off with her coat. Perhaps they *were* standing a little too close together. Did his hand linger on her shoulder, or am I just imagining that because I'm trying to make the pieces fit?

I put the book of paintings back where I found it. Why am I doing this to myself? The worst thing I can do is speculate like this. Chances are I've got it completely wrong. Ross has never given me cause to be jealous. Just because Catherine is an attractive woman, it doesn't mean he fancies her. It's me he loves. Me he's going to marry. Not that he's mentioned that lately. Not once. In fact, the last time I brought it up, he changed the subject pretty much straightaway. I didn't think anything of it at the time. After all, we've got enough to worry about right now with a baby on the way, but still, we could at least be *thinking* about it. We could at least be making plans.

I should get out of here and go downstairs, stop torturing myself with all this crap, but something is gnawing away at the back of my mind and I find myself walking over to the chest of drawers instead, slowly opening the one at the top. I know it's an invasion of her privacy, but it's like an itch I have to scratch. A compulsion to find out more about this woman I've invited into my home. Invited into my life. I don't even know what I'm looking for. Some kind of evidence that she and Ross are having an affair?

What if she isn't sorry about the past at all? My eyes drift back to the discarded bed shorts and camisole top. Has this been her plan all along, to steal Ross from under my nose as some kind of twisted revenge?

I take a couple of deep breaths to steady my nerves, but whatever I'm hoping to find, or rather, hoping I *don't* find, it isn't here. All I can see is underwear and T-shirts, balled-up socks and pairs of tights.

I'm wasting my time. Letting my jealousy rear its ugly head again, just because there was a bit of tension between the two of them this morning, which, knowing me, I probably imagined in the first place.

Even so, I don't stop looking. The next drawer is full of gym wear, everything all jumbled up and plonked in any old how. It makes me remember that time Alice and I searched through Catherine's bedside cabinet at Riley Road, when we were looking for her contraceptive pills. She's no tidier now than she was back then.

The bottom drawer is equally messy, and rammed full of jumpers and jeans and a couple of hats—a woolen beanie and a navy baseball cap. It's the same one I saw in her car when she took me for my scan. Only now I see something I didn't register before. The red letters ICL on the front.

Imperial College London. It's where Ross did his medical training.

43

I turn the baseball cap over in my hand. I'm pretty well acquainted with Ross's possessions by now, and I've never seen this before. He does *have* a baseball cap. A plain black one. He wore it the first time he met my parents. Dad teased him about wearing it the wrong way round. Said he looked more like a skateboarder than a GP.

I bring it toward my nose and inhale the fabric. Nothing. Just a slight mustiness. A faint trace of smoke. Stupid to think it might smell of him. Stupid to even entertain the possibility of it being Ross's baseball cap. Stupid. Stupid. Stupid. It's a coincidence, that's all. Catherine is a nurse. She's bound to know other people—other doctors—who went to ICL. It's a famous London medical school, for God's sake. She must have got it from one of them or picked it up from somewhere.

I study the cap for a little longer, then toss it back in the drawer. This stops now. I'm going to go downstairs, clear up the breakfast things, and then I'm going to go for a nice long walk and forget all about this nonsense. This is what jealousy does to you. It drives you crazy. Makes you lose your mind.

After I've washed up, I take the cards that Ross has left on the table, together with the framed photograph of his mother, and put them on the mantelpiece in the living room. He was really pleased with the vinyl I bought him, but I could tell that it was this photo that touched him the most. It must have been so hard for him, losing his mother at such a young age. I can't imagine how sad he must have felt.

Now that the photo has been enlarged, I can see the similarities between the two of them. The high forehead. The long, straight nose and square jaw. His mother was what some might describe as a *handsome* woman. She's not wearing any makeup and her hair is tied back off her face in a rather severe bun, but she clearly liked her jewelry, if that striking pendant round her neck is anything to go by.

I've left the two photos that Catherine gave me a few days ago propped up against the mirror. I really ought to get these framed, too. In fact, that's what I'll do now. I'll walk to Blackheath Standard and go to that gift shop I passed a while back. I look at the photos once more and my eyes wander to the figure of Sheena Dawson as she chats with the woman in the next-door garden. I still can't believe that Mum and Dad lived in Riley Road. Catherine said that her mum was almost back to her old self by the time Alice and I met, and then she got depressed again. I can't see her face because her back is turned to the camera, but the woman she's talking to is smiling broadly, which must mean they were sharing a joke about something.

That's odd. I peer at the photo in my hand. The neighbor is wearing a pendant that's almost identical to the one Ross's mother is wearing. It's a turquoise oblong that looks like it's made out of glass or resin with swirling shapes inside, a little like a lava lamp. I look from one photo to the other. No. It isn't *almost* identical. It *is* identical. What are the chances of that?

I study the neighbor's face. She, too, has a long, straight nose and square jaw, and she's the same coloring as Ross's mother. My mouth goes dry. But Fiona Murray had been dead for almost twelve years when this photo was taken, and she lived in Aberdeen. It's not her. Of

course it isn't. It's obvious she's a different woman. There is a like-
ness, though, and what with the pendant . . .

A strange and troubling thought enters my mind, making the hairs
on the back of my neck stand up. I go into the study and pull out
Ross's old photo album. He doesn't have many pictures of his mother
and the one in the frame is the clearest, from what I can remember,
but it's not his mother I'm looking for. It's his aunt. Ross once told me
that when she first took him in, he couldn't bear to look at her, because she reminded him so much of his mother.

I turn the stiff cardboard pages that have browned with age and
examine the old photos stuck under the sticky plastic. There are several of Ross in his school uniform as a solemn-faced little boy.

Something frightening is ticking away at the back of my mind. All
these coincidences keep stacking up. Things that on their own aren't
particularly odd, but that taken together add up to something very
odd indeed.

Catherine working at Ross's GP practice out of all the possible GP
practices in the country where she might have ended up. Mum and
Sheena Dawson being best friends. The ICL baseball cap in the
drawer upstairs. And now this: the neighbor who looks a bit like his
mother and who's wearing an identical pendant. It's the sort of thing
a grieving person might do, isn't it, wear something that belonged to
her late sister?

But Ross's aunt lived in Sittingbourne, in Kent. That's where he
went to live when his dad couldn't look after him anymore. At least,
that's what he told me.

With trembling fingers, I examine every single photo in the
album, making sure to look not just at the subject of each one, but at
what's in the background, too, and on the edges of each shot, to see
if something—anything—jumps out at me.

When it does, it's like a blow to my solar plexus. I double up in
shock and the photo album shoots off my knees and lands on the
floor with a dull thud.

44

It's a group photo. Ross and the "old gang" from ICL. He's kneeling down at the front in the middle, his head turned to one side, mouth open wide in what looks like either a laugh or a yell. The others are gathered around him. A loosely arranged huddle of confident-looking men and women—mostly men—in their twenties.

Several of the faces at the back are partially or completely obscured by the heads and shoulders in front of them. But there's only one figure I'm interested in right now, and that's Ross. Because of what's on his head: a navy baseball cap worn the wrong way round, the straight red lines of the letter "I" just visible where his head is turned.

I stare at it in disbelief. There must be hundreds of those same baseball caps in circulation. Thousands, even. It doesn't prove anything. Of course it doesn't. So why is my heart hammering like a Kango drill? Why is sweat breaking out in the small of my back?

My horror mounting, I race back upstairs and into the spare room, pull open the bottom drawer. I pick up the cap and examine it once again. It must be pretty old, because the cotton is soft and worn. I turn it inside out and my heart misses a beat. Panic explodes in my mind. The label is small and soft as silk, frayed at the edges. Whatever was printed on it has long since faded, but two small marks remain. The capital letters R and M, written in black biro.

I dry-retch over the open drawer.

Ross Murray.

Back in the study, my mind gibbers with theories. Perhaps Catherine gave him a lift somewhere, something to do with work, and he left it in her car. Maybe it was the same night she accompanied him on that home visit. That's where they could have eaten their takeaway. I don't expect Catherine would mind a few stray chips in her messy Peugeot.

But then, why would Ross have been wearing a baseball cap to do a home visit? A cap I've never seen. And why wouldn't she have given it back to him? Why would she hold on to it like this, unless . . . unless it *means* something to her.

Maybe Ross *did* know Catherine before she started working at the surgery. Maybe they went out together once and that's why she has it. It would still mean he's been lying to me, that *both* of them have been lying to me. But that's a hundred times better than him knowing her since he was a child, living *next door* to her. I don't even want to think about the implications of that.

There's only one way to find out whether the nightmarish scenario unfolding in my mind can possibly be true, and that's to find the paperwork relating to the sale of his aunt's house. I never questioned him at the time. Why would I? It was already in progress when we first got together. The money came through a few months later. It was Ross's money. Ross's inheritance. I had no reason to disbelieve him when he told me her house was in Sittingbourne, that that's where he'd lived with her as a child.

Each drawer contains foolscap suspension files, meticulously organized with clear plastic tabs labeled in Ross's neat capital letters. I think of the R and M on the label inside the baseball cap and my mind spins. My hands are shaking as I flip the files toward me, one after another, scanning each label. I can't afford to break down. Not yet. I need to focus on the task in hand. Only then will I be able to reject this strange and frightening story taking shape in my mind. The story that can't possibly be true.

There's so much filed away in here: bank statements, utility bills, stocks and shares, letters about the mortgage on this place, warranties for household appliances. My fingers walk their way toward the back of each drawer. House deeds, tax returns and correspondence from HMRC, life-insurance documents, envelopes full of receipts, his birth certificate and passport, his medical degree certificate and all the rest of his academic qualifications in hard-backed brown envelopes.

A little voice tells me to slow down, to be as methodical as I can. Neither Ross nor Catherine will be back for hours. I have to keep calm and remember to breathe. I'm pregnant. I need to think of the baby and not get too stressed.

I'm on to the third drawer now. This one seems to be full of documents relating to his parents: power-of-attorney forms and bits and pieces from his father's nursing home in Aberdeen; his mother's birth, marriage, and death certificates. Maybe this is where I'll also find . . .

Yes. Here it is. At last. A file labeled "Aunt Jessie."

I take a few long, deep breaths and steel myself for what I might find. The only noises in the house are the ticking of the clock in the living room and the faint burble of the radio in the kitchen. I lift out the wodge of papers in the file and take them over to the swivel chair, sit down with them on my lap, trying desperately to hold myself together, to tell myself that all will be well, that my life isn't falling apart. That his aunt Jessica's house was in Sittingbourne, just as Ross told me.

Except it wasn't. I know that now. I know it beyond a shadow of a doubt. Because here in my hand is a property description from an estate agent in Chelmsford. The address screams at me from the page: 22 Riley Road. The house next door to the Dawsons. I can even see half of Alice's front door.

Ross's aunt lived at 22 Riley Road. She knew the Dawsons, used to chat to Alice's mum over the garden fence. Catherine and Ross have known each other since before Alice and I were even born. A sob erupts out of me. A rasping, primal sound I've never heard before. He's been acting all this time, playing me for a fool, manipulating me. Catherine, too. But why? What do they want with me after all this time?

45

THEN: AFTER

WEDNESDAY, OCTOBER 10, 2007

It's a chilly autumn morning and the whole of Year Nine is assembled outside the main entrance of the school, facing the green area where Alice's memorial tree is about to be planted. Mrs. Peacock told us yesterday that the tree is called *Prunus avium*, or wild cherry, and gave us all a factsheet about it. It's said to be one of our prettiest native trees and can grow up to eight meters in ten years. I must have read that factsheet at least twenty times. I practically know it off by heart.

I look down at my shoes, which, despite all my best efforts, are already badly scuffed at the toes. In ten years' time, I'll be twenty-three. An adult. But Alice will still be thirteen. She'll always be thirteen. While Alice is frozen in time, the tree will continue to grow, blossoming every year in April, the month of her birth.

There's a horrible lump in my throat. I keep trying to swallow, but the lump is getting bigger. It's like when I have a sore throat and it hurts to swallow, which makes me want to swallow all the more, even when I don't need to.

Mrs. Peacock told us yesterday that the spot they have chosen to plant the tree is sunny and sheltered, which means that the fragile clusters of white flowers won't get blown away too soon, and even when they do fall onto the grass, there will be a carpet of petals to remind us of Alice. Mrs. Peacock didn't need to raise her voice to get our attention like she usually does. She didn't need to tell us to be quiet. She only had to say Alice's name and everyone fell silent and sad.

With the nail of my index finger, I pick the skin away from round the edges of my thumbnail. I'm making it red and sore, but I can't stop doing it. We're all getting a bit restless now. The gardener was late this morning and we're waiting for him to finish digging the hole. It has to be bigger than the root ball of the tree and he is already sweating with the effort.

At last, it's ready. I've been so worried that Alice's sister might turn up, but she's not here, thank God. Her mum isn't here either. Only her dad. He's standing with the gardener and Mr. Davis, the head. His hands are folded across his chest and he keeps stamping his feet and coughing. I'm glad I'm not standing near the front, because I don't want to catch his eye. A couple of times he's looked over in this direction, but I made sure to move my head so that I was directly behind the girl in front and he couldn't see me.

Heather Langton nudges my elbow. "You okay, Lizzie?" she whispers.

I nod, tight-lipped. It's nice of her to ask, but I wish she wouldn't. All I want is for this to be over so we can go back inside. I've been dreading it all week. I know these rituals are supposed to be important, but I'll be relieved when they're all over.

At last, Mr. Davis clears his throat and asks for hush. He tells us that Mr. Baines, the gardener, and Alice's father are now going to plant the tree. The last few murmurs peter out as Mr. Baines holds the sapling in place and Mr. Dawson picks up the shovel. The sun glints off the shiny metal.

Now all we can hear is the sound of the shovel slicing into the mound of soil and the soil falling into the hole. It makes me remember the day Alice was buried and, for one hideous moment, I imagine her hand thrusting up through the soil, her finger pointing straight at me. The shock of it makes me flinch violently and the girls standing near me shuffle quickly out of the way, as if they think I'm about to have a seizure.

Wouldn't that be a nightmare? Having another seizure while Alice's memorial tree is being planted. I can just imagine what Melissa and Bethany and some of the others would say if that happened. They'd say I was spoiling Alice's day on purpose, that I was hogging all the attention and making it about me.

Please God, don't let me have a seizure today. Not while Alice's dad is here, planting her tree.

When the tree has been firmed in and the two men stand back, Mr. Davis gives a speech, similar to the one he gave at Alice's memorial service, but shorter. He says that while the tree is growing there will be a mesh guard around it, to protect it while it's still young and delicate. We should avoid getting too close to the tree until it is established, he says, but that as long as we are careful and respectful, this section of the school garden will be a place to visit and feel close to Alice.

A shiver runs down my spine at this last mention of her name and I have the weirdest sensation that she is standing right behind me, that I can feel her icy breath on the back of my neck, and I know that as long as I live, Alice will always be with me. Always weighing on my conscience. I don't need a special tree to remember her by.

46

NOW

Somehow, I get to my feet, my legs weak and unsteady, my breath ragged with shock and fear. Why would Ross do that? Why would he fake a whole relationship? He can't have been lying about everything, surely. I'd have known if he was. I'd have sensed it, wouldn't I?

I grab the sheet of paper from the floor where it's fallen from my hands and put it with the others, stuff them back into the hanging file marked "Aunt Jessie." Shut the drawer, heart pounding.

I pace the hallway. I can't just stay here, as if nothing has happened. And I can't confront Ross and Catherine either. I have to get away from them. Get away from this house and work out my next move.

I call Mum, but her phone rings out. They'll be at the airport now, waiting for their flight, maybe even boarding the plane. I bet she hasn't even got it switched on. She's hopeless with it. Hopeless. Only turns it on when she wants to use the bloody thing. I try Dad's number, too, on the off chance that he even has it with him, but the same thing happens. Fuck! Just when I need them the most.

They warned me about Catherine, but I didn't listen. I try to imagine their reaction, their shock and disbelief, when they find out she's entangled with Ross, has been from day one, and that far from being the "safe pair of hands" they imagine, Ross has duped me from the very start. Duped them, too. And when they find out I've invited her into my home . . .

My home. Who am I kidding? This isn't my home. It never has been.

Cathcrine has burrowed her way back into my life like an invasive weed. If only I'd listened to my initial misgivings. If only I'd trusted my instincts. She has seized on my vulnerability and my need for friendship. Manipulated her way into my affections.

All those little quirks I chose to ignore. Because I actually felt sorry for her. The way she stood in front of the fridge this morning and stared at the contents, as if it were *her* fridge. *Her* kitchen. The way she eats her cereal on the settee instead of sitting up at the table. The way she watches telly with us in the evenings sometimes, as if she has a perfect right to intrude upon our personal space, to play gooseberry.

Now, of course, I know the truth. The only gooseberry in this house is me. That's why she was acting so weird this morning. She's tiring of the pretense, starting to let her true self show through.

I go upstairs and into the bedroom, reach up and pull my rucksack from the top of the wardrobe. Stretching for it sends a shooting sensation down the side of my stomach. *Calm down, Lizzie. Think of the baby. Think of the baby.*

Who else can I phone? Why haven't I made any friends here yet? I've been so complacent. So utterly reliant on Ross. *Think, Lizzie. Think.*

I unzip my rucksack and start flinging things in. No wonder Ross looked so appalled when I told him about the pregnancy. He looked shattered. Undone. I put it down to shock at the time. But he *was* shattered. A baby clearly wasn't part of the plan. But what the hell *is* their plan?

Whatever it is, I'm in danger. I have to get out of here and find somewhere safe. A hotel, maybe? A B & B? There's hardly any money in my account, just what Ross transfers over to me each month for shopping and bits and pieces, but it should be enough for one night in a Travelodge or somewhere like that, maybe even two. It'll tide me over till I speak to Mum and Dad and they come home.

I open drawers and stare at the contents. How do I know what I'll need? I'll need everything, surely. How can I ever come back? But there's no way I can pack everything. I have to focus on the most important things. A change of clothes. Some toiletries. My glasses. My phone and charger. My meds. Should I take my personal documents? Shit! This is going to take longer than I thought. It's like one of those anxiety dreams where I need to pack really fast and I can't think where to start or what I'll need.

Except this isn't a dream. Something terribly wrong is happening here.

It's only when I'm pulling out the box file under the bed where I keep all my admin, and riffling through it, that the perfect solution pops into my head. A wave of relief washes through me. I've still got my front-door keys for the house in Dovercourt. I meant to give them back to Mum and Dad the last time we visited, but I completely forgot. Thank God I did!

I'll get a bus to Woolwich and take a train into town, go to Liverpool Street and from there to Dovercourt. When Mum and Dad get home from New York, we'll work out what to do.

I zip up my rucksack, pausing in the doorway for one last look. And that's when the tears finally break. When the full horror hits me in one vicious blow. My whole life with Ross has been a sham. How many lies has he told me? Has he ever loved me at all?

Oh my God. The young man Catherine was with, the day Alice and I followed her from Nando's. The young man in board shorts. He was wearing a navy baseball cap the wrong way round. It must have been Ross. I clamp my hand over my mouth and think of the way Catherine's head disappeared in the car, my dawning realization of what was going on in there. Alice and me giggling so much we almost choked on our sweets.

My eyes tremble and blur. I can't stay here a minute longer. I need to leave. I reach out a hand to grab the doorframe, but it looms at a strange angle and I miss it completely. My ears pound. The room suddenly looks all jagged and angular, like a cubist painting. Something strange is happening. Something strange and, at the same time, frighteningly, sickeningly familiar.

PART THREE

No story is the same to us after a lapse of time; or rather we who read it are no longer the same interpreters.

—George Eliot

For months after it happened, I was terrified that someone would find out it was me who ran into Sue Molyneux, who almost made her lose the baby. Lose Lizzie. Catherine said that if I got caught I'd be convicted for attempted murder and sent to a children's prison.

I later discovered that this wasn't true. For a start, I was only nine when it happened, and nobody under ten can be charged with a crime. What's more, there's no such thing as attempted murder of an unborn child. In the eyes of the law, an unborn child is not a person. So even if I'd been ten, the most I'd have been charged with is Actual Bodily Harm, that's if they could even prove it was intentional. And how could they? Catherine had burnt the only piece of evidence that existed—that childish declaration she'd made me sign in her bedroom, which seemed so meaningful and portentous at the time.

When I found this out and told Catherine, she went scarily still and I knew I shouldn't have said anything. She told me it didn't make a jot of difference. There were other punishments I would receive. I'd be put under a Child Safety Order and Aunt Jessie would disown me.

She said I'd probably be taken into care and the police would always be monitoring me for the rest of my life.

Especially when they found out about the "other things" I'd done.

That was the threat she always hung over me. Telling her parents and Aunt Jessie that I'd touched her private parts. Even though she'd told me to do it. Even though she'd shown me exactly what to do and liked it just as much as I did.

I had a profound fear of being taken into care. If it weren't for Aunt Jessie taking me in when Mum died, I'd have almost certainly ended up in a children's home, or been farmed out to foster parents. I don't like to think of that time very often, trapped indoors with my grieving father, wondering whether I'd get beaten for nothing at all, wondering whether there'd be anything for supper that night or whether I'd have to make do with a tin of cold baked beans again.

Aunt Jessie wasn't the most maternal of women, and even she wasn't averse to giving me a good slap if I did my chores badly or forgot to do my homework, but I knew where I was with her, and if I followed her rules, things were fine. Sometimes, when she was in a good mood and her face was soft and calm, she looked so much like my mum.

Despite the threats, Catherine was my best friend. I was a strange, awkward boy and having someone like her looking out for me meant I never got picked on. Back in those days, Riley Road and the rest of the estate could be a pretty rough place to live if you didn't have an ally. And Catherine Dawson was probably the best ally you could have.

It wasn't her fault she was so screwed up. Her mother was too absorbed in her own pain to give her daughter the love and attention she craved. And as for Mick, he did what so many men do when things get tough at home. He threw himself into his work and his hobbies, withdrew into his own little world. So when I came along Catherine turned her full attention on me. She gave me the love I needed in the only way she knew how. In fits and starts.

I adored her. I hated her. I needed her.

You may wonder why I let her take the lead. Why I surrendered all

sense of myself on the altar of her desires. I wonder it myself some-
times, but I never had a choice. Not really.

Some people are like that, aren't they? They take you over, every
little bit of you, and even though it rankles and you try to resist, deep
down you know there's no point because the sad truth is, you rather
like it that way.

I liked it that way.

Until I didn't, and by then it was too late.

47

At first, I think it must be the hiss of rain, or the rustling of leaves. It's a comforting sound, the sort of sound that might lull someone to sleep. I try to open my eyes, to drag myself back to consciousness. There's a reason I need to wake up. An important reason. If only I could remember what it is.

The noise continues, so close it might be just outside the window. I turn my head toward the streetlight that shines through the gap in the curtains. Streetlight? How can it be nighttime already? Then I recognize the noise. It isn't the hiss of rain or the rustle of leaves. It's whispering. The whispering that's haunted me all my life. My parents whispering behind closed doors. Police officers whispering in corridors. Schoolfriends whispering behind my back.

It's coming from beyond the curtains, which now I realize aren't my bedroom curtains at all, but curtains around my bed. A hospital bed. The vestiges of a dream hover at the back of my mind. A nightmare about Ross and Catherine.

I struggle to sit up, but I'm so groggy I can barely move. It feels as though I'm shrouded in gauze. Every muscle in my body aches. Every sinew. Every bone.

I run my hands over my stomach, pressing ever so gently, and am, at last, rewarded with a faint sensation of movement. I exhale in relief, but the feeling is short-lived. My temples throb with the worst headache I've had in ages. There's no saliva in my mouth and my tongue feels swollen and sore.

I sink back onto the pillows, defeated. A feeling of despondency settles like sediment in the pit of my stomach. The thing I most dread must have happened again. Another seizure.

Hands pull the curtains aside and Ross appears, his eyes tired and dull, the corners of his mouth pulled down in a worried, tense expression that turns into a smile when he sees me.

"Hello, sleepyhead. How are you feeling?"

He perches on the side of my bed and strokes my cheek and, as he does so, the dream comes flooding back. Pulling my rucksack down from the top of the wardrobe. Flinging things inside. The old, familiar anxiety dream, but a particularly nasty one. The discovery that he didn't love me, after all. That he and Catherine were laughing at me behind my back. Conspiring against me. I hate those bloody dreams.

I squeeze his wrist and kiss his fingers, tears brimming at the sight of him, so solid and loving, so absolutely here and on my side. The man I love. The father of my unborn child.

"I came home and found you slumped on the floor by the bedroom door," he says. "Oh, Lizzie. Lizzie, darling."

Something about his voice unsettles me. It's that awful dream. For some reason, I can't stop thinking about it. Nasty snippets keep arriving in my head. His baseball cap in Catherine's drawer. His aunt living on Riley Road. It's still so vivid and painful. So random and bizarre.

I let him hold me against his chest and stroke my forehead. I always have dreams like that when I'm worried about something. And I *am* worried about something. I'm going to have a baby, the most momentous, life-changing experience I can possibly imagine, and I've just had another seizure. No wonder I feel so weird and disoriented. No wonder I feel so scared.

They keep me in hospital overnight. More tests. More scans. I drift in and out of sleep, only waking when I hear the clank of a trolley, or when a nurse comes round to do my observations. I want to be at home with Ross, in my own bed. I can't believe I missed his birthday evening—the trip to the cinema and the meal out I'd planned. But at the same time, I'm also glad to be here, being monitored. Because I'm terrified it'll happen again. I know the dangers. The risks. And all that matters now is having my baby. A healthy baby, with no complications. Sleep drags me back down.

I'm discharged the next day, but it's ages before we can actually leave because my phone's gone missing. Ross says he distinctly remembers putting it in my bag when he drove me to A & E yesterday, but we can't find it in the ward anywhere. We look through the cabinet next to my bed. We look in the bed and under it. We even take the pillowcases off, just in case it's got caught up in one of them, but it's nowhere to be seen. Ross fills in a lost-property form, but I don't hold out much hope of it being found. Things get nicked in hospitals all the time.

When we finally get home, it's as if I've been away for far longer than one night. The house feels different, smells different. Familiar but strange at the same time. Just like a dream. He follows me upstairs. I take each step slowly, gingerly, one hand steadying myself on the rail. I still feel shaky and tired. Ill at ease.

And I'm so pissed off about my phone. I know it can easily be replaced, but I can't remember Mum and Dad's mobile numbers off by heart—I stupidly never wrote them down anywhere—so I can't let them know what's happened. Although maybe it's better they don't find out straightaway. They've been looking forward to their week away for ages. I don't want to spoil it by alarming them, and anyway, I'm fine now. I can tell them when they get home.

The first thing I see when I go upstairs is the emptiness of the spare room. The door is wide open and all of Catherine's things have gone. I pause a moment, to take this in.

"She had another call from the landlord of her new place," Ross says when he sees me looking. "The current tenant has left earlier than expected, so we've got our house back at last."

I step over the threshold and reacquaint myself with the room now that it's been cleared of her possessions. A faint trace of coconut oil lingers in the air. The carpet needs a vacuum.

"Oh, right. That's good."

I'm surprised, especially after her saying she might have to stay for even longer, but I can't pretend I'm not relieved, especially after that horrible dream about her and Ross.

Ross puts his hands on my shoulders and kisses me gently on the lips. "Why don't you get into bed and rest while I make some tea?"

While he's downstairs and I'm changing into a clean pair of pajamas, the dream invades my mind once more. I look up at my rucksack on top of the wardrobe and remember the shooting pain in my side as I stretched up for it. But that was in the dream, wasn't it? It didn't really happen.

That's odd. Something about the rucksack doesn't look right. It's pushed way too far back. I always make sure it's right at the front so I can easily pull it down when I need it. Maybe Ross was going to use it to put my things in for the hospital and changed his mind, brought them in a carrier bag instead.

I have a sudden urge to check inside it. Being back here in the bedroom makes the dream seem real, as if it actually happened.

I stand on the chair I use at my dressing table and reach for the rucksack. It's light and empty, as I knew it would be, and I make sure it's positioned at the front so I can get it down next time I need it. That's when I notice a slight bulge in one of the compartments at the side. I wonder what that is.

I unzip it and draw out a handful of blister packs of my meds. What are *they* doing in here? There's something else, too. My passport and some folded-up sheets of medical information. An uneasy sensation uncoils in the pit of my stomach. Why on earth would I have put my passport in there? I always keep it in the box file under my bed.

Images from the dream race through my mind. My hands flicking through papers. The baseball cap in Catherine's drawer with Ross's initials on the label. The file marked "Aunt Jessie." I feel a sudden chill. Something dark and twisted is coming into focus. My stomach falls away as the fog I've been drifting through ever since waking up in hospital finally clears. That was no dream. Oh my God! It really happened.

My stomach pitches with shock as the hideous truth begins to emerge. I must have been trying to leave before I had the seizure. Ross must have seen my rucksack when he came home and found me passed out on the floor. Did he realize I was trying to escape?

The stairs creak. I stuff the tablets and passport back into the compartment and get off the chair, just managing to put it back in front of the dressing table before Ross opens the door, my heart thumping so loud and fast I'm amazed he can't hear it. The knowledge is like a bad drug speeding through my veins, turning my blood to ice.

I pretend to be putting something away in a drawer. I have to keep calm and act normal or he'll know something's up. I have to pretend that nothing has changed. That I'm still the same old Lizzie he thinks he knows. The one who thinks his aunt Jessie lived in Sittingbourne. The one who has no idea how long he's really known Catherine Dawson.

Oh God. So he knew who I was right from the start! His confusion at the party when I dropped the tray of wine—the whole thing was an act. And his questions when all the guests had left. He already *knew* all the answers.

He rests the tray of tea on top of my dressing table and runs the tip of his finger down my cheek. That sweet, intimate gesture I've always loved. Is it nothing more than a calculated display of affection?

Fury swells inside me. He's been playing a part all this time. The consummate actor. Nothing about our relationship is real. Everything that anchored me in this house, this life, is slipping away from me. Everything I know about him—everything I *thought* I knew about him—is gone in the blink of an eye. Ross has unraveled before me, been replaced by a clone of himself.

"Glad to be home?" he says.

Something about his voice is slightly off, at least that's how it sounds to my suspicious ears. My fury turns to fear. What the hell is happening here? I don't trust myself to speak, and yet I must or he'll realize something is wrong.

"Can't wait to get into my own bed again," I say. Can he hear the tremor in my voice?

I hold my breath, bracing myself for his reaction, but he carries on chatting as if nothing is wrong. My mind whirls as I climb under the duvet. Even if he did look in the rucksack, he'd have only seen a few bits and pieces. Some items of clothing. He might have thought I was getting it ready for a yoga class or something. He obviously didn't look in the compartments or he'd have emptied them, too, put everything back in its right place. And even if he did, even if he knew for sure that I was trying to leave, he'll be assuming my post-seizure brain has forgotten all about it.

There's a menace about him now. An indefinable quality that must have been there all along, only I never noticed it before. I never saw it because I was blind to his flaws. Blind and stupid. A gullible little fool. If only I hadn't been so out of it in hospital, I could have alerted someone. Told them I didn't feel safe. They'd have helped me. Now, with no way of contacting Mum and Dad until they're back from New York, I'm on my own.

48

Ross hands me a mug of tea, but I can barely hold it. I'm always weak and shaky after a seizure, and tired. So terribly, bone-achingly tired. Too tired to think straight, but I must. I've got to force myself to stay awake.

He takes the mug out of my hands and pours some into the empty glass that's still sitting on my bedside table from two nights ago.

"Here," he says, putting the mug down next to me. "It should be easier for you to hold now."

He fusses with my pillows. If I didn't know any different, I'd be thinking how attentive and kind he's being, how lucky I am to have him looking after me.

He carries the glass of tea over to the tray on the dressing table. "Try and get some more sleep, and maybe you'll feel like something to eat when you wake up."

I nod. I just want him to go away and let me think. I can't even bear to look at him. I have to get out of here as soon as I can. But right now, I doubt I'd make it to the bottom of the road before collapsing. He'll stop me if I try to leave. I can barely walk I'm so exhausted.

Perhaps I should call the police on the landline when he goes down-stairs. Tell them I'm in danger.

But *am* I in danger? Catherine has gone now. Moved out. Maybe that was another lie he told me. Maybe he *asked* her to leave. After all, he wasn't exactly pleased when I offered her the room. And they were definitely being snippy with each other yesterday morning. Maybe they aren't the couple I think they are. Maybe she's using him to get at me and he's just been going along with it.

But why? What kind of person would do that? He isn't a little boy anymore. He's a grown man. A doctor. What possible motivation could he have had for colluding with her in this? Whatever *this* is.

The only motive I can think of is revenge. Revenge for Alice's death. Has Catherine managed to convince Ross of my guilt, per-suaded him to string me along in order to undo me somehow?

Besides, if I phoned the police, what would I say? My fiancé has been lying to me. He didn't tell me he's known one of his colleagues since they were children. She's the sister of my best friend who was killed by a train. She's never liked me and blamed me for her sister's death, but now I'm friends with her. Or rather, I *was*.

They'll think I'm a lunatic. That I'm having some kind of psy-chotic episode. Ross will be the sensible, respectable GP who tells them I've been under a lot of strain recently, what with the unex-pected stress of the pregnancy. He'll tell them how disoriented and poorly I always am after a seizure. They'll only have to take one look at my pale face and wild hair to believe this. And the hospital will confirm my recent admission.

But when Ross plucks the phone from its cradle on his way out, my fear intensifies.

"I'll take it downstairs," he says. "So that it doesn't wake you if it rings," and before I have a chance to synchronize my brain and my voice, the door closes softly behind him.

I sink back onto my pillows in frustration. It wouldn't have worked anyway. The story sounds absurd. It *is* absurd.

The only thing I can do right now is think. Decide where I'm going to go when I'm strong enough to leave the house. I must have had a plan yesterday, when I packed that rucksack. If only I could remember what it was.

I start to mentally retrace my steps, thinking of every single thing I did from the moment I watched Ross and Catherine drive off in the morning, right up to the point when I pulled the rucksack down and started flinging things inside. After that, my mind is a blank.

I huddle down under the duvet, drawing it round my neck for comfort. Where was I going before the seizure put paid to my plans? I'd have rung Mum and Dad, wouldn't I? It's the first thing I'd have thought of doing. I can just imagine Dad's fury with Ross for deceiving me. I might be twenty-five but he still thinks of me as his little girl. I dread to think what he'll do when he finds out.

But I can't have spoken to them, or left a message, because if Dad thought for one second that I was in danger, he'd have booked them on the first flight home. I know he would. And then he'd have driven me home to Dovercourt. My eyes fill with tears as I think of him. Dad will sort this out. I know he will. He and Mum might not have been entirely honest with me about their friendship with the Dawsons, but that's nothing compared to what's happening here.

Something clicks at the back of my mind. Home. Dovercourt. Mum and Dad's house. Of course! I still have the key! I don't have to wait till they come home from New York. Was that the conclusion I reached yesterday?

At last, the panic in my chest starts to subside. I have a plan. Somewhere to go. I only have to stay here long enough to regain my strength. I'll leave tonight, when Ross is asleep. I'll be safe if he thinks I don't know about him and Catherine, or that my seizure has made me forget.

I just have to pretend for a little while longer.

49

The room is almost dark when I wake up. It takes me a few seconds to remember where I am and what's happened. Catherine must be home from work. She's in the living room with Ross. I can just make out the faint murmur of their voices over the TV. The thought of the two of them down there, while I'm in bed, woozy and defenseless, nauseates me.

Wait a minute. She's supposed to have moved out. She *has* moved out. So why is she downstairs?

I get up, slowly and carefully. I feel raw and tender, the discomfort in my body mirroring the anguish in my head. The shock of betrayal. The anger. The fear.

I need to act normally. Prove to them that nothing is different. That I'm not in the least bit scared. Because if they *did* look in that rucksack, or I left something out in the study, if they have the slightest whiff of suspicion that I was intending to leave, I'll be in real danger if they think I still remember.

My head is telling me to get dressed and leave right now. But they'll hear me go down and I don't have the strength to argue with them. I certainly don't have the energy to run away. I have to keep the pretense going for a little while longer.

I stand in the semidarkness of the landing and peer over the balustrade into the hallway below, straining my ears to hear what they're saying, but the only thing I pick up is the tone. The conspiratorial tone of two people who don't want to be heard but who obviously have a great deal to say to each other.

I give up trying to eavesdrop and go and wash my face. One glance in the mirror tells me I look as bad as I feel. I'm pale as a ghost and there are dark shadows under my eyes. My hair is wild and uncombed, my lips dry and parched. I drag a brush through my hair and put some Vaseline on my lips, rub my cheeks with my fingers to try to get some color in them.

When I come out of the bathroom, I nearly jump out of my skin. Catherine is standing there, stock still, as if she's been listening outside the door. It's as much as I can do not to cringe at the sight of her.

"God, sorry!" she says, stepping back. "I didn't mean to frighten you." Her face is the picture of concern, but it isn't real. I know that now. She still thinks I killed Alice.

"Lizzie, how *are* you?" she says.

That feeling I had when I first saw her in the hall, the night of the party, comes reeling back. The shock. The revulsion. But now it's stronger than ever. I want to push her away from me, to pummel her chest with my fists and scream at her to get the hell out of here, but all I can do is smile weakly and pretend that I'm glad to see her. Surely she can see the suspicion in my eyes?

"I thought you'd gone," I say, my pulse racing. It's taking all of my efforts to keep my voice warm and natural. I feel like I want to vomit.

"I have, but I left my hair straighteners behind. I popped round to pick them up. Oh, Lizzie, I was so worried when I found you lying on the floor."

"Oh, was it you who found me? I thought Ross said—"

"Well, I got home from work first. Ross came in a few minutes after. You poor thing. But Ross tells me the baby is fine, that they've checked you over and no harm has been done. What a relief."

Sweat prickles at the back of my neck. Nothing about her seems genuine anymore. When I think of how remorseful she's been, how keen to get close to me, to be my friend. How *could* I have been so easily fooled?

"Thank goodness you found me when you did," I say, trying to arrange my face into an expression of gratitude, aware of a pulse throbbing in my left eyelid, a flush of heat staining my cheeks. She'll notice it, surely she will.

Ross has now come upstairs and is standing with us on the landing.

"The important thing is that we *did* find you," she says. "And that you and the baby are both fine." She glances at Ross. "It's been a worrying twenty-four hours, that's for sure."

I watch their faces. Is that some kind of coded joke between the two of them? Were they really worrying about my health, or were they more concerned about whether I was on to them?

Ross nods in agreement. He looks paler than normal. Weaker, somehow. I may be clutching at straws, but I have the distinct impression he's scared of her, too, that for some inexplicable reason, he's dancing to her tune. He might be the big, strong, rugby-playing doctor, but Catherine is firmly in control here. I'm in no doubt about that. She has some kind of hold over him, I'm sure of it.

She goes into the spare room and comes out again with her straighteners.

"Can't live without these things," she says, smiling broadly. "See you tomorrow at work, Ross. And Lizzie, I'll ring you in a few days. When you're feeling better."

"Yes, that'll be nice," I say, knowing that, in a few days' time, I won't be here. Can she see it in my face?

We all troop downstairs and say goodbye.

"Catherine?" I say, as she's about to leave, trying to keep my voice as light and casual as I can. "Did you give Ross the spare keys back?"

She pauses for a beat too long. A flicker of irritation passes across her forehead, but then she delves into her handbag and produces them with a flourish. As the front door closes behind her, Ross visibly relaxes.

Maybe I should confront him right now? Tell him what I know. All the time I've been with Ross, I've never been scared of him. He's made me feel safe. Protected. Maybe it *was* all acting, but I can't believe he'd willingly do anything to hurt me or the baby.

But every time I'm about to say the words, something stops me, because however hard I try to convince myself that he's on my side, I realize I don't know this man at all. I have absolutely no idea what he's capable of. And do I really *want* him on my side, after all the lies he's told me?

No, I am *not* going to rock this boat until I'm well and truly on dry land. He's still deceived me in the most insidious way. He's still an unknown danger to me and the baby.

I watch, surreptitiously, as Ross gets ready for bed. I'm pretending to read, but every so often I raise my eyes to steal a glance at him as he discards his clothes onto the chair. This will be the very last time I see him do this and, despite everything, I feel a rush of emotion. Love, it seems, cannot be turned off like a tap, no matter how serious the betrayal, no matter how deep the hurt.

I scan back over those early moments in our relationship. How giddy and swept up I'd been in the romance of it all, how much I'd wanted to be loved. Our first meeting in the café in Dovercourt. The subsequent walks on the beach. Was spilling his coffee on my boots a deliberate ploy? How did they know where to find me?

He gets into bed and spoons my back, his arm resting gently on my bump, his breath warm on the nape of my neck. How is it possible to love someone and hate them at the same time, to hold two different versions of them in your head?

His hands move slowly and gently up to my breasts, just as they've done so many times before. I want to push him away. I want to scream at him to stop, to get up and leave right now, but all I can do is lie here, entwined with this stranger. This imposter. Allow him to make love to me as if nothing has changed.

I could say no. Tell him I'm too tired. Too ill. Because I am. I'm both of those things. He's never pressured me into sex, not once. But something tells me that now is not the time to refuse, that keeping him onside and confident of my love, my desire for him, is more important than ever. Sex is a language all of its own. If my body fails to communicate in its normal way, he'll know something's wrong.

So I let him enter me for the last time, willing myself not to cry. I let him push into me again and again, arching my back like I usually do, pressing into him and going through the familiar motions. I even make the same noises. The little sighs and gasps. Because I can play-act, too. I have to.

When it's over, I lie with my back to him, tears flowing silently down my face. I wish I could shower every last molecule of him out of my body.

Except I can't, can I? I'm carrying his baby. Our baby.

My baby. My little girl. I place my hand protectively on my tummy and tell myself to be strong for her sake. Under my bed is a canvas tote bag I packed earlier, with my purse, my old house keys, the meds I found in my rucksack, and a change of clothes. There are so many other things I'd like to take with me, but the most important thing is to get away. As fast as I can, unencumbered by possessions that will only slow me down.

As soon as I think it's safe, I'll get up and creep downstairs. Change into my jeans and jumper, grab my coat from the hook, and get the hell out of here as fast as I can.

50

All the time Catherine was here, Ross's sleeping pattern was badly disrupted. He'd tossed and turned, sighed and fidgeted. Tonight, though, he falls asleep almost straightaway and is snoring within minutes. Even so, I want to be absolutely sure he's in a really deep sleep before I venture downstairs.

I ease myself gently into a sitting position and pinch the flesh of my forearm with my fingernails, keep them embedded so that I don't fall asleep while I'm waiting. I'll have a nasty bruise in the morning.

Eventually, when I see the rapid movement of his eyes beneath his eyelids, I reach down to the side and slide out the tote bag from beneath the bed. Then I get up carefully and approach the bedroom door, my eyes not daring to leave the sleeping form of Ross, whose right shoulder is sticking out of the duvet. He's turned away from the door, thank God. I'm glad I can't see his face.

I depress the handle as quietly as I can and step into the darkness of the landing, my ears pricked for sound—a change in his breathing pattern, the squeak of the mattress. Nothing. I close the door softly.

This is it. I'm going. The next time I return, it'll be with Mum and Dad, to get the rest of my things.

With trepidation, I hold the stair rail and lower myself onto the top step. Every single creak, every single breath, sounds magnified in the silence. I pause after each couple of steps and listen. By the time I approach the bottom, I'm rigid with tension.

The shrill ring of the landline jolts through me like an electric shock. I stumble down the last few steps, frustration and fear like a physical pain in my chest. Fuck! There's no way he'll sleep through that.

For a few seconds, I'm paralyzed by indecision. Either I leave right now in my pajamas, knowing that Ross will wake up and find me gone almost straightaway, maybe even come running after me, or I answer the phone myself and make out I was on my way down for a glass of water.

But it's too late. The phone stops ringing and I hear Ross's voice from upstairs. The bedroom door opens and the landing light comes on. Shit! I should have just gone while I had the chance.

Suddenly, he's at the top of the stairs. I head for the kitchen, heart thumping. I'm going to have to wait till morning now, when he's gone to work. I should have done that anyway. It's madness to be creeping about like this in the middle of the night like some kind of criminal, but the urge to leave was overwhelming. It still is. It isn't till I'm standing at the kitchen sink that I realize I still have the bulging tote bag over my shoulder.

I open the cupboard where we keep the saucepans and stuff it right at the back, out of sight. Then I quickly run the cold tap and take a glass from the draining board, hands shaking so much it's a miracle I don't drop it.

Ross comes downstairs and into the kitchen. He's listening intently, with only the occasional interjection of a "Yes, I see, thank you," or "Okay." At last, the call finishes. He drops the phone into the pocket of his dressing gown and rubs his hands over his face.

"That was the nursing home," he says. His voice is weary and re-signed. "My dad's just died."

"Oh no, I'm so sorry." The words are automatic, because I *am* sorry. Whatever lies Ross has told me, this isn't one of them. His relationship with his father was complicated, I know that. But I've heard it said that loss can hit a person harder in such cases and, by the look on his face, that's true.

He moistens his lips with his tongue. "I'm going to have to go to Aberdeen to sort things out." He glances at the kitchen clock. "I'll try and get a couple more hours' sleep and then I'll drive to the airport, catch the first flight up there. The sooner I can sort things out, the better."

I step toward him and give him a hug. Actually, this has worked out much better for me. If Ross leaves for Aberdeen first thing in the morning, I can pack properly. I can make sure I've got everything I need and call a taxi when I'm ready. Now that Catherine is out of the way, I don't have to worry anymore.

"Actually," he says, "why don't you come with me? We could make a weekend of it." I go very still in his arms. "I don't like the thought of leaving you on your own, not when you've so recently had another seizure."

I take a step back and shake my head. "No, you go on your own. I'm not sure I'm up to rushing around yet." I try to keep the desperation out of my voice. "You don't mind, do you?"

He takes my face in his hands and looks deep into my eyes. I used to think it was so romantic when he did this, but now it seems false. Controlling. He kisses me gently on the lips.

"You don't have to come to the nursing home if you're not feeling up to it. We can check in to a hotel and you can stay there and pamper yourself. Order room service. We can eat out in the evening. Go somewhere nice. You've always wanted to see the place where I was born."

Shit. How ironic that when I wanted to go to Aberdeen with him before, he put me off. Now, when it's the very last thing I want to do, he's all up for it. The thing is, if I say I'm too poorly for the journey, he may well delay going up for a couple more days. With no way of speaking to Mum and Dad until they ring me, I'll be stuck here with him.

"I'd love to come with you, Ross, I really would. But I've got an antenatal appointment with the community midwife tomorrow and I don't want to rearrange at such short notice."

I turn away from him to pick up my glass of water, praying he won't notice how my cheeks have started to redden at the lie.

"Oh, I didn't know about that," he says. He's tugging gently at his chin when I face him again. "But they won't mind, will they?"

"No, but I will. Especially after what's just happened. I don't want to have to wait for the next appointment. It might take weeks." I put my hands on the front of his shoulders. "Besides, I want to spend a *proper* weekend in Aberdeen with you, look round the city together. We can go up another time, when you can spend more time with me."

He sighs, but I think—I hope—I've convinced him.

"I guess you're right," he says.

I smile. "I'm always right."

Ross pours a finger of whiskey into a tumbler. "To the aul' bastard," he says, raising his glass and giving me a sad little smile.

I raise my water in the air and we chink our glasses.

"To the aul' bastard," I say, looking deep into Ross's eyes.

Catherine went crazy when I asked her to leave. When I told her to leave. Crazier than when she'd found out about the pregnancy even, and that was some kind of crazy, let me tell you. I told her I couldn't keep doing this for the rest of my life—indulging her vengeful fantasies—and that it was time I stood up for myself. I was developing feelings for Lizzie. Uncomfortable, messy feelings. The sort of feelings I'd never experienced before, but that somehow felt . . . right. Playing the loving fiancé role was becoming both easier and harder than it had ever been. Easier because it came so naturally now. Harder because I didn't actually want to play anymore.

Sometimes, at work, I'd draw Lizzie's photo toward me—the one I kept in a frame on my desk. It's a casual, unposed snap that captures her mid-laugh, her blue eyes smiling in the sun, a pretty smattering of freckles across her nose and the tops of her cheeks. Who'd have thought that Lizzie Molyneux would turn out to be so beautiful? No wonder Catherine hated it. No wonder she used to turn the photo facedown whenever she came into my consulting room.

She said she'd tell Lizzie everything and I said I didn't care. I was *going to tell her anyway. Tell her how I'd been manipulated and controlled since I was a little boy. Catherine didn't like that. She didn't like that one little bit because it was true and there was nothing she could say to make it otherwise.*

I felt invincible then. Able to deal with whatever crap she threw at me, even when she ambushed me in the middle of the night wearing nothing but her silky bed shorts and beckoning me into her bed, because I knew damn well that if I didn't make a stand, I'd never be free of her. Never.

And it was Lizzie I wanted now. Lizzie and the baby.

51

I wake from a deep, dreamless sleep. The early-morning sun streams through a gap in the curtains. I blink and turn away from the light. It feels like I've been asleep for years and years, curled up in the same fetal position.

I squint at the time on Ross's clock radio: 9:27. I've slept right through the night. I'm still here. I struggle into a sitting position and swing my legs over the side of the bed. Fuck!

But as soon as my feet touch the floor, the memory lands like a dart behind my eyes. I fall back onto the bed, relief flooding through me. Ross's father has died. He's gone to Aberdeen. I can get up when I'm ready and pack properly, call a taxi to take me to the station. I'll be home in Dovercourt by the early afternoon.

I roll onto my back and stretch out like a cat. I can't believe I fell asleep again, not with all the drama last night. But after Ross and I came back to bed, he talked to me about his father and what kind of a man he was, what it was like for him in the days after his mother died. It was the first time he's ever spoken to me in detail about that part of his life. It felt almost as if he was working himself up to something more, maybe even a confession, and I wanted so much to hear it. I wanted so much to understand.

But his voice was deep and low, a soothing monotone in my ears as he stroked my back gently with his fingers. I must have drifted off. My body, still tired after the seizure, and my mind, no longer fraught now that I knew I'd have the house to myself in the morning, must have taken the decision for me and switched off, allowing me to sleep deeply and recuperate.

I get up out of bed and take a long draft of water from the glass on my bedside table. Then I go into the bathroom. I ought to shower. I feel hot and sticky; grubby, too. But I make do with a quick wash instead. I know I don't need to rush anymore, but that doesn't mean I want to stay here any longer than I need to. I can shower when I get to Mum and Dad's.

The thought of showering in their bathroom, stepping out of the cubicle on to the tufted white bath mat and drying myself on one of their fluffy tumble-dried towels, safe in the knowledge that I'm back home, makes me weak with longing. The sooner I call that taxi, the better.

Back in the bedroom, I change into a summer frock. Something loose and cool and comfortable. Then I pull down my rucksack and drag my suitcase out from under the bed. I won't be able to pack everything, but at least I can take more than one change of clothes this time.

It's actually a good thing that Mum and Dad won't be there when I arrive. I'm not sure I could cope with their shock and anger. Their disappointment. I need time to let my own feelings out, to nurse my conflicted emotions in private, before having to deal with theirs, too.

When I've packed everything I can, I zip up the case and rucksack and start to carry them downstairs. All I have to do now is retrieve my tote bag from the saucepan cupboard where I stuffed it last night, pack the rest of my medication, and call a taxi. I'll write a note to Ross while I'm waiting for it to arrive.

God knows what I'll say. He needs to be in no doubt whatsoever that we're over, that there's no way back from this. And I don't want him guessing where I've gone and turning up on Mum and Dad's doorstep while I'm on my own there.

I'm about halfway down the stairs when I sense something different about the house. A slight change in atmosphere. As if I'm not alone. Blood pulses in my ears. Every hair on my body stiffens.

"Ross? Are you still here?"

No reply. Of course there isn't. Ross left hours ago. I'm imagining things. I carry on down and dump my case by the front door.

I reach for the phone on the hall table, but my hand pauses mid-air. It's not there. Why isn't it there? It was definitely there last night, because the sound of it ringing almost made me fall down the last few steps. Maybe Ross used it this morning, to phone one of his colleagues and let them know he wouldn't be in. He's probably left it in the living room, like he usually does, but when I look for it, it isn't there. I wrinkle my nose in distaste. I can still smell Catherine's coconut oil from when she was here last night.

I go into the kitchen to use the extension there, but that one's missing, too. Why are *both* the phones missing? For fuck's sake, I'm going to have to use the one in the bedroom. I turn back into the hallway and head for the stairs. Which is when I see that my front-door keys aren't in the little dish by the phone where I keep them.

Ross must have taken mine by mistake. He's done that before, ended up at work with both sets in his pocket. Not that it matters. It just means I won't be able to lock the house when I leave. Even so, I wanted to take them with me, so that Dad and I can come back at some point and get the rest of my things. Maybe it doesn't matter. Whatever I can't take with me can be replaced. All that really matters is leaving.

Hang on, though, where are the spare keys? I took them off Catherine last night, didn't I? They should be in the dish, too. He can't have taken *all three* sets.

I try to open the front door, but I can't. I rattle the handle. He's locked it. I run back to the kitchen and rattle the handle of the back door, but that's locked, too, and the keys aren't in the door, where they usually are.

Exasperation turns to rage. White-hot fury. Ross has locked me in the house and taken all the phones away, knowing I don't have my mobile either. How dare he do this to me? How fucking dare he! Oh my God. All that searching for my phone in the hospital, then Ross filling in the lost-property form. What're the odds he never put it in my bag in the first place?

I move swiftly into the living room, my anger now transmuting into a calm, steady determination to get out of this house by any means possible.

The curtains are still drawn, so I yank them back. But even as my fingers close round the brass handle of one of the windows, I know it won't open. The little keys are missing.

I press my forehead into the glass. Solid, triple-glazed, energy-efficient window units. It was one of the things Ross was so pleased about when he first bought the property. Will anyone even hear if I bang on them and shout? Because that's what I might end up doing. Unless the ones upstairs are still unlocked. With any luck, he's forgotten about those and I can alert a passerby, get them to call the police.

I turn to leave the room. I'll get out of this house if it kills me.

I stop dead in my tracks. Terror squeezes my heart as I see her, sitting in the armchair in the far corner.

"Going somewhere, Lizzie?" she says.

52

My flesh shrinks at the sound of her voice. She's moving something on the armrest of the chair. Pushing and pulling it backward and forward like a child with a toy car. I stare at her, open-mouthed. It feels like all the air has been sucked out of the room. It's the toy train I saw on the wall, all those weeks ago, the day I went to the university. Was she behind the phone calls, too? She must have been.

I gape at her in dismay. My mind is awhir. Did Ross set me up for this? But no, he wanted me to go with him to Aberdeen. Why the hell didn't I say yes? Now I'm trapped. Trapped with the woman who's waited twelve years to exact her revenge. The woman who has preyed on my vulnerability and need for friendship from the very first time she set foot in this house. I think of her tears in the study the night of the party. Crocodile tears. All that hatred is still fresh in her mind. It always has been.

Escape strategies spark in my mind like fireworks, but they all fizzle out, one by one.

"I'm not trying to sell you anything, I promise," she says.

I frown, confused. What does she mean? And why is she speaking like that, in an Australian accent? It sounds strangely familiar.

She leans forward, smiling sweetly. "I just need five minutes of your time."

Of *course*. Ruby Orchard. The reporter I put the phone down on. There was never any story about Elodie Stevens. It was another one of Catherine's strategies to draw me toward her, to reel me in. And it worked, didn't it? I took the bait, like she knew I would.

My body is rigid with tension. "How did you get in?"

She smiles again. But now it's the kind of smile that Melissa Davenport and Bethany Charles used to give me. On the surface, it's just an ordinary smile, but there's cruelty lurking beneath.

"I had the foresight to get another set of keys cut."

Of course. It was probably the first thing she did.

Panic is rising inside me, but I won't let her see it. I won't. I straighten my spine and force myself to hold her gaze.

"I want you to give me my keys and leave right now."

She wags her finger at me as if I'm a naughty little girl. "Don't give me orders, Lizzie. They're not *your* keys anyway. And if anyone's going to leave this house, it'll be you. But only when you tell me the truth."

A fist of anger clenches inside me. "You can't intimidate me anymore, Catherine. I'm not that frightened little girl you used to terrorize in the middle of the night."

She raises her eyebrows. "You mean that frightened little girl who pushed my baby sister in front of a train? No, you're not her anymore. You're all grown up now, aren't you, Lizzie? But you're still a liar. And you're still a murderer."

Her words expand in the room. She takes a step toward me. My heart thuds in my neck, my ears, but I stand my ground.

"What do you hope to achieve by this? It won't bring Alice back." I sound a whole lot braver than I feel.

She regards me with distaste, as if I am something unpleasant she is forced to look at. Her top lip curls. "What really happened that day, Lizzie?"

"I can't remember. You *know* I can't remember. You're a nurse, for Christ's sake! You know about epilepsy. Why are you doing this to me?"

"But you *do* remember having an argument, don't you? You mentioned it to Ross."

I close my eyes. It was that conversation I had with him after he found Catherine's flowers in the bin and we started talking about the accident. I blurted it out. He didn't seem to take any notice at the time, so I stopped worrying and forgot all about it. But he must have picked up on it. He must have fed the information straight back to her.

The thought of the two of them together, plotting against me, brings on a fresh wave of pain and sadness. That's what's been happening this whole time: He's been studying me, waiting for me to slip up. And yet, I'm sure it wasn't *all* pretense. It can't have been.

Catherine leans in toward me, her face so close to mine I can smell the coffee on her breath. "What were you arguing about? What *didn't* you tell the police?" Her voice is pure acid.

My breath judders in my chest.

Her jaw hardens. "Was it the same argument you had after the disco? The one where you said you wished she was dead?"

I stare at her in disbelief. The silence between us is solid. Oppressive. How does she know about that? She wasn't there.

Catherine juts her chin at me. "Just because you saw me slap her that time, it doesn't mean she didn't love me. It doesn't mean she didn't confide in me when she was unhappy. I was like a mother to her."

The corners of her mouth turn down into a sneer. "You've lied about your seizures before, haven't you? Used them to get out of things you couldn't face. Like that school trip you didn't want to go on."

Heat floods into my cheeks. "That was just the one time. I did it for Alice. It was Alice who didn't want to go."

"And nor did you. She told me the next day. I caught her trying to forge Mum's signature on a note to Miss Nandy. Alice was never a very good liar." She narrows her eyes. "Unlike *you*." Her face is hard and unforgiving.

"And you!" I retort. "You've lied to me ever since the party. And Ross has lied to me even longer."

Something is starting to unfold in my brain. A dawning realization. His anger when I told him I'd offered her our spare room. His awkwardness the whole time she was here. The look on his face yesterday evening, when the three of us stood on the landing. And last night, after the phone call from the nursing home. The way he talked to me about his past while we lay in bed.

It might just be wishful thinking. Desperate thinking. For all I know, he's as mad as she is, or why else would he have deceived me like this? But a small voice keeps telling me that, despite everything he's done, he isn't like her. He's different.

"He doesn't know you're here, does he? You didn't leave of your own accord. He *told* you to go."

Her face changes. She looks defensive all of a sudden. I'm right. It hasn't all been a pretense for him. He *feels* something for me. I *knew* it. That's why he wanted me to go to Aberdeen with him. I feel a sudden pang of regret. He'll be mid-flight by now, his legs stretched out under the seat in front, plugged in to his iPad. That's why he unpacked my rucksack and put it back on top of the wardrobe, why he didn't ask me where I was going. Because he didn't *want* me to remember. He didn't want me to go.

And that's why Catherine is here now. That's why she's let herself in. Because she knows she's lost him.

I fight back nausea at the thought of what she might do. If she blames me for Alice's death, she'll blame me for losing Ross, too. And now she has me exactly where she wants me. Trapped in the web she's so meticulously and stealthily spun.

"It's only because of the baby," she says. "He doesn't want *you*."

My hand moves instinctively to my belly, and so do her eyes.

"You're just like your mother. A filthy bitch in heat."

I reel at her words. "What's any of this got to do with my mother?"

"Everything!" She spits the word out. "It's got everything to do with her." She fixes me with an icy stare. "You really have no idea, do you?"

I stare back at her. "No idea about what?"

She inhales, sharply. "Your mother wanted something my mum already had."

I don't understand what she's saying. She isn't making any sense.

"Something she couldn't get from your beloved 'father.'" She makes finger quotes round the word and does that nasty little smile again. "All that Bible shit she used to spout. What a fucking hypocrite!"

I feel as though I'm on the brink of something dark and chaotic. Something unspeakable.

"He was infertile, your dad. You didn't know that, did you?" She laughs, but it's a horrible, mirthless laugh. "No, of course you didn't."

Her words don't compute. All my thoughts up to this point collide in a big messy jumble, then vanish. My mind goes blank. I can't move.

"You're lying!"

"I'm not. Why do you think my mum was so depressed?" Her voice sharpens. "Because she was betrayed by her best friend and her husband. That's why. It doesn't get much worse than that, does it? Except in this case, it does. Mum was so happy when she found out Sue was pregnant because she knew how desperately she wanted a baby of her own. She knew it was probably her last chance. But then she worked out whose baby it was and by that time, Mum was pregnant, too." She shakes her head in disgust. "Nice work, Dad."

I try in vain to control my breath, to understand the full extent of what she's saying. There's a terrible emptiness inside me. Like an ache that keeps on expanding till it's all there is. My entire world has been thrown into the air and now that the pieces are falling, none of them are landing in the right place. I feel cut off from my own body. Frozen in shock and . . . and grief. My dad is not my real dad. I clamp my hand to my mouth and stagger back. Mick Dawson is my biological father.

53

I press my lips together and shake my head, as if, by continuing to deny it, I can make it go away.

I wrap my arms round my chest. This means that Alice and I were half-sisters. Oh my God. This means *Catherine* and I are half-sisters, too! The shock of it is turning into a physical pain, as if I'm being held in a vise. When finally I manage to speak, it's like the words are being squeezed out of me. My voice is thin and reedy.

"But . . . but why didn't they tell us? Why didn't we know?"

Catherine shakes her head, a bitter smile on her lips. It seems impossible that we're related. Impossible.

"Because that's what they agreed," she says. "Your parents and mine."

I lower myself slowly onto the settee. My parents' deception goes deeper than I thought. I've been living in a bubble all this time. Sealed off from the truth. Even when I found that card and they finally had the chance to come clean, they *still* didn't tell me. All that stuff Mum said on the phone about Sheena accusing her of being a stuck-up busybody might well have been true, but it wasn't the whole story, was it? It was nowhere near.

Catherine goes on talking. "I wasn't meant to know, but I was good at listening in. Ross and I worked it all out. We were an ace team of detectives, the two of us."

The nauseous feeling that's been swirling around at the back of my throat suddenly gets a whole lot worse at the mention of Ross's name. All those times he's sat with my parents, chatting away with them, drinking Dad's whiskey, paying compliments to Mum. He hasn't just deceived me, he's deceived them as well. All the time, he knew their guilty secret. Even if he *does* regret tricking me, even if he really does love me now, it's too much to forgive.

"Mum didn't want you to be part of our lives, couldn't bear to be reminded of the betrayal. And that suited your parents, too. They had their precious baby at last, and that was that. They moved away and it was all just swept under the carpet."

My head is screaming at me that it's not true, that it's all a product of her sick, twisted mind, but my heart knows different. My heart *knows* she's telling the truth because it all makes perfect sense. The connection I felt with Alice. How instant our friendship was, how profound. The way my parents never approved of us being friends. The conversations we could never have. How odd they've been acting lately.

Catherine stares in the direction of the window, her eyes glazed. "I used to pretend she was mine, you know. Alice. Mum got better, eventually, started being a mother again, but Alice belonged to me. She always did. She was the only good thing to come out of that whole sorry mess."

My lower lip starts to wobble as things fall into place. I know what she's going to say even before she says it.

Her eyes refocus on me, narrow into hate-filled slits. "Then she met *you* and everything changed. She didn't need me anymore. And you can imagine what it did to my mother when she found out who you were. It dragged all that heartache up again, sent her spiraling back down into depression."

Her fists clench. "And we both know what happened next, don't we?"

She takes a step closer. "So now you will tell me, once and for all, what happened that day. From the very beginning, right through to the argument and the moment you decided to kill my sister."

She lowers her voice. "I told her everything that day, before the two of you went on your stupid walk. I thought it was about time she knew the truth. If you hadn't killed her, she'd have told you, too. She'd have told you that she was your sister. How does that make you feel?"

Her words land like a blow, but I force myself to hold her gaze.

"I didn't kill Alice. I never touched her. You have to believe me. We were arguing, yes, but I didn't push her. I had a seizure. I blacked out."

"Don't lie!" she hisses through bared teeth. "You couldn't stand it that Alice was so much prettier and more popular than you. You were eaten up with jealousy. Admit it."

My eyes swim with unshed tears. I'm damned if I'll cry in front of her. "You're wrong! I loved Alice. She was my best friend."

But even as I'm saying these words, I know that Catherine's right. I *was* jealous of Alice. Of *course* I was. I hated the fact that she was everything I wasn't: pretty, confident, popular. I hated the fact that she'd danced with Dave Farley even after he'd humiliated me in front of everyone. And I hated the way she kept doing that annoying little smile, the one she'd been doing ever since we set off on our walk, because I was so sure it was about him, and what had happened. I was so sure she was going to tell me he'd asked her out, and then it would all be over. I'd have lost her.

Catherine gives another of her scornful laughs. "Your best friend? You mean like your mum was my mum's best friend?" She scowls. "Like mother, like daughter. Jealous, bitter bitches."

"No! That's not true! It was a silly row. We were thirteen, Catherine. Thirteen! We were children." My words tumble out in juddery gasps. "I'd never have done anything to hurt her. It was an accident. A terrible accident!"

But how is she going to believe me when I don't even believe myself? All those nightmares I've had over the years, horrible scenes of us fighting on the track, of me pushing and shoving her in fury. The shock and fear in her face. I've always told myself they were another symptom of post-traumatic stress, but what if those things actually happened?

I thought my discovery about Ross and Catherine was a dream, but it wasn't, was it? That turned out to be real. So maybe the nightmares are real, too.

Maybe they're memories.

54

A sudden pain shoots up the side of my abdomen, like something tearing the muscle apart. It disappears almost as fast as it arrived, but whatever it was, it's a stark and visceral reminder that I need to protect myself and my baby. I need to get away from Catherine. Get away from this house.

I stand up, slowly, trying to ignore the trembling in my legs. Catherine's gaze travels down to my bare feet. Her eyes widen in surprise. And that's when I feel it: a trickle of something wet reaching my inner ankle.

I look down in horror. I'm bleeding.

"I need to call an ambulance. Where's the phone? Give me the phone!"

But Catherine is just standing there, arms folded.

"For God's sake, Catherine. Can't you see what's happening? I need to get to hospital. I need your *help*."

An expression of distaste slides across her face. Then, in a sudden but entirely controlled movement, she walks over to the window and closes the curtains. "Sometimes these things are meant to be," she says. "They're nature's way of telling you that something's wrong."

"What are you *talking* about? I'm four and a half months pregnant. I need to get to a hospital. What's *wrong* with you? Where's the fucking phone?"

My whole body is shaking. "Please, Catherine. You've got to help me. I'm high-risk, you know I am. This shouldn't be happening."

I feel dizzy and weak, so I sit down again. I need to keep calm and still. I need to rest. I need to be in a hospital!

She nods, slowly. "Yes, you're quite right."

My hopes soar. She isn't a monster, after all. She's going to help me. She *has* to help me.

"It *shouldn't* be happening," she says. There's a glassy indifference in her eyes that scares me. "You should never have got pregnant in the first place." Her face hardens. "And neither should your mother. If Ross had done the job properly, you wouldn't even *be* here."

My heart is racing so fast it hurts. I cross the palms of my hands on to my chest and press them down. Once again, my mind struggles to make sense of her words. "What do you mean? What are you saying?"

"He was meant to push her harder, to send her flying, but the little fool messed it up." She sneers. "I should have done it myself."

It takes several seconds for her words to sink in. When they do, a wave of revulsion almost knocks me back. "You mean . . . You mean Ross was the child my mum tripped over? You mean that was *deliberate*?"

She nods. "I dared him to do it, and he did. Now you're going to lose *your* baby and I'm going to watch it happen."

Sweat pours from my head. I was wrong. She *is* a monster. They both are.

My brain is a jumble of thoughts that slowly start to arrange themselves. So Ross was one of the "noisy urchins" my dad used to complain about. My parents were an older childless couple when they lived on Riley Road. No wonder they were irritated by all the kids on the estate. Mum and Sheena's friendship was already on its last legs when Mum tried to talk to her about Catherine's feral behavior. Meanwhile, Sheena was getting close to the woman next door. Ross's aunt Jessie. So when she found out about Mum and Mick, I can only imagine what the fallout was like and the sort of things the young Catherine and Ross might have heard.

Catherine leans over me. "I only ever wanted the truth about how Alice died. And then I wanted Ross to break your heart in two, like you broke mine. And my mum's." She points to the beads of blood soaking into the carpet between my feet. "All this is a bonus," she says. "You might have Ross, but you're not going to have this baby. Soon you'll know what it's like to lose someone precious. Not that it'll come anywhere near the pain you've caused me. I had thirteen years with Alice."

I want to punch her in the face. I want to pull her hair out and claw at her eyes, but that tearing sensation is back. I double over in pain.

"Call a fucking ambulance!" I scream, but she just laughs. A vile, hateful laugh.

"You think that little twinge is bad. You wait till the big ones start rolling in."

Oh dear God. She's unhinged. She must be. Something Mum said comes back to me. She said Sheena was always blowing hot and cold and that it wasn't her fault—she was ill. What if she was ill long before Mum betrayed her? What if her demons came from something a lot more serious than heartbreak? The betrayal would have been devastating, of course it would, but surely her depression wouldn't have lasted all those years? Did she have some kind of personality disorder, too?

Does Catherine suffer from the same thing? My brain frantically searches for the right words to reason with her. The words that will make her help me.

"But this is Ross's baby, too," I say. "You might hate me, but you love him, don't you?"

"He's made his choice," she says. "And it wasn't me." Her voice almost breaks. Is this the chink in her armor?

Her shoulders slump. All that righteous anger she's been holding in her body, all that venom, has drained away as if a valve has been opened. She wrings her hands and sways backward and forward on the balls of her feet.

"But you said he only wants me because of the baby. It's you he loves, Catherine. You he's always loved. He's just doing what he thinks is the right thing."

She gives me a suspicious look. "You're just saying that because you want me to help you." She laughs through her nose. A dismissive exhalation. "Believe me, it'll be better for everyone if you lose this baby. You're not fit to be a mother. No child would be safe with you. You've said as much yourself."

I blink back the tears. She knows my deepest fears, because I, like the trusting fool I was, shared them with her. All the advice she gave me, the encouragement. It was all just more of her bullshit.

Well, two can play at that game.

"Ross doesn't love me," I say. "I've always known that, deep down. I always knew he was out of my league. In normal circumstances, he'd never have looked twice at someone like me. Don't you think I know that? I've seen the way he looks at you."

A faint smile plays on her lips. She likes what she's hearing. She's a narcissist.

"He kept making excuses for not making love to me. Saying he was too tired. That he wasn't in the mood. It's a miracle I got pregnant at all."

"You can hardly blame him for that, can you?" she says.

I shake my head, sadly. "No, I can't. Not when he had someone like you. You're so . . ." I clench my toes. "You're so lovely. I bet he wishes this was your baby. Yours and his." The words stick in my throat, but I force them out. To my ears, they sound flimsy and fake, but I have to try. "He called out for you sometimes, when he was sleeping."

The lie hangs between us and, for a second, I wonder if I've gone too far. She holds my gaze. Her expression doesn't change, but the quality of the silence *does*. Emboldened, I carry on.

"You're my sister, Catherine. My flesh and blood."

She bristles at the words. That was a mistake. I shouldn't have said that. I quickly change tack. "Ross's baby is part of *you*, too. This baby will be your niece."

There's a pause. Something unreadable flickers in her eyes.

"I'm so sorry Alice died," I say. "And you're right. I *was* jealous of her. Because she was everything I knew I'd never be. Just like *you're* everything I can never be. And I *was* shouting at her that day. But I didn't push her, Catherine. I didn't push her under that train. I promise you. I had a seizure, and when I woke up . . . when I woke up, she was gone."

Catherine's eyes are wet with tears, only this time, I'm pretty sure they're the real thing. I've only one card left to play.

"This baby is part of Alice, too."

Her forehead pleats into a frown. She looks troubled by this.

Another drop of blood rolls down my inner thigh. "Please, Catherine, I'm begging you. Help me save her."

She contemplates me through narrowed eyes. "I've never thought of you as family," she says. "I never wanted to acknowledge your existence. I blamed you for everything. You and your mother."

It's on the tip of my tongue to ask her why she never blamed her father, but I stop myself just in time. I don't want to aggravate her, not now I've come this far. She's wavering and I don't want to give her any reason to turn on me again.

"I wonder what Alice would say, if she were here now?"

She looks up, sharply, as if she's never considered this before. Something in the atmosphere has shifted.

I need to choose my words carefully. My baby's life may depend upon them. Mine, too. I think of the Bible I found in her room. The one she's kept all these years. The inscription on the inside cover. It's worth a try, isn't it?

"And what about your Nanny Dot? She'd want you to help me, Catherine. I know she would. She'd want you to save this baby." My voice falters. "Save your niece."

She blinks, uncertainty in her eyes. I watch her throat move as she swallows, see the frown give way to something unexpectedly tender. Then the tenderness turns to panic and suddenly she's reaching for my wrist and checking my pulse. She's helping me to my feet. Terror and relief collide in my head like two opposing currents. She might be deranged, but she's a trained nurse, and right now I need her.

A car door slams outside. I hear feet running up the path to the front door. A key turning in the lock.

"Lizzie? Lizzie, where are you?"

It's Ross! I thought he'd be 30,000 feet in the air by now, but he's here, in the house. He bursts into the room, breathless and agitated. He stops dead in his tracks. His face pales as he takes in the blood dripping slowly onto my feet and into the carpet, Catherine still clutching my wrists.

His fists clench at his sides. I've never seen him like this. He is livid. White with rage.

"What have you done to her?"

"It's okay, Ross," I say, flashing him a warning look. "She's helping me. She's taking me to hospital."

But he isn't looking at me. He isn't listening. He strides across the room and yanks Catherine's hands from my arms. He grabs hold of her by the shoulders and pushes her against the wall, pins her there, his arms outstretched, the muscles taut through the sleeves of his shirt.

"Ross, what are you doing? We need to go to hospital. Just drive me there now and we can sort this out later."

"Get in the car, Lizzie," he snaps. "Get in the car and we'll go."

But he's still pressing her shoulder blades flat against the wall, his face barely inches from hers. Now his hands are round her neck.

"I can't do this anymore, do you hear me? I've had enough of all these stupid mind games. You can't control me anymore."

His fingers tighten round her neck. Her eyes widen like a startled deer's. She tries to push him away, to claw at his hands, but he's too strong for her. She can't get away from him. The muscles on his arms bulge as he gouges his thumbs into the cavity between her collarbones. Her eyes are wild and unfocused as she struggles to escape.

I pull at his arms, try to wrench them off her, but it's hopeless. He's like a man possessed. I grab handfuls of his hair and tug as hard as I can. It's the only thing I can do.

"Ross! No! Stop it! Stop it now! She's my sister, for Christ's sake. She's ill. She needs help."

All this time, I've thought of myself as vulnerable. Not a victim of my epilepsy—never that—but *tormented* by it. But Catherine is tormented by something far, far worse. I see that now.

At last, he releases his grip on her neck, and she gasps for breath. I stagger backward, then sink to my knees, blood pounding in my ears. If I had any strength left in my legs I'd run, screaming, into the street. But I'm weak and woozy. I'm going to faint.

I watch through partially closed eyelids as he cradles her face with his hands and kisses her on the mouth, caresses her neck where he's hurt her. What in God's name . . . ? Is he really doing this? Is he really doing this now, while I'm bleeding on the carpet, about to lose our baby? Jesus Christ. He's as twisted and evil as she is. He tried to hurt my mother. He tried to kill me while I was still in the womb!

But he isn't kissing her anymore. He's sobbing. Sobbing like a little boy. I've never seen a man cry before. Not like this. His whole body is heaving and shaking. Catherine looks over his shoulder at me, her face triumphant. Bile rises at the back of my throat.

Then Catherine's face changes. His hands are round her neck again, and this time I know he won't stop. Oh God, no. Please no.

I scramble to get up off the floor, but it's no use. My brain is closing down, like a blind being pulled against the light. Hot tears stream down my face. I'm dissolving into nothingness.

The last thing I see is Catherine sliding down the wall and crumpling onto the floor like a rag doll.

55

I come round in the car, dizzy and bewildered. I'm strapped into the backseat, wrapped in a large bath towel. I don't have any shoes on and there are bloodstains on my feet. My knickers are wet and there's a dull ache in my pelvis. A heavy weight pressing me down into the seat.

I shut my eyes against the sun. Dreadful images swirl in the blackness. Catherine's startled eyes. Thumbs gouging into a neck.

I jolt forward, then slump back.

Ross sees me in the rearview mirror. "Don't panic, darling. We're almost there," he says. "You fainted."

Our eyes meet in the glass. He's just strangled someone to death before my eyes. Ross has just killed Catherine.

I'm numb with shock.

When we arrive at A & E, Ross carries me through the entrance. He speaks to the person on reception.

I keep opening my mouth to tell them what's happened, but the words won't form. I'm like a fish, drowning in air. I feel detached from reality, as if I'm floating above myself, watching the action unfold from afar. It's all happening to someone else, not me. Everyone's voices sound distant and muffled, as if my ears are blocked, as if the walls and floors of the hospital are made of cotton wool.

I'm taken straight through to the triage nurse and, from there, into a cubicle, where Ross lays me gently on a bed and covers me with a blanket. He hovers over me. The picture of love and concern. The doting fiancé who arrived in the nick of time. And I hover over the two of us: a watchful, disembodied presence, unable to break through.

The nurse asks me questions and, somehow, I manage to answer him: hoarse, monosyllabic responses confirming my name and age, my dates. My voice belongs to someone else. It's the voice of a robot.

I think of Catherine, still crumpled, lifeless, on the living-room floor, the bruises from Ross's fingertips a purple choker at her neck. I'd talked her round. It was going to be all right. She'd have got the help she needed. He didn't have to do it.

He didn't have to do it.

An obstetrician checks me over. She is kind and efficient and my eyes will her to see all the words I can't say, but I'm not getting through to her because Ross is doing all the talking for me. Now I'm having my bloods taken. I'm being wheeled away for a scan. I'm being taken to the antenatal ward.

Someone brings me a cup of tea and some biscuits. Ross strokes my hair with the same hands he used to strangle Catherine, and *still* I can't speak. He kisses my forehead and whispers apologies in my ear and tells me he is free at last and that he's never felt happier and more hopeful in his entire life and that, between us, we'll get through this. He will *sort things out*, he says, as calmly as if he is telling me what he intends to cook us for dinner. I just need to trust him, he says.

Trust him. Oh my God. The enormity of what he's done crashes about in my head. Who *is* this man? Do I know him at all?

At last, when the curtains are drawn around us and we are left on our own, a sentence begins to form in my mouth. "But what—"

He puts his forefinger to his lips and tells me to hush. Then he holds my hands in his and starts to speak. His hands are warm and dry. His voice is controlled and calm. It's the sort of voice a doctor might use with his patients. Ross *is* a doctor. Authoritative, but gentle. No hint of unnecessary emotion.

"She's the most vindictive person you can imagine," he says.

All I can do is blink at him. Why is he talking about her in the present tense when he knows she's dead? I moisten my lips. He must think I'm going to say something, because he puts his forefinger on *my* lips now, pressing them gently shut.

"She'd never have let me go. Never. She'd have ruined everything, don't you see? She'd have accused me of inappropriate behavior at work. Or worse. Much worse. She's threatened to do it before. She'd have said I raped her. And they'd have believed her, wouldn't they? Because that's what she's like. She'll convince anyone of anything. It's what she does. She's controlled me from the start. Made me do things . . ."

He releases my hands and rakes his hair with his fingers. It's the first sign that he's in any way perturbed by what's happened. I think of him sobbing onto her neck, then gripping it with his fingers, squeezing the life out of her. My pulse begins to race.

"I'd have been suspended at first. Then I'd have been arrested and it would have gone to trial and I'd have been sent to prison. I'd never have been able to practice as a GP again."

What in God's name is the matter with him? Doesn't he realize that all these things are going to happen anyway? He's just killed a woman in cold blood.

I nod, as if what he's saying makes perfect sense. As if I understand and am on his side. It's quite clear from what he's saying that his overriding concern in all of this is himself. I listen to him speak, listen to his insane justification for murder, and I don't interrupt him anymore, because, really, what's the point? He's as sick as she is. As she *was*.

Finally, he gets ready to leave. He's reluctant to go, but he has no choice in the matter. Visiting hours are over and the nurse is adamant that I need to rest. Besides, as Ross himself says when she goes away, there are certain things at home that he needs to "sort out." We look at each other for the longest time when he says this. I don't respond, but I make a small movement with my mouth. Not quite a smile, but it's enough to reassure him.

The phrase and its implications chill me. All he's thinking about are the practicalities of the situation. He really does think he can "sort this out." As if Catherine's dead body is merely a problem to be solved. What does he think he's going to do with her?

I wait for a full five minutes after he's gone before reaching for the call button at the side of my bed. I don't think the nurse believes me at first. I can't say I blame her. It sounds preposterous. Like some horrific fantasy I've just made up. But eventually, I get through to her and she rushes off to phone the police.

I close my eyes against the bright lights of the ward and Catherine's body slides down the wall once more.

———————
———————

If I let myself relax, properly relax, so that my limbs are light and tingly, so that I have the sensation my body is floating on air and that I am at one with the universe, my mind slows, and the enormity of what I've done loses its power to haunt me. For however many minutes I remain in this state, I am free.

Free from the past. Free from her.

But the mind has a habit of breaking through, of striving for the clarity of conscious thought. Something will bring me back—the slam of a heavy door; the clanking of a guard's keys; my cellmate's fart—and my focus will return. A crescendo of shame and disgust.

I made a mistake. A colossal mistake. I underestimated Catherine Dawson. As soon as she got to work that day and found out that I'd had to fly to Aberdeen, she knew there was a good chance Lizzie would be on her own in the house. I should have realized that would happen. I should have made Lizzie come with me.

When I phoned the surgery again from the airport, to let them know I'd be staying in Scotland overnight and that they'd better get cover, one of the girls on reception let slip that it was going to be a hectic couple of days now that two members of staff were off at the same time.

"Oh yeah?" I said. "Who's the other one, then?"

As soon as she said the name Catherine, I knew. My heart pounded against my rib cage. My brain raced. That's when I started running back to where I'd parked the car, all thoughts of the flight I'd just booked and my father's body abandoned in the rush to drive back home. Back home to Lizzie.

The rest, as they say, is history.

I underestimated Lizzie, too. She's stronger than I thought.

56

I'm sitting on the floor in the middle of my parents' living room, surrounded by brightly colored wrapping paper. Toby gurgles contentedly as Dad dangles a piece of red ribbon in front of him as if he's a kitten that will swat at it. He's wedged between Dad's legs, the lights of the Christmas tree dancing in his eyes. Not quite the little girl I was expecting—so much for my gut instincts—but my love for him is fierce, has been from the moment I first set eyes on him. I wouldn't swap him for the world.

Dad lifts Toby's right arm and makes him wave at me. Dad is wearing one of those ludicrous Christmas jumpers with a reindeer's head on the front. Mum bought it for him as a joke. She always buys us funny things along with our proper gifts. I got a pair of novelty elf slippers with curled toes and bells on the end.

Not that we laughed as much as we normally would. Not that we laughed much at all. We're just going through the motions, really, because what else can we do? And besides, this is Toby's first-ever Christmas and, although he's only four weeks old and won't remember a single thing about it, we will. Because in a way, it's *our* first

Christmas, too. Our first Christmas as an altered family, but a family nonetheless.

I *will* forgive them. In time. I think a part of me already has. They are my parents, after all, and I love them. None of this would even have happened if they hadn't yearned for a baby. If Mum hadn't taken matters into her own hands and slept with Mick Dawson as a means to an end. If Dad hadn't loved her so very much and understood her desperate need for a child of her own. If he hadn't been selfless enough to swallow his pride and become my father. My *real* father. Because let's face it, never mind the biology, that's what he is. That's what he's always been.

Whatever misguided motives they had for not telling me the truth, I have to accept that they thought they were doing it for the right reasons.

Unlike Ross.

Ross. My toes clench in their stupid elf slippers. I promised myself I wouldn't think of him today, but how can I not? The mind has a knack for making you think of things you'd rather not. Another letter from HMP Wormwood Scrubs arrived last week. He said all the same stuff he said in the last one, but this time he's included a long confession, written out like a story, so that I understand exactly how it happened. *Why* it happened. I haven't read it yet. I will, though. Eventually.

Will knowing the details make any difference to the way I feel about him? Somehow, I doubt it. Because the man I fell in love with doesn't exist. He's a figment of my imagination, of his and Catherine's devious little plan. He's a projection of my own romantic longings.

When they led him away at the end of the trial, I felt sorry for him, naturally. Prison must be a dreadful experience. But seeing him in that courtroom was like looking at a stranger.

I never knew Ross Murray at all.

I like to think about the sort of man he *could* have been, if he'd never gone to live with his aunt Jessie in Riley Road. If he'd never met Catherine Dawson and been taken over by her. Because I caught a glimpse of that man. He was always there, somewhere. And that man loved me. I have to believe that.

I *do* believe that.

I screw my eyes tight shut and force myself not to think of his hands on Catherine's neck. If only he'd been strong enough to walk away. To carry me into the car and let her go. Maybe, in time, I might have forgiven him. Not enough to stay with him—never that—but enough to let him see his son from time to time, to have some kind of presence in his life. And I'd have spoken up for him if she'd done what he thought she might do, if she'd tried to level some kind of sexual allegation at him.

A fresh spasm of horror ripples through me when I think of Catherine's blood-engorged face, her dead, staring eyes. My therapist recommends doing something physical whenever my mind insists on returning to that moment, on replaying it over and over. So I clamber to my feet and start tidying up some of the wrapping paper still strewn about the floor. Folding the pieces that can be recycled and setting them aside in a neat little pile. My world might have changed beyond all recognition, but life goes on. It has to. And sometimes it's little tasks like these that keep me sane, that quieten the noise in my head.

Dad watches me, a mixture of sadness and pride in his eyes. He's told me he doesn't mind if I want to contact Mick Dawson in the future, if I need to talk to him and tell him that I know. But I don't want to. I know I can't speak for my future self, but I'm pretty sure that I won't change my mind. It's one of the reasons I didn't go to Catherine's funeral. Because I didn't want to see him, and I don't expect he and Sheena would have wanted me there anyway. Both their daughters are dead and I was with them both when they died. I still can't get my head round it, so most of the time I don't even try.

Mum and Dad want me to move back in with them permanently, but I've said no. It would be so easy to let them carry on looking after us, to stay in this little cocoon of love, but after everything that's happened and what's brought me to this point, I know it's time for me to live on my own, to be independent at last.

If Ross hadn't insisted on transferring the deeds of the house in Charlton into my name, I wouldn't have been in a position to turn them down. But now that the paperwork is finally completed, I'm going to put the house on the market and buy a place of my own here in Dovercourt. I'll be near enough to Mum and Dad that they can be part of our lives and watch Toby grow up, but we won't be in each other's pockets all the time. I'll make sure of that.

Dad didn't want me to have anything to do with the house at first, but then he came round to the idea. "You're right," he said. "Why the hell should he get away with not providing for his child? He owes you and Toby this for what he's done. As long as he doesn't think he has any kind of hold over you when he comes out. Because if he comes anywhere near you or Toby, I'll . . . I'll . . ."

Once upon a time, I suppose he might have said something like "I'll kill him with my own bare hands," but in the circumstances he couldn't quite bring himself to finish the sentence.

It's going to be tough, walking back into that house, but it's got to be done if I'm ever going to move forward. I need to collect the rest of my things and get it ready for the estate agents to take their photos. Dad's already bought the paint to cover up the stains in the hallway.

When things have settled down, I'm going to apply to the local university, too. See if I can do a part-time English degree. And in the meantime, Toby and I will camp out in my old bedroom. It'll give me time to get used to being a mum.

What will I tell him as soon as he's old enough to understand? Because I *will* tell him. Some of it, at least. I'll tell him that once upon a time I had two sisters—Alice and Catherine—but that now they're both dead. That once upon a time I loved his father so much, I wanted to be his wife, but he turned out to be a liar and a murderer. And that's the brutal truth.

I swallow hard. Because here's the thing: I am also a liar. I'm almost certainly a murderer, too. Will I tell him that? Somehow, I don't think so. We all have things in our past we're ashamed about. Things we'd rather others didn't know.

Mum calls to us from the kitchen. She wants me to put Toby in his baby chair and she wants Dad to carve the turkey. The table is already laid. I helped her do it earlier while Toby was sleeping. There are four Christmas crackers waiting to be pulled. One for each of us in this strange little group we call a family.

"Here you go, Pumpkin," Dad says, handing Toby over like the precious Christmas gift he is.

I take him in my arms and kiss his downy little head as he snuffles into my neck. When I think of how close I came to losing him . . . how close Mum came to losing me.

My darling Toby. My little boy. We're a team now, the two of us. So much stronger than we look.

THREE MONTHS LATER

I've been expecting it to look the same, but it doesn't. This ugly concrete-and-steel footbridge is new and it takes me a while to process the change, to reconcile it with the image I've had in my head all these years. The image that comes back to me in dreams. Just one of many images that continue to haunt me.

It was Dad who suggested we come here. For closure, he said, although I'm not sure such a thing exists. He hasn't accompanied me onto the footbridge. He's waiting at the bottom of the steps, Toby strapped to his body in the baby carrier. This time last year, Toby was the size of an apple pip. I didn't even know I was pregnant. Now he weighs six kilos and can push himself up on his arms when he's lying on his tummy.

I can imagine how secure he feels, snuggled against Dad's broad, warm chest, and I wonder if that's how Dad carried me once. The little girl who wasn't his, but whom he loved just as much as if she were. Still does.

I stop and lace my fingers through the steel mesh that's here to stop people launching themselves off, or daredevil children from climbing down. I can't toss the flowers I've brought with me onto the track, as I'd planned, but maybe that's just as well. I dread to think how much worse I'd feel if I were leaning over the edge, my sight unencumbered by this metal latticework.

My forehead presses into the cold steel and I peer down. This is as close as I can get to the actual spot where it happened. My breath comes fast and shallow.

Somewhere above my head, a crow screeches and I'm tumbling back in time, wrestling with Alice on the track. It wasn't the stuff of nightmares, that fight. It really happened, and now it's happening all over again. My world has contracted to this one point in time and space. We're swiping at each other with our hands, slapping the air and what bits of each other's flesh we can find. We keel over in slow motion, arms flailing, legs buckling, mouths open in shocked concentration.

It seems to last forever, this dance of ours, as if regaining our balance is simply a matter of time and finding the right steps. Needles of light glint sharp and silver off the tracks. Her face is so close to mine I can see the raised blue vein throbbing at her temple. The raw pinkness at the back of her throat.

Now more memories emerge from the darkness. Is that what these are? Memories? I can't be imagining them; they're too real. Too familiar. Like phantoms long repressed.

I used to wonder about all those missing pieces of my life, the things that happened to me before seizures. I used to think, if only the memories would return, somehow the picture would be complete and I'd be whole again. But what if the thing I can't remember is just too awful to contemplate? Aren't I better off *not* knowing?

My fingers clench tighter and I lean against the steel cage, willing my mind to return to the here and now. This can't be what happened. Please God, tell me it can't! I might have hated her in that moment, but I wouldn't have hurt her. I couldn't have!

Her eyes are frantic, her voice beseeching, just like the nightmares that have plagued me all my life. My grip tightens and the steel mesh digs into my fingertips as the scene plays out in my mind. I lash out at her, striking the tops of her arms, her face. She tries to grab me, but I'm too wild, too strong. I can't hear her voice, only a buzzing noise getting louder and louder till it feels like it's coming from inside my body, but I know she's still screaming at me. I can see the black gaping hole of her mouth. The fear in her eyes. The fear.

My stomach contracts in a violent retch and I spit the saliva that's flooded into my mouth onto the concrete between my feet, hoping Dad's too preoccupied with Toby to notice what's happening. I glance down at him, relieved to see his back is turned and he's swaying gently from side to side. He's probably singing to him, but I can't hear him from all the way up here. All I can hear is a strange whooshing noise that isn't, as I first thought, the wind whistling through the trees, but the sound of my own blood magnified in my ears.

I sink to my knees, hot tears coursing down my cheeks, my nose all stuffy and blocked, as I finally realize what my subconscious has been trying to tell me all these years. I didn't push Alice. We weren't fighting at all. We'd been arguing, yes. A childish spat that spiraled out of control.

Maybe it was the stress of the quarrel, but I must have stumbled onto the tracks in those surreal few minutes before a seizure, that briefest of periods when mind and body separate, when consciousness tilts and fades. Whatever we'd been screaming at each other up to that point is irrelevant. It always has been. It *was* fear in her eyes when we were struggling. But she wasn't frightened *of* me like I've always suspected; she was frightened *for* me.

I wasn't fighting her on the track. I was having my seizure on the track. Alice was trying to save me. She always looked out for me, made sure I was safe. Somehow or other, she found the strength to push me onto the ballast. And that's where I finally came to.

But it was too late for Alice.

All my life I've wanted a sister. Was that why the two of us became such instant friends? Was there an invisible thread between us, binding us together from the start? Was that why our friendship seemed so natural, so right? All the laughter we shared. All the fun. If only I hadn't seen that flicker of a smile on her lips. If only she hadn't hinted at having a secret, we might never have started arguing in the first place. But once again, I let my stupid jealousy get the better of me and started yelling at her. Saying horrible, mean things.

Now, of course, I know exactly what she was smiling about. Catherine had broken her thirteen-year silence and told Alice what she knew. Told her we were sisters. There was me thinking that Alice was being all mysterious about Dave Farley and working myself up into a jealous fury, when all the time she'd been trying to find the right way of telling me we were related.

Alice was excited. Happy. All she wanted to do was share the news.

Alice, my best friend.

Alice, my sister.